Praise for Anita Shreve's

A Change in Altitude

"No one is better at gently, but thoroughly, probing the interior life of her characters than Anita Shreve. In *A Change in Altitude,* she traces the effects of distrust and tragedy on a newlywed couple also trying to deal with life in a strange country."

— Mary Foster, *San Francisco Chronicle*

"Anita Shreve is a master of domestic drama...grounded in the pointed and complex everyday relationships that bind close friends and family....Kenya is unfamiliar literary territory to Shreve, but the book's theme is one that she tackles often: how a pivotal event in someone's life can change all that follows."

— Jim Concannon, *Boston Globe*

"Anita Shreve's salad years as a journalist for a Nairobi magazine lend a roiling authenticity to this tale of loss and disillusionment....The first, most psychologically fraught of the book's three parts hurtles along in the rip-snorter mode of *King Solomon's Mines.*" — Jan Stuart, *New York Times Book Review*

"Truly gripping....The emotional power of watching a young couple battling to mend their tattered partnership is undeniable....This is the sort of fiction that compels you to go a stop further on the bus than you really need to."

— Fiona Atherton, *Scotsman*

"Enthralling. . . . Prepare to cancel all your appointments as you race through this dramatic saga." —Eliza Borné, *BookPage*

"Shreve abandons her usual locale, the chilly shores of New England, for the heat of East Africa, showing herself a more expansive writer in the process. . . . Her waspish insights into the mindset of the colonial alpha male lend the novel a sophisticated edge." —Emma Hagestadt, *Independent*

"Shreve moves relentlessly from plot point to plot point. . . . She knows how to keep a reader engaged. . . . Shreve packs an impressive amount of sympathetic and intelligent detail into this narrative." —Valerie Sayers, *Washington Post*

"Another fine novel by an author who never loses her capacity to surprise and enlighten. . . . It is only in the final few pages that the alert reader will become aware that the whole book is actually a sustained engagement with *To the Lighthouse*." —Giles Foden, *Guardian*

"In Shreve's latest novel, mountain-as-metaphor looms large. . . . Her command of the land, the language, and post-colonial society is evident. . . . Shreve takes readers from Nairobi's lush suburbs to its fetid slums, from the drawing-room world of the white gentry to that of its black servants." —Olivia Barker, *USA Today*

"Things go terribly wrong on a mountain climb. . . . As Margaret finds herself stepping beyond the post-colonial cocoon, she's susceptible to both perilous politics and adulterous passion." —Sherryl Connelly, *New York Daily News*

"Highly reflective.... A rough parallel develops between *A Change in Altitude* and *Out of Africa*.... A good, absorbing story, assisted by Shreve's effective evocation of Nairobi and its environs.... Africa itself becomes a character."

— David Hendricks, *San Antonio Express-News*

"A winner.... An unusual kind of page-turner, part whodunit, part adventure story.... Readers will vicariously enjoy all facets of this adventure in Africa from the safety of their own armchair."

— Diane Makovsky, *Fredericksburg Free-Lance Star*

"When tragedy occurs in the mountain's icy crevasses, Patrick and Margaret have to confront the fissures that rapidly begin to appear in their own marriage.... A perfect companion for those chilly, curl-up-on-the-couch nights."   — *Redbook*

"Shreve's narrative gift is so highly developed that it gets the upper hand.... She asks readers to think about whether you can separate 'actions' from 'unintended consequences.'"

— Kate Kellaway, *Observer* (UK)

"A great novel.... With sparse, crisp dialogue, great emotional insight, and compassion tempered with a beautiful portrayal of Kenya, Shreve brings us 'out of Africa.'"

— thereviewbroads.com

"Shreve is a master of psychological suspense.... The climb is superbly dramatized.... I could not put the novel down.... Shreve grapples with subjects and themes that matter.... She delves deeply into marriage, a rich, bottomless subject."

— Ami Sands Brodoff, *Globe and Mail*

A Change in
Altitude

A Change in Altitude

A NOVEL

Anita Shreve

BACK BAY BOOKS
LITTLE, BROWN AND COMPANY
NEW YORK BOSTON LONDON

Back Bay Books / Little, Brown and Company
Hachette Book Group
237 Park Avenue, New York, NY 10017
www.hachettebookgroup.com

Originally published in hardcover by Little, Brown and Company,
September 2009
First Back Bay trade paperback edition, May 2010

Back Bay Books is an imprint of Little, Brown and Company. The Back Bay
Books name and logo are trademarks of Hachette Book Group, Inc.

Author's Note: This is a work of fiction. The events described are imaginary and
the characters are fictitious. It is not intended that any reader infer that these
settings and incidents are real or that the events actually happened.

Michele Magwood's interview with Anita Shreve, which appears in the
reading group guide at the back of this book, was originally published in
The Times (Johannesburg) on October 3, 2009. Copyright © Avusa, Inc.
Reprinted with permission.

Library of Congress Cataloging-in-Publication Data
Shreve, Anita.
    A change in altitude : a novel / Anita Shreve. — 1st ed.
        p. cm.
    ISBN 978-0-316-02070-1 (hc) / 978-0-316-02071-8 (pb)
    I. Title.
PS3569.H7385C47 2009
813'.54—dc22   2009024011

10 9 8 7 6 5 4 3 2 1

RRD-IN

Printed in the United States of America

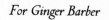

For Ginger Barber

Part One

"We're climbing Mount Kenya. Not this Saturday, but the next."

Patrick made the announcement as he moved into the guest room of the Big House, the plumbing in their own small cottage currently disabled. Patrick spoke of the climb without fanfare, as he might a party in two weeks' time. They were young, each twenty-eight. They'd been in the country three months.

Despite the heat, Patrick's shirt still held its creases. James, whose black skin shone blue in the planes of his face, washed their clothes in a bathtub, hung them to dry, and pressed them with an iron that made the fabric hiss. Not even the equator could undo James's creases.

Patrick set his doctor bag and his briefcase on the floor. He had shaved his beard as a gesture of respect but wore his black hair longer than most.

"Arthur's arranging it. It takes four days. Porters will carry the provisions."

When Margaret and Patrick's toilet in the cottage had ceased to function, they'd temporarily moved in with their landlords, Arthur and Diana, who lived two hundred feet away in the larger house on the property.

"We'll camp?" Margaret asked.

"There are huts."

In a few minutes, Margaret would dress for dinner. Under her palm, she could feel the distinctive stitching of the white coverlet. "I'd better buy hiking boots," she said.

Beyond the casement window, there was birdsong, noisy until early evening, when the day would be snuffed out, at the same hour, every day, summer or winter. In Africa, Margaret often felt dazed, as if something shiny had hurt her eyes.

"Who will go?" she asked.

"Arthur and Diana. You and me. Arthur mentioned another couple, but I forget their names."

"You can take the days off?"

Patrick shrugged his shoulders, indicating a flexible schedule. He moved to the bed and sat beside Margaret, making a deep V in the soft mattress. Despite the heat, he wore long trousers, another gesture of respect. In Kenya, African men emerged from mud-and-wattle huts in suits to drive matatus or to sell scrap metal or to cut meat. To dress casually was to flaunt the ability to do so, as well as to advertise oneself as an American. Only American and German tourists dressed like children.

"You okay?" Patrick asked.

His eyes were light blue, sensitive to the sun. When outdoors, he always wore dark glasses.

"I'm fine," Margaret said.

"You seem quiet."

"How was your day?"

"I was mostly at the hospital. What time is dinner?"

The house ran with the precision of a father's watch. They had been Diana and Arthur's guests for five days, a decent plumber apparently difficult to obtain. First a message had to be sent—the plumber didn't own a telephone—and the problem described. A fee would have to be negotiated, and then transportation sorted. The particular plumber Diana liked was said to be visiting his wife in Limuru. It was unclear when he would return.

Margaret wanted to ask if another plumber could be found, but to do so would be to seem ungrateful for the hospitality. Patrick and Margaret were, after all, being housed and fed.

"Seven," Margaret said of dinner.

Patrick asked her if she had ever climbed a mountain. As he did so, he took her hand. He often took Margaret's hand, in public as well as in private. It meant *I am suddenly thinking of you.*

Though Patrick and Margaret had been together for two years—married five months—entire landscapes of their individual pasts were unknown to the other. Margaret told Patrick that she had once climbed Mount Monadnock, a lesser New England peak. Patrick said that he hadn't ever climbed a mountain, being a city boy from Chicago.

The smell of boiling horse meat made its way into the bedroom. It was an awful smell, and Margaret was certain she would never get used to it. The meat was for the dogs.

"Do we need, I don't know, instruction?" Margaret asked.

"I'm sure Arthur will have it all in hand."

The meat would be something James had purchased at the duka earlier in the day, the blood soaking the *Kenya Morning Tribune* used to wrap it. It would not be any different from the beef Margaret bought for Patrick and herself, the steaks too fresh, not aged, and therefore tough, tasting of animal. "How tall is Mount Kenya?"

"Seventeen thousand feet, give or take."

"That's over three miles high."

"We're already a mile above sea level just sitting here. And I think we probably gain some altitude driving to the mountain."

"So Kilimanjaro is higher?" Margaret asked.

"Higher but easier. I think you simply walk to the top. In large circles. It takes a while, but most amateurs can handle it. It's supposed to be fairly boring."

Patrick changed out of his brown leather everyday shoes, which were covered with mud. If he left the shoes outside the door in the evening, they would be clean in the morning.

"We don't walk?"

"We climb. We hike. Parts of it will be rough."

Margaret imagined Diana's Land Rover, packed with gear, journeying through the shimmering lime-green tea plantations she'd seen only from a distance.

The guest room seemed to have been designed for a writer or a scholar. Margaret sometimes sat at the heavy carved desk, on which an antique typewriter had been placed. She'd tried it once, wincing at the hard thwacks the keys made, as if something delicate and tentative were being announced with a tattoo.

The desk chair had carved arms and a nearly silver patina. On the walls were photographs of people she could not identify, a wooden shield that had perhaps been used in battle, and a sunburst design of spears. The books were leather-bound and uniform and, to judge from their condition, often read. Margaret imagined an early settler, the books all there were available to him of the printed word in Nairobi, reading and rereading them by lantern light. She sometimes held one in her hands.

On the other side of the room was a skirted dressing table of the sort one used to see in old movies. On its glass surface were cut-crystal jars with silver tops. Perhaps the room had belonged to Diana's parents when they built the house in the late 1940s. They'd come out from England after the war to try their hand with horses. Margaret picked up a picture of the couple, extravagantly dressed, looking as though they were about to head off to a party at the Muthaiga Country Club. The father's face was weathered; the mother had a small, sweet smile. Diana, as a child, would constantly have heard that she resembled her father.

Margaret thought about the story of the young Masai who'd been invited by an American benefactor to use his wit and innate intelligence to make a go of it in New York City. Two months after the young man's arrival, he jumped to his death from his tenth-story apartment window. She thought the Masai's heart must have grieved for the Rift Valley or that his senses had been violated by the city's gray geometry. The anecdote was meant to be a cautionary tale, though Margaret was never quite sure what exactly was being cautioned. One shouldn't be taken out of one's environment? Or, if so, might one, at any moment, be subject to dangerous derangement?

Already there seemed to be an inability to adapt. Once, when Patrick and Margaret left town for a long weekend to travel to the Serengeti, they returned to a cottage from which the contents of their bedroom had been emptied. The only thing not touched was Margaret's underwear drawer, in which she had kept their passports. This proved a lesson they'd been taught at the beginning of their stay: keep your valuables in your underwear drawer; no African man would touch a woman's underthings. The police came, looked at the bedroom, pointed to a broken window, and said, Aha. It wasn't an inside job. Did anyone dislike them? Wish them harm? The case was never solved.

Patrick and Margaret bought a new bed and had a lock installed between the bedroom and the living room. They later learned from the inspector that nearly everyone had those sorts of locks; hadn't anyone ever mentioned them to the couple before? It was their third theft in six weeks. Margaret's wallet had been stolen from her straw bag at the market, and one morning, as Patrick had walked out of the cottage on his way to the hospital, he'd found their secondhand Peugeot on cement blocks. All four tires had been taken during the night.

Margaret understood the thieving in a purely intellectual way. The distance between those who were comfortable and those who were not was a precipice an expatriate stood upon, the ground beneath subject at any moment to erosion. In her body, she knew fear; morally, the thieving felt like reparation. She had learned to tuck her purse under her arm and disliked herself for doing it. She tipped James generously for washing their clothes. She was fairly certain this was not the custom, but it made her feel better. James never refused the money.

Patrick wouldn't ask Margaret what she had done that day, the question a prickly one, because she hadn't yet found a job. He didn't seem to mind, but she did. If he *had* asked her, though, she'd have told him that she had walked the dirt roads of Langata with her camera, taking photographs of the askaris in their long greatcoats, their pangas at the ready, or of the signs that read *Mbwa Kali,* Fierce Dog, at the gates of large houses. She also snapped pictures of the delicate falling branches of the jacaranda and of the scarlet-orange-pink bursts of color in the bougainvillea, a plant that grew like a weed and covered stone walls and rooftops. The other doctors at the hospital, she knew, viewed Patrick's residence in Langata, an expatriate haven, as suspect. But Margaret had fallen in love with the cottage in Langata quite by accident.

The Peugeot had stopped along a paved road as she was on

her way to view a flat. Arthur, finishing his workday, had slowed down to inquire if she was all right. She might have guessed at his motives—a mixture of protectiveness and perhaps opportunity: a young white woman in a skirt, stranded at the side of the road behind a white Peugeot, newly purchased but decidedly second-hand; perhaps a lemon. The Peugeot had simply ceased to move, giving no warning.

Arthur rolled down his window and called across the front seat, "You all right?"

Margaret walked to the place where he had parked, white face trusting white face. Had he been an African, she wondered later, would she have waved the man away? Arthur would not take no for an answer, and she was grateful for the help. He tried to start the car in case the problem was simply a lack of petrol; Margaret was, after all, a woman. He would call from his house, he said; he was headed home. He knew of a mechanic who would take care of her. He used those words. *Take care of you.*

Margaret studied the man. He had mud-brown hair and dark eyes, a cleft in his chin, and white teeth inside an easy smile. The bottom half of his face didn't seem to match the top.

In Arthur's Mercedes, Margaret was introduced to the sudden beauty of the manicured gardens and the tall hedges of Langata, a kind of suburb of Nairobi. He turned and stopped at the bottom of a long drive. An askari, greatcoat over his bare legs, hopped up to open Arthur's gate. Arthur never acknowledged the man. The path to the house was lined with jacaranda petals that made a purple carpet to the front door. The two-story home was made of stone with mullioned windows. All around her was a busy foreground of bright blossoms Margaret didn't know the names of. Beyond the garden was a striking expanse of cornflower sky, as saturated a color as she had ever seen. It must have to do, she thought, with the equatorial sun, a distinctive angle of light.

Arthur, offering Margaret a drink, made the appropriate calls. The car was being towed to a garage, where mechanics would repair it. Margaret became aware of her own bare legs, particularly when Arthur's wife, Diana, clearly disconcerted to see a visitor she hadn't been told about, entered the room. The wife took note, she saw, of the drink. Arthur explained, and Margaret was treated to Diana's first smile: a sudden sharp surprise. Margaret called Patrick at the hospital to tell him that they'd been invited to dinner in Langata. She had to make the call with Arthur in the room and so sounded more enthusiastic than she actually felt, perhaps even a little breathless. Margaret could hear Patrick's gentle complaint at the other end.

At dinner the first night, another invitation was extended. A guesthouse on the property was vacant. Arthur named a sum less than the one Patrick and Margaret had been prepared to pay for the flat she'd intended to view. Diana suggested that Margaret and Patrick, who'd taken a bus out from Nairobi, stay the night and view the cottage in the morning, when they would be able to see it in the daylight. In bed that night, Patrick was wary—perhaps he had heard, before Margaret had, the faint tumble of a lock. They held each other tightly on the foreign mattress as if reestablishing themselves as a couple, as if an act of resistance were called for.

In the morning, they viewed the guesthouse, a white stucco cottage with a red tiled roof, surrounded by pink and orange bougainvillea. The cottage had a sitting room with a small table swathed in a vermilion-and-yellow khanga. The kitchen had a

Dutch door; the bedroom had a bathroom. The floor was polished wood in an intricate parquet pattern. The walls were white; the windows, mullioned glass. Even in America—or especially in America—Patrick and Margaret had never lived in such a beautiful place. Before the car had given out, they had been living over a nightclub at the Ngong Road Hotel. Prior to that, they had endured a grim stay at the Hotel Nairobi, where the sink and toilet had been encrusted with filth, where cockroaches had fled whenever Margaret had opened the bathroom door. She thought that Patrick must have seen, that morning, her desire for the cottage, and so he gave up his mild political objections.

The guesthouse was far enough away from Arthur and Diana's house to suggest a measure of autonomy. Diana insisted that the two couples would hardly ever see one another: Arthur worked all the hours of the day as head of sales at Colgate-Palmolive; Diana bred Rhodesian ridgebacks and had little time for people. All this seemed fine. Or Margaret made it so.

That afternoon, James had taken a photograph of Margaret and Patrick. The picture was of Margaret in a chair just beyond the Dutch door of their new cottage in Africa. She had on a white sundress. Her skin was a deep red—Indian red, her mother used to call it. Margaret's hair was dishwater blond, though dishwater didn't really resemble her hair color, a light brown with hints of brass. Her skin seemed painted on and shiny.

Behind her, Patrick was standing in a short-sleeved white shirt with a tie. He had a healthy-looking tan and hair that might or might not have been washed in several days. In the picture, it looked lank. His face was in shadow, sunglasses shading his eyes.

James was serious when working Margaret's Nikon, but he grinned as he handed the camera back to her.

At the Big House, James cooked the meals, set the table, served the food, cleared the dishes away, and then washed them. Patrick and Margaret didn't have servants. Only recently had Diana sent James over to the cottage to wash their clothes. Though Margaret had been advised early on to hire someone to do the chore, the task seemed too intimate to farm out. She had tried to wash the clothes in the bathtub, but she hadn't been able to get all the soap out. When Patrick developed a rash around his neck, Margaret capitulated. She cooked and served their dinners, however, and Patrick did the dishes. It seemed a straw victory. Not to employ a servant was to deny an African a job.

At dinner on the evening of that first mention of the climb, Arthur, his wet hair still grooved from his comb, spoke of hypoxia.

"The lungs fill up with blood," he said, setting Patrick and Margaret straight. "Typically four or five people a year die climbing Mount Kenya. Usually it's the fit German climbers who hop off the plane in Nairobi, head straight for the mountain, and practically run up it. They often get into trouble because they haven't allowed their bodies to acclimate to the height and the thinner air. The slower you climb and the longer it takes, the better off you are."

"I should do really well, then," Margaret said.

Arthur ignored the joke. "As we climb, we'll come across park rangers. They'll be in pairs, and they'll go right up to your face. They'll fire a series of questions at you: What's the date? What time is it? Where do you live? And if you can't fire answers back at them, they'll each take an elbow and run you straight down the mountain whether you want to go or not. It's the only cure."

Margaret was thinking that Arthur, by nature, wasn't an

alarmist. Though he could be condescending—she sometimes thought he viewed condescension as a minor sport—he and Patrick had had lively discussions that had lasted late into the night. Patrick would not concede a point if he had facts to back it up.

"We'll leave Nairobi midmorning," Arthur continued. He had on a white shirt, the sleeves rolled to the elbows, a striped tie. He had a pallor that seemed unusual in Africa, a perpetual five o'clock shadow emerging from his skin.

Diana had on a blue cotton sundress. Her skin had the patina of an outdoorswoman. She had recently cut her bright blond hair, a practical gesture that lent her a gamine look.

"We'll take the Thika Road and have a comfortable night, I should think, at the lodge in Naro Moru," Arthur said. "Then we'll make our way to Park Gate, where we'll leave the Land Rover. At the gate, we hire the guide and the porters who will carry the food and gear. They're meant to be very good, by the way. Then it's straight up to Point Lenana. It's one of the steepest and fastest ways up, but an amateur can make it. It'll take four days, three nights, not including our stay at the lodge."

The meal was lamb with mint sauce. The table was elaborately set in the English mode. Beneath Margaret's place was a mat depicting Westminster Abbey. Patrick had St. Paul's. Each diner had his own silver saltcellar and tiny spoon. Arthur was generous with the wine, which he poured into cut-crystal goblets. The dinner plates might have been Wedgwood or Staffordshire. The ones in the cottage were mismatched and had chips in them.

Two children appeared from behind a door. Edward and Philippa, nine and seven, were being raised by an ayah named Adhiambo. The children came and went in school uniforms as if they lived in Kent and not just one road removed from a forest with antelope and lions and buffalo. Diana believed in bringing up children the British way, without excessive praise.

Adhiambo stepped from behind the door as well. She had a red head scarf over her hair and a pink sweater that might once have been part of a twinset. Her hips were wide, but she was young. Twenty-three, twenty-four, Margaret thought, though she was hopeless at decoding African ages. Adhiambo had a deep scar on her chin and a shy smile that revealed a row of gapped teeth. In her eyes, though, there was something Margaret couldn't iden-tify — something resilient or simply persistent.

"Say good night to Mummy," Adhiambo said to the children.

In their pajamas, they went to their mother for hugs and kisses that looked real and needy, small blots on a stoic ledger. Arthur demanded kisses and hugs as well. Margaret knew this already to be the evening ritual. Philippa looked like her father, with her long brown hair; Edward, a towhead, resembled Diana before the weathering. At first, Margaret had found the gender mismatch disconcerting. Diana mentioned riding; Arthur, tennis. Within minutes, the children and their ayah were gone.

"Bring gaiters for the vertical bog," Arthur continued. "Hats and gloves and parkas for the cold."

"What bog?" Patrick asked.

"Bog." Arthur seemed uncharacteristically at a loss for words. He held his arms wide. "You know . . . mud."

"Sunglasses to avoid snow blindness," Diana added. She seemed distracted by activity in the kitchen. Earlier, she had got-ten up from the table. James and Adhiambo weren't the only ser-vants. There were several men who worked in the kennels, as well as the askari at the gate. "And be sure to break in your boots."

Patrick shot a glance at Margaret.

"I don't have boots," she said. "I'm going to buy some tomorrow."

Arthur calculated. "You've got ten, eleven days. That should be sufficient if you work at breaking them in. Wear two pairs of socks."

"I might have boots that will fit you," Diana offered, stealing a glance at Margaret's feet in her sandals. She frowned. "Maybe not."

Margaret saw, in the doorway, James patiently waiting to clear the plates.

After-dinner drinks were offered in a room Diana called the drawing room. Margaret had a brandy while trying to describe to Arthur a "rusty nail," Scotch laced with Drambuie. Diana sat across from Margaret on an oversize chintz sofa and appeared to be impatient *to get going,* though going where Margaret wasn't certain. It seemed Diana's natural state. She lived not for the moment but for the one anticipated. Diana wasn't beautiful, but she was pretty. Margaret had guessed Arthur and Diana to be in their early to midthirties.

"How did you two meet?" Margaret asked.

Arthur, at the drinks table, answered without hesitation, as if repeating a marital legend. "We met at a party in London. Within five minutes, we'd worked out that each of us secretly yearned to go to Africa. In Diana's case, to return to Kenya, where she'd been raised. In my case, to get as far away from bloody London as possible."

Margaret noted that neither Arthur nor Diana looked at the other while Arthur told his brief story. Perhaps Diana wasn't listening. Perhaps she rued confessing that yearning.

Arthur raised his glass. All present raised theirs as well, though a toast had hardly been offered. Arthur, also, seemed a man on the move, having to harness an energy too great for the occasion.

On the marital balance sheet, Margaret guessed that Diana thought herself from better stock than Arthur. Margaret wondered if this counted for a lot. In her own marriage, Patrick was third-generation Irish, his distinctive gene pool noted for its fondness for medicine, the pointed chin, the black hair that didn't gray until well into the sixties, and the surprise of the pale-blue eyes. Beauty depended upon how these features had been arranged, and Patrick seemed to have gotten a goodly share. Patrick's father, a gynecologist, still had a brogue, a lovely accent that put all of his patients at ease.

As for Margaret, she came from a middle-class, suburb-north-of-Boston, Unitarian background with some history. A distant relative of hers had been commissioned as an officer during the American Revolution. Her mother had a plaque attesting to this fact hanging behind her bedroom door, though she was a rabid Democrat and had been since FDR.

Arthur turned his attention to Patrick. "So what's going to happen to all of us when Kenyatta dies?"

"I'm very surprised we haven't had this conversation already," Patrick answered.

The British seemed to have an unquestioning sense of legitimacy in Kenya. Americans did not. Margaret guessed the difference to be Vietnam.

Idly, while Kenyatta was being dispensed with, Margaret counted seventeen different patterns on the various fabrics and dishware. She looked around her at the room: the windows were casements, like those in Margaret's cottage, but there the resemblance between the two buildings ended. The furniture in the drawing room had carved legs and ornate surfaces, mass as well as decoration.

"Who's the other couple?" Margaret asked.

"On the climb? Saartje and Willem van Buskirk. I didn't tell you?" Diana seemed puzzled at this omission.

"He's part of the Hilton Group," Arthur said. No mention was made of what Saartje did. "We'll have them over this week for a planning session. You'll like them. No-nonsense. Very down-to-earth. I should think Willem has done Mount Kenya before."

"I don't remember that," Diana said.

"He used to climb in Switzerland before they went out to Bombay."

Diana nodded, and Margaret worried about the pace of the climb if one of their party was experienced.

"In addition to the hypoxia," Arthur continued, "almost everyone gets AMS of some form or another. Acute mountain sickness. Headache. Fatigue. Vomiting. Dizziness."

"This is supposed to be fun?" Margaret asked.

"I'm telling you all this because we're going to have to diagnose each other," Arthur said, a touch sternly. "Watch for signs."

Margaret nodded, suitably chastened.

"The huts fit between ten and thirty," Arthur went on. "One usually sleeps on cots. There are latrines, if you want to call them that. Not a trip for the squeamish."

"The Kikuyu think the mountain is sacred," Patrick offered, and Margaret was glad for the respite from the images of misery. "Their god Ngai is said to reside there. They call the mountain Kirinyaga."

*   *   *

Margaret had been taking a photograph of a physician, a man who had recently set up a series of free clinics for babies and toddlers to receive vaccinations and medical care in Roxbury, Boston's poorest neighborhood, not least because it was almost entirely black. Her paper, a Boston alternative weekly, had given Margaret the assignment that morning. She was having trouble presenting the doctor in a flattering pose: his glasses were magnifying lenses, and the overhead hospital light was too bright. Finally getting enough shots to ensure at least one her editor could use, Margaret realized that there was another doctor standing in the doorway, watching the shoot. When Margaret asked her subject where she might get a Tab and a sandwich, the man in the doorway answered first. "Come with me," he said. "I'll take you to the cafeteria. I'm headed that way myself."

Margaret packed up her equipment while the two physicians conferred about a matter she wasn't privy to. Then she followed the second doctor out the door and along a hospital corridor. "Patrick," the man said, turning and putting out his hand.

"Margaret," she said.

Patrick told Margaret over tuna on rye that he was completing a fellowship in equatorial medicine. He'd become interested in tropical diseases in medical school and had visited Africa twice. She thought he was a beautiful man, and she was fascinated by the unusual planes of his long face. Perhaps, she thought, she had fallen in love with those planes before she'd fallen in love with the man. Before coming to Africa, Margaret had photographed his face at least a hundred times. At first, Patrick was intrigued, then merely patient, and then mildly annoyed, as one might be with a child who wants to play the same game again and again.

When Patrick asked Margaret if she wanted to go to Kenya with him, she said yes with enthusiasm. Her job at the alternative paper wasn't progressing, and she was tired of photographing congressional meetings and folksingers in Cambridge coffeehouses. Patrick had attached himself to Nairobi Hospital, which he could use as a resource for as long as he wanted in exchange for conducting free clinics around the country when asked to do so.

Margaret and Patrick were hastily wed in a backyard in Cambridge. Margaret wore a long white cotton dress and wound her hair into a French twist. After the ceremony, they and their guests drank champagne on plastic deck chairs and an ornate sofa brought outside for the occasion. Patrick and Margaret sat in the sofa's plush center, fending off witty barbs and occasionally gazing at the stars.

At a good-bye dinner at her parents' house the night before Patrick and she were to fly out of Logan to Nairobi, Margaret couldn't imagine how she could go a year without seeing either them or her twelve-year-old brother, Timmy, born sixteen years after Margaret—a happy accident, her mother had explained. She pleaded with them to come visit her in Africa. No one in the family had ever used the word *love* before, though the connection among them was fierce.

On the plane, Margaret was mildly homesick. During the flight across the alien continent, the sun rising, her face pressed to the window, her breath fogging her vision, Patrick held her hand. If he was apprehensive, he didn't say so.

From the plane, she saw all the places she had read about in preparation for the trip: the Nile River, long and brown; Lake Turkana, once Lake Rudolf; the Rift Valley, vast and barren and unearthly; and then suddenly the Ngong Hills and the plateau on which Nairobi had been settled. In the distance, Margaret could see, rising above the clouds, Mount Kenya, and even, to the south, Mount Kilimanjaro. Before the plane set down, Patrick presented her with a silver ring, a small diamond at its center, something he hadn't been able to manage before the wedding. They landed on Margaret's birthday.

On the morning after the Mount Kenya climb had been proposed, an iridescent peacock greeted Margaret at Diana's front door. The bird, seen so close, seemed otherworldly, fraudulent. The peacock eyed her with indifference. What must it think, she wondered, of her own dull plumage?

Overhead, a jacaranda tree had again laid down its royal carpet. The air felt cool and rinsed. Margaret had on a belted white cotton jacket over a yellow cotton dress. She would have to take the jacket off at ten a.m. At noon, she would want to be indoors. By three, she'd be fantasizing about a cold swim at the InterContinental. The jacket would go back on at six thirty, and by eleven, Patrick and she would be sleeping beneath a pair of down comforters. It was all a matter of altitude, Patrick had once explained.

Margaret inhaled the scent of burning leaves as she made her way to the car Patrick had left for her. He had taken the bus into town more than an hour earlier. The Peugeot was parked beside the cottage with the still-defunct plumbing. Margaret slid into the front seat, the floor tinged here and there with red marum. She set her straw bag on the passenger seat to her left. When she'd first arrived in the country, it had taken her nearly a week of trial runs to feel even mildly confident about driving on the left side of the road.

The scent of the smoke she'd brought with her into the Peugeot made her lean back and close her eyes. She wondered if Matthew, the gardener, burned marijuana leaves with the debris, as if the ganja were no more valuable than twigs. Absurd, Margaret thought, though she was fairly sure that something soporific was in the smoke. She inhaled deeply. The scent was both nostalgic and exotic.

A knock at her window startled her. Arthur, in suit and tie, motioned for her to roll down the window.

"The Mercedes won't start. I've called for a mechanic. I need a ride to the office. I have to leave the Rover for Diana to get the kids and so forth."

There could be no thought of refusing him.

"Get in. One good deed deserves another."

Margaret moved her straw bag. Arthur slid in, putting his arm across the back of his seat, a proprietary gesture that caused him to have to face Margaret. Arthur reestablishing the alpha male. She knew with certainty that if Patrick entered a car with a woman not his wife behind the wheel, there would be no proprietary arm. Patrick, unlike Arthur, would face pleasantly straight ahead.

They passed the duka and its gathering of African men in pressed shirts and pants, most smoking, many laughing. The men, Margaret knew, worked as servants and were meeting for a morning break after having done the shopping for the day. Most would have been up since four thirty, preparing meals for dogs and families. Were the Africans in the area mostly Luo, like James? She would have to ask. Already Margaret understood that though the country was deeply misogynistic and acutely aware of class as defined by money, the true animosity that kept man from man or woman from woman was tribal. Turkana, Nandi, Kalenjin, Kisii, Kipsikis, Kikuyu, Luo, Masai, and others. In Africa, a native man with dark skin was identified by tribe.

"I think it's fair to say you haven't mastered the roundabout yet," Arthur commented, eyebrow raised, as Margaret stopped for a matatu, listing and overloaded, moving into their lane.

"They're counterintuitive."

"To Americans. You call them something else."

"Rotaries."

"I think you need more practice."

"Thank you for noticing."

He made a *pshaw* sound that was distinctly British and couldn't be spelled. It meant *Don't be silly. Don't be ridiculous. Don't be so touchy.*

"Where can I drop you?" Margaret asked.

"At Mather House. I hope Diana told you that Saartje and Willem are coming to dinner tonight? We're meant to discuss the climb."

Arthur gestured toward the road Margaret should take.

"She did, and I'm on my way to buy boots."

"You'll conquer Mount Kenya."

Margaret was taken aback. "I don't think I'm capable of conquering anything, least of all a mountain. In any event, I didn't come here to conquer."

"Where are you from?"

She glanced briefly in his direction. He was studying her, as she had suspected.

"I grew up in a small town north of Boston. Went to college near Boston. Been living in Boston ever since."

"Why Boston?"

"It's close to my family, and it's a city."

"You're not for the rural areas, then."

Margaret laughed. "I guess not."

"Never been to Boston," he said in that accent of his that suggested a manufacturing town in the north of England. "Spent a lot of time in Arizona, though."

"Arizona?"

"Diana's parents moved there about ten years ago. They have a kind of mini-estate — I suppose you'd call it a ranch — just outside Phoenix. Diana's father plays golf. They went for his health. The climate. He's developing emphysema. Still smokes a pack a day. Prides himself on having cut down from three."

Once again, Margaret glanced in Arthur's direction. He was staring out his window. There was about him a quality of smugness that might attract a European woman but might put off an American.

She had conquered her third roundabout in twenty minutes when Arthur gestured. "It's just there."

She entered a circular driveway on the outskirts of the city that led to an office complex. It resembled a school built in the 1960s — concrete and utilitarian, without any attempt at charm. "Well." Arthur seemed reluctant to leave the car. "You're off to buy boots."

"Yes."

"Go to Sir Henry's." Arthur took a small notepad from an inner pocket of his jacket. He wrote down the address and handed her the slip of paper. "Ask for Tommy. He'll take care of you. Tell him Arthur sent you."

There it was again. *Take care of you.*

"That's it?" Margaret asked. "Just *Arthur?*"

"He'll know who it is."

* * *

Askaris stood guard in front of the shops on Kimathi Street. Margaret tipped a parking boy eight shillings, the equivalent of a dollar, to watch her car. She passed a Scandinavian store in which an African man was polishing silver. A sign in the window read *50 Shillings* but seemed unattached to any object. Next to the Scandinavian shop was a store called Crystal Ice Cream. The special that day was a serving of vegetarian Samosas. A man hawked and spit on the sidewalk, and Margaret had to maneuver around the glob. Farther along, another man was selling curios. She stopped merely to be polite but found a small gold-colored teapot and wondered to whom she might give it. At the bank stood a flank of askaris with drawn pangas and what looked to be ferocious guard dogs on leashes. Margaret noted that the many Africans who wanted to get into the bank passed the dogs with excessive caution.

She glanced at the scrap of paper Arthur had given her. Sir Henry's, she calculated, must be at the other end of Kimathi. She crossed the street and strolled, looking for the address. When she came to the intersection of Kenyatta and Kimathi, she saw men lying on the grass divider, some asleep. Barely avoiding them, other men in white shirts and ties were watering the grass and the bases of the palms. She walked by a gentleman in a white kaffi-yeh, followed by several women in the long black bui-bui that covered them head to toe, their faces veiled. Margaret could not imagine the discomfort the noonday equatorial heat might cause beneath that thick fabric.

In front of a shop called the Village, she eyed a simple four-bead necklace. The asking price was two hundred shillings. In the reflection from the window, she could see a tall, thin Masai with large holes in his ears pass behind her. He wore only a red blanket and carried a spear. Beyond him was a white teenager in a lime-green T-shirt pausing on a motorcycle at a light. The light turned, and she sped off.

An African woman at the charity sweepstakes booth barked in English and reminded Margaret of auctioneers in America. When the woman leaned back, Margaret saw that she was pregnant. Behind her was a Woolworth's in which one could buy cooking pans, secondhand books, used tires, and Cuisinarts. Margaret went inside and bought a guidebook to Mount Kenya. As she left the store with her purchase, she saw a mother and her three children sitting on the sidewalk with their backs to the wall. The woman was in the same dress she'd worn every time Margaret had seen her. The baby, who had on a dirty shirt and nothing else, stood up, squatted, and shat on the sidewalk. Beside the woman was a tin cup with a few shillings in it. Margaret still held her change in her hand and dropped it into the tin. *"Asante sana,"* the woman said with little energy. Before, when Margaret had passed by and put something in the cup, the beggar had put her hands together as if in prayer, repeating *"asante sana"* until Margaret was out of earshot. Patrick had warned her never to give money to the beggars, that by doing so, one could stir up a mob scene, other beggars rushing toward the point of donation.

An unexpected thirst caused Margaret to make a detour and cross the street to the New Stanley Hotel, a tall, white building filled with tourists. She noted cameras, safari jackets, binoculars, maps. As families waited for the zebra-striped minibuses to arrive, she heard English from the tourists, Swahili from the porters. In one family, the father, an older man of about fifty, counted the number of film canisters he had in his pockets. His wife had on a polyester blouse. The couple had two sons, one a teenager who looked bored already. The other, a boy of about ten or eleven, was dancing up and down, eager to see the lions.

In another familial grouping, a Midwestern woman was worrying her teeth with a toothpick. She said she was in a tizzy from the effort of trying to pack the contents of her four suitcases into two, the limit while on safari.

"I'm still not calmed down," she said.

"What day is the inaugural address this year?" the man next to her asked.

"The inaugural address?"

"Jimmy Carter? In America?"

"How should I know?"

Another man set a suitcase among the others to be collected.

"I just brought this tiny suitcase," he said. "What you see me in is what I'll be wearing for three days."

What Margaret saw him in was a pair of blue sneakers, brown-and-white patterned trousers, and a red polo shirt with white piping.

"I hear there's more ivory there," he said.

More than where? Margaret wondered.

She had a tall glass of iced tea at the Thorn Tree Café. She couldn't remember when iced tea had ever tasted so good. She fingered the mint and read the notes tacked onto the message board beside her. *Shenaz, I am needing my washing machine back. Peter Shandling, if you get this message, please call Mark at New Stanley House. Needed: Cocktail waitresses for Swiss embassy party on the 19th. Ask for Roger at the InterContinental.*

At the Thorn Tree Café, an African woman was not allowed to sit at a table without a man. If she did, she would be asked to leave. It didn't matter if the woman was a banker or an editor or owned her own shop and felt as desperate as Margaret had for a tall glass of iced tea. If the woman was an African, it was assumed she was a prostitute.

A dark man in an embroidered kaffiyeh wore a jacket with a Nehru collar. Margaret was having trouble observing the man because he was openly staring at her.

From where she was seated, Margaret heard five languages she could identify: English, Swahili, Urdu, German, and French. She thought there must have been at least four or five others just beyond her hearing and comprehension.

Margaret examined the menu. The prices were impressive. Didn't the tourists realize they were being fleeced?

At the next table, a foursome explained their dining instructions in exaggerated detail to the waiter, as if he might not understand English. When the waiter left, a woman at the table rolled her eyes.

At Margaret's left, two African students spoke in excellent, if accented, English. She missed most of the conversation but heard something that unnerved her. The government had rounded up fifty students at the university, one of them said. The students had been massacred and tossed into a mass grave.

Margaret was stunned. Was this a rumor, or was it true? If it was true, why didn't Patrick and she and everyone else know about it? Why wasn't it on the front page of the newspapers? Margaret sat still and listened for more, but the students had gone silent. Possibly one of them had seen her cock her ear in their direction. Maybe the other had cautioned silence.

*   *   *

Margaret searched for the boot shop and twice missed it, its discreet sign not intended to lure customers. She entered through a polished wooden door and took off her sunglasses. She guessed the enterprise to be as close to a bespoke shop as one could find in Nairobi. The men behind the counters and on the small floor were white. She saw immediately that women's clothes were displayed as well as men's. She wouldn't mention Arthur's name, even though, at dinner, she might have to say she had and had therefore received excellent service.

Margaret was allowed to browse before being accosted. In the end, she had to ask for help. She needed hiking boots, she explained. She was to climb the mountain in ten days' time and wanted something sturdy but flexible so that her feet wouldn't hurt. The slender young salesman snapped his fingers. An African associate brought out a device meant to measure her foot. She took her sandal off, exposing dust-covered skin.

"May I have a cloth?" Margaret asked.

It seemed not to be an unusual request. Two cotton cloths, one damp and one dry, were presented to her on a brass tray. After she washed, the African disappeared and the British salesman gently took her right foot and placed it in the measuring device. His hand on her heel and sole felt soothing. He asked her to stand up, and he recorded her size, a number she didn't understand. She was asked to sit and did so. When the man returned, he had a pair of silk socks that he gently pulled over Margaret's feet. It felt like a brief massage, and already she was wondering if she might not need another pair of shoes. The lambskin lining of the boots caressed her leg to midcalf. Patiently, the salesman tightened and tied the laces. The procedure was repeated with the second boot.

"I think you should walk around the store now," the salesman suggested. "Take your time. The fit of the boots is critical on such a climb."

Margaret walked the narrow aisles of the shop as if floating. She doubted she had ever owned a more comfortable pair of boots, or even shoes. Once, she bent down to touch the soft leather, and when she stood up, the salesman smiled.

"They're wonderful," Margaret said.

"They're sturdy in the soles and around your ankles. You could easily climb Mount Kenya in those."

Margaret gave a slight nod.

"You don't want to make the climb, do you?"

She was surprised. "No."

"You've been talked into it."

"Kind of."

"You'll do fine. It will be hell, but it will end, and you'll have done it, and you'll never have to do it again."

"How did you know that I didn't want to do the climb?"

"Women often come into the shop needing hiking boots. They all more or less have the same expression on their faces."

"And what would that be?"

"Fear."

He took off the boots and then the socks, and Margaret's feet felt as though they'd been plunged into cold water. When she reached the counter, the salesman handed her a piece of engraved letterhead with the price discreetly written in pencil. Why pencil? Was Margaret meant to bargain? The sum made her swallow, but she had no hesitation as she wrote the check. Patrick would understand.

The salesman concluded the transaction, coming around the

counter with the package in which the boots had been neatly wrapped and tied.

"It has been a pleasure serving you," he said with a slight bow.

"Thank you."

"Are you a tourist?"

"My husband is with Nairobi Hospital."

The salesman smiled. "Then I hope either you or your husband will return to our shop."

"I think we might."

Margaret was almost out the door when she decided.

"Is your name Tommy?"

The salesman looked surprised but answered, "Yes."

"Arthur sent me," she said.

Margaret returned to Crystal Ice Cream and ordered a pair of vegetarian Samosas and a Fanta. When the Samosas were handed to her on a paper plate, she took her food to a small table with a red Formica top. Next to her were two Asian men — Pakistani or Indian — who were sucking the marrow out of chicken bones and then eating the bones themselves.

Margaret took her plate back to the counter and asked for a bowl of ice cream. As she sat again at her table, one of the Asian men looked over. She wondered if it was odd to see a grown woman eating ice cream. In a city with so many different cultures, it might take years to learn the proper mores. As she slipped the banana-coconut onto her tongue, she knew there wasn't a chance of cream in the icy concoction. The name *Crystal* took on new meaning.

Margaret walked back to the place where she had left her car and was startled to note that there was no Peugeot where it was supposed to be. She thought she must be disoriented and examined each of the twenty vehicles parked along the side street. The boy to whom Margaret had paid eight shillings to watch her car was sitting on a fence—in her sight but ignoring her.

"Excuse me," Margaret said in English. "Aren't you the boy I paid to watch my car?"

The boy seemed not to have heard her. She repeated the request in Swahili. *"Nataka gari, tafadhali."*

"No, miss," he said quickly. "No, miss."

Margaret examined his face, his small body, his bare chest. She couldn't say for certain that he was the boy, though she trusted her instincts. "I want my car," she said calmly.

Again, he appeared not to understand her. Impatient now, Margaret repeated the sentence in Swahili.

"No, miss," the boy said, shaking his head. "No, miss."

Margaret thought she saw something of fright in the boy's eyes and made the statement again, this time in a slightly louder voice. An older and taller boy, muscled and fingering a baton, emerged from an unmarked doorway.

"You have problem, miss?" the larger boy asked. He had on a white undershirt and a pair of dark-blue trousers and seemed to possess an unexplained authority.

Margaret felt her hands go cold.

"Yes," she said as calmly as she could. "Around ten o'clock this morning, I parked my car, a white Peugeot, just here, and I asked this boy to watch it. I gave him eight shillings to do so."

The older boy spoke to the younger boy in a language Margaret didn't understand. The older boy turned toward her with exaggerated politeness.

"No, miss. Though I do not doubt that you believe you

are correct, you are much mistaken. There has been no white Peugeot of your description on this street all morning. My brother is extremely certain."

The taller boy took a step toward Margaret. Would he hit a white woman?

"This is infuriating," she said, her heart beating as if she were already climbing Mount Kenya. "I know what I did. I need that car. What's the point of paying eight shillings to someone to watch the car if it's not going to be here when I return?"

The street was empty. Margaret knew the older boy had seen her glance around. He turned toward the younger boy and argued with him in an angry voice. The young boy looked down at the sidewalk, seemingly repentant.

"My brother is very sorry to be infuriating you. I apologize for him since he is too stupid to do so himself. But I urge you on to find your white Peugeot, a kind of automobile which has not been seen on this street since before five o'clock this morning."

Margaret knew he wouldn't tell her what had happened to the car. She didn't have enough money in her straw bag for that kind of information.

She stood her ground for a minute, maybe two, and then walked away. She knew that they were smiling and that the minute she rounded the corner, they would put their hands over their mouths and laugh.

Margaret meant to go directly to the police station. But first she investigated all the side streets off Kimathi in case she hadn't been paying attention when she had parked the car. She found two white Peugeots, but neither of them was hers. She thought about what might turn out to be an hours-long rigmarole at the police station and felt exhausted. She walked on until she reached the New Stanley Hotel. She went into the Thorn Tree Café and used the telephone attached to the message board. She bent her head to the pole, the flat of a tack making a small dent in her forehead. She called Patrick at the hospital.

"The car's been stolen," she said.

"It's not supposed to be like this," Patrick insisted, fists hard on his thighs. He sat across from Margaret at a table at the Thorn Tree. She knew he meant that the thieving wasn't part of his participation in Kenya, his hope for Kenya. That it had happened to them—and four times—hurt him. Patrick's anguish, which was real enough, had turned his skin blotchy. They were drinking Tuskers, which were not delivering on promised consolation.

Patrick raised his eyes to hers. "You all right?" he asked. Earlier, when he'd made his way to her table, she'd stood and embraced him, and he hadn't let her go until she'd stopped shaking.

"I am now. I'm just wondering what they'd have done if I hadn't backed off."

Patrick took in a sharp suck of air.

"I just dread the red tape at the police station," Margaret said, trying to change the subject. "You must have gone through it with the tires."

Patrick nodded. "I'll call Arthur from here. He'll give you a ride home."

"He can't," she said. "I gave him a ride in."

"You gave Arthur a ride to town?"

"His car wasn't working. Diana needed the Land Rover for the kids."

Patrick took a long pull on the Tusker. "What do you think of Arthur?"

Margaret was surprised by the question. It seemed literally to be out of order, something they might have discussed in fifteen minutes' time. She assembled her answer, unsure of Patrick's reason for asking.

"He's smug and a bit arrogant. I can't tell if he's like that around us because we—I—am a naive American. Though I suspect that's his nature. Sometimes I think he means well, and sometimes I think we're a kind of plaything for him—a dog's squeaky toy."

"But the fact is," said Patrick, "this country needs the Arthurs of this world in order to stay afloat. They need his company's capital, too. It's common knowledge that when Kenyatta goes, the tourism will collapse. They're desperate for some kind of industry—not just coffee or the distribution of crafts."

"So you like Arthur," Margaret said, somewhat amazed that her husband could so quickly make a cost-benefit analysis of a human being. She wondered if he had ever done the same with her but then dismissed the idea.

"I reserve judgment on pretty much everyone until he or she has done something egregious."

"What about Diana?" Margaret asked.

"Diana's elitist and deeply preoccupied."

"With what?"

"Her dogs."

Margaret laughed. She took a sip of Tusker and leaned back into her chair. The café was half full, the expats having the edge.

"Come back with me to the hospital," Patrick said, opening his wallet. "We'll get you a ride from there, and then I'll tackle the police."

She glanced at a nearby table and saw what looked to be a student drinking a cup of tea and reading a textbook. She thought about the rumor she'd overheard just hours earlier. She leaned forward and lowered her voice. "Patrick, do you know anything about fifty students being massacred and thrown into an unmarked grave?"

Patrick's body went still, as if each muscle were shutting down, one by one. "Where did you hear that?" he whispered.

"Here. I overheard two students talking at the table next to me."

Patrick moved closer. "What else did you hear?"

"Why?" She studied Patrick's face. "It's true, isn't it?"

He looked away.

Margaret reached out and grabbed his arm. She felt something like aftershocks on the surface of his skin.

"Why hasn't it been reported in the press?"

Patrick was silent for a time. "No newspaper in this country would print that story."

"Why not?"

"The press, Margaret, is controlled by the government. Anyone who printed something like that would be out of a job and probably arrested."

"Couldn't *we* get the story out, then?" she asked, having no clear idea of what she was suggesting. "Feed it to the *New York Times*? Or anyone? I mean...this...this is huge, isn't it? Fifty students in a mass grave?"

"We'd immediately be deported. Or worse." He did not define the *worse*. "I have only hearsay myself, and I can't reveal who told me, for obvious reasons."

"It doesn't feel right," Margaret said, shaking her head. "This is crazy."

"It feels crazy if you're an American on American soil. It's easier to understand if you're sitting at a café in Nairobi."

Margaret wondered if that was true. "Isn't it worth it to be deported in order to bring this thing to light?" she asked. "Why were they killed?"

"They're rumored to be part of a student group protesting the arrest of the novelist Thomas Oulu. He's being held without benefit of trial."

"Why?"

"For writing material the government considers seditious."

"These protesters, they're just kids, though."

Patrick looked off and then leaned in close to her. "If I say one word to the *Evening Standard,* just to use that as an example, I can't be sure the editor won't pass this information on to someone in the government. In fact, he'd almost have to if he was even considering investigating the story. And if he did, I would be arrested, and possibly you, too. And I'm guessing it wouldn't take them too long to work out who my source was. That man would be arrested, possibly executed. His family would almost certainly suffer reprisals. But let's say I don't do that. Let's say I leave this country voluntarily and go directly to the *New York Times.* They, too, are going to want my source—a source I can't give them. And if they miraculously decide to pursue this story anyway and assign someone to investigate, will anyone with certain knowledge speak to an American reporter? Fear of family reprisals keeps most Kenyans mute."

"Maybe you underestimate the skills of good reporters."

"Do I?"

"When did you know?"

The student at the next table glanced up at Margaret.

"About a week ago," Patrick said, again keeping his voice to a whisper.

"And you didn't tell me?" she asked.

"I don't think I'd have told you until I knew it was true. And maybe not even then. I wish I didn't know."

"How can you live with this knowledge?"

Patrick spoke fast. "The same way I can live with the knowledge that the Mathari slum is a hellhole, that it's not an uncommon occurrence for a panga gang to stop a vehicle at night and machete all the passengers, and that ruthless corruption from the top down will get significantly worse when Kenyatta dies."

"And yet you were eager to come here. For what?"

"To do my bit? To selfishly study something of great interest to me? To further my career?"

"You do it to save lives," Margaret said.

"I hope so."

She smiled.

"You all set?" he asked.

Margaret gathered up her straw bag and the package of boots she had bought earlier. Patrick stood and left some shillings on the table.

As she and Patrick left the café and passed through the lobby, she slid her hand up under his rolled shirtsleeve. It felt safer there.

Arthur seemed mildly amused. Diana was appalled. A cloud had burst and was sending down a drenching rain so dense and thick Margaret couldn't see a single thing beyond the windows. They were sitting in a small room off the drawing room that hadn't yet been identified. Tea had been brought in by James, and Diana was pouring. Margaret noted that her own hands were trembling and wondered, *Why now, when I am safe?*

Patrick sat across from Margaret, having just returned from changing a shirt that had soaked through in the run from the car to the house. Diana had driven into the city to fetch them. Margaret had waited in the car with her while Patrick had gone into the police station to file the paperwork.

"You poor dear," Diana had said repeatedly, as if Margaret were her niece.

On the way home, with Patrick in the backseat, the storm had started. It would stop, Margaret knew, as suddenly as it had begun, and within minutes the sun would light up the wet landscape so that it glittered with hidden jewels scattered in the trees and sprinkled along the grass. She had been frightened as Diana had driven through the heavy rain, unwilling to stop and wait it out. Visibility had been nil.

"The point is," Arthur was saying, "that you're supposed to give the parking boys five shillings to watch the car, with the promise of five more shillings when you return. Thus ensuring that the vehicle will be there when you want it."

Margaret wondered if she could have negotiated that bargain in Swahili. She had a silent go at it, drawing a blank with the subjunctive.

"What is it now? Four times you've been robbed?" Arthur counted, trying not to shake his head and smile. Margaret hated the man in that moment.

"I've been paying the boys eight shillings the whole time we've been here," Margaret said in her defense, immediately regretting it.

"My point exactly."

"Arthur," Diana scolded.

"It'll turn up," he offered in a more conciliatory tone. "They always do. Some wog needs a car to go visit his wife at the shamba. He can't possibly hire a car on his own, so he makes a deal with the parking boys. That older boy you spoke of? He's fifty shillings richer tonight. Well worth it to him. It would have cost the wog half his wages to pay the boy, so I'm guessing his errand was urgent. A sick child? A need to deliver money fast? A family dispute that might turn violent? Who knows?"

"And when he's done," Diana said, "he'll abandon the car within walking distance of a matatu so he can get back into the city. It almost always works like that."

Margaret's hands were shaking so much, she didn't dare pick up her teacup. Arthur, always vigilant, noticed.

"I think we can segue right into whiskey," he declared. "What time is it?" He stood and checked his watch, as if the time made any difference. He put his hand briefly on Margaret's shoulder, making it clear that he was *taking care of her*.

Margaret welcomed the whiskey. She pondered getting tipsy. It seemed as good a way as any to introduce herself to Saartje and Willem, who were arriving at seven. Get mildly looped, have a bath, meet Saartje and Willem. At least it was a plan. She picked up the copy of the *Kenya Morning Tribune* that was on the table. Patrick watched her as she examined the front page. Margaret hoped Saartje and Willem were the forgiving kind. There was something profoundly humiliating in having one's car stolen. It suggested a naïveté that went beyond mere nationality.

"Well, here's some good news," Diana said. "The plumber has been found and is coming tomorrow. I can't promise he'll get it fixed in one day, though, God, I hope so. Otherwise, he'll be sleeping here, too. Well, not here."

Margaret understood. The plumber would sleep with James in the cement box just behind the garage that James shared with the evening askari. It was thought to be an excellent arrangement: one worked days, the other nights. Margaret had never been in the cement hut, though she was curious.

"Great," she said, trying not to sound too relieved.

"Except they do the cattle rustling with automatic weapons now," Willem was saying while Arthur chuckled.

The meal, a *joint,* as Diana had referred to it, with gravy and potatoes, had revived Patrick. His skin looked tanned and healthier now. Margaret knew she'd had too much to drink and was showing it by slurring certain words. She tried to say as little as possible. Patrick glanced at her several times during the meal, assessing her condition. He was forgiving her, Margaret knew, because of the incident with the parking boys. Saartje seemed a bit cool toward Patrick and Margaret, though it was clear she was fond of Diana. The bond, the glue, that cemented the two couples was there, Margaret thought: Saartje and Diana. Willem played manager in chief, which, in fact, he was. In the matter of climbing Mount Kenya, Arthur deferred to Willem, which made a pleasant change. Diana, of course, deferred to no one.

Saartje, too, had weathered skin but was tall and lovely with nearly white-blond hair, turquoise eyes, and full, unpainted lips. Willem was overweight and nearly bald, and seemed the prototypical burgher, partial to beer and sausage. Saartje was taller than her husband, which only emphasized Willem's robust figure.

In the drawing room after dinner, Diana and Saartje, the two blondes, sat close together on the claret-striped sofa. Willem leaned over the coffee table with papers spread out before him. Patrick was languid in a wing chair, his reclined body making a diagonal line. Arthur seemed to have no seat at all, supplying and resupplying drinks, fetching guidebooks he just knew he had somewhere. He was serving Margaret rusty nails, which he'd already learned to make for her. She thanked him for that effort and success, though she wondered at his motives. Margaret loved the familiar smoky taste of the first drink but was wary of the second. For just a moment, her vision blurred when she swung her head in Patrick's direction. But then a double image coalesced, and all was well.

"We leave Nairobi at nine in the morning," Willem said. "That's Saturday, the twenty-second. We'll spend the night at a lodge at the base of the mountain. I've made all the arrangements. Got us quite a deep discount, too."

Thanks were expected and received.

"I'm driving," Diana said. "If we use the Rover, and I'm assuming we are, I'm driving."

"Yes," Willem said, adding that the Rover would fit all six of them with the gear tied down on top. "The next morning we'll make our way to Park Gate to pick up the porters. One per couple, then a guide and a cook. Five in all." He paused. "Oh, and a word to the wise? Don't show up Sunday morning with a hangover. Won't do you any good on the climb. Staying hydrated is key, and starting off with a fuzzy mouth will make the first day a nightmare."

"Arthur," Diana said, and left it at that.

"On Sunday, we walk from Park Gate to Met Station. Helps with the acclimatization. Who's provisioning the food?"

"I will," Patrick said. "I assume there's a decent list some-where?"

"I have recommendations," Willem said, lighting a cigarette. "And I'll tell you this about food. We don't want to skimp here. Last time I did the climb, we subsisted on dried food. Bloody awful. We'd be eating the crud and look over at the next party, and they'd be having hot soup and coffee."

"I'll keep that in mind," Patrick replied. Margaret noted that he hadn't broken his diagonal to volunteer.

"Staying at Met Station will be tough. The altitude plays with your sleep. I highly recommend Nytol. But we'll get to the meds in a moment. Who's doing meds?"

"I will," Margaret said. It seemed a chore she could handle.

Willem handed out paper and pens for everyone to take notes with. Margaret wrote on hers: *Meds*. She knew Patrick would help her.

"You'll each be responsible for your own gear, though the porters will carry it. Sleeping bag. Foam mat. Parkas. Rain gear. Hats and sunglasses are a must. The sun is brutally strong when it comes out, even if you don't feel the heat. Snow blindness is sometimes a real problem. Wear wool or synthetic socks. Never cotton. Speaking of which, always walk with two pairs of socks. If one gets wet, you can just peel it off. Keep your essential stuff in your backpack, since you might get separated from your porter for several hours."

"How's that?" Margaret asked.

Willem turned to her and smiled. He smiled a lot, Margaret realized, a great big Dutch burgher smile with lots of teeth. "They might go ahead and set up camp," he suggested, "when the trail is fairly obvious to us, for example."

She nodded. She hoped she wasn't exaggerating the earnestness of the nod.

"The Teleki view is astonishing," Willem said. "After that, we make a brief descent and then a very tiring climb to Mackinder's Camp, where we'll spend the night. Saturday. Sunday. Monday. Monday night. We want to get there quickly and have an early night. We're supposed to wake up at two a.m. the next day."

"Ouch," Patrick said.

Margaret couldn't shut her eyes, even for a moment. Sharp focus was required to keep the room from spinning. She wished she could ask for a thick piece of cake to absorb some of the alcohol, but they'd already had the dessert, a sherry trifle. It was the third or fourth they'd had at Diana's table. Perhaps Margaret could find some of the leftovers in the kitchen, though probably not. James almost certainly had cleaned up by now. He might even be asleep in the concrete hut at the back of the garage. Diana and Saartje were laughing at something Margaret hadn't heard. They were drinking crème de menthe in champagne glasses. Margaret could smell the sickening liqueur from where she sat.

"Day three of climbing. The scree and the glacier." Willem stubbed out his cigarette. "We climb in darkness most of the way. I don't generally like to do the glacier in the dark, so we'll leave a bit later. Three o'clock would be good. That way, we'll just get to it at daybreak. The glacier will be bloody."

Margaret thought about the notion of a glacier on the equator. Did it melt and freeze, melt and freeze? Or had it been frozen for eons?

"I won't lie. The scree is brutal. You're looking at three hours of very steep climbing and deep breathing. It's usually there that the AMS kicks in. The guide and the porters will see us across the glacier. Mind what they say. They've done it hundreds of times. We'll all be clipped into a guide rope, anchored by the guide and the porters. The guide will have a pickax with which to make the footprints that we will follow. It's scary as hell and thrilling. We traverse the glacier at a steep angle, and, believe me, it's a long way down." He took a sip of his drink. "Then it's off to Top Hut. Those who are fit enough at that point will attempt the summit. Let's see. There are six of us? Only two will make the summit."

"What will happen to the rest of us?" Margaret asked.

"You'll be moaning on your cot with headache, or you'll be hurling. Of course, one hopes for the former. Misery enough, the headache. Takes about forty-five minutes straight up through a snowfield to make it to the top. Quite a reward if you get there."

"Well, isn't that the whole point?" Diana asked. "To get there?"

"Do you think so?" Arthur countered. "I should have thought the climb itself was the point. To have done it, I mean."

"Right now, I wouldn't mind having done it," Patrick said.

Margaret smiled at her husband.

"And then we have to go down," Arthur said, clearly relishing that part of the trip.

"Swift descent," said Willem. "Be careful on the scree. Easy to break an ankle there. Now the medical. Two really severe conditions: HAPE and HACE. HAPE is identified by bloody frothing at the mouth. HACE by ataxia, slurred speech, general confusion. No cure but to get off the mountain as soon as possible. And sometimes even that doesn't work. HAPE is deadly serious stuff."

Margaret thought, but didn't mention, that she might be having a touch of HACE at that moment.

"So here's what we need," Willem said, turning to Margaret. "Aspirin for fever and headache, ibuprofen for muscle aches, paracetamol for colds, Diamox as a prophylactic for AMS, Imodium to stop you up if you get the runs, oil of cloves for dental use, and water-purification tablets."

"I thought we were carrying our water," Saartje said, her first foray into the conversation, though she'd said plenty to Diana.

"The porters can't possibly carry enough water for all of us for four days. We'll be getting our water from streams."

"Not actually," objected Arthur.

"Yes, actually," said Willem.

"Right."

"So where were we?"

"Water tablets," Margaret said, reading from her list.

"Oral rehydration salts for the replacement of fluids, and the Nytol for sleeping, of course."

"Somebody better bring the booze," Saartje said. "This whole thing sounds bloody boring."

"It is, in a way," Willem agreed. "Boring. There's a lot of time at the huts to kill. You think you'll want to play cards or drink or talk, but you won't. You'll just want to eat and sleep. And definitely no booze. Surest way to kill yourself up there."

"I suggest we do a practice try on the Ngong Hills," Arthur offered. "Break in our old boots, get our legs under us. What do you say?"

"When?" asked Diana. "I have a client coming from Mombasa on Saturday."

"Sunday?"

"Sounds fine to me," Patrick said, looking at Margaret.

For a moment, Margaret wondered what all this had to do with parking boys and mass graves and infants shitting in the streets. The room spun out of control, and even the hardest focus on Patrick's face failed to make it stop. She prayed for him to notice.

Margaret slept, then woke, then slept again. When she woke for the second time, she needed water and went into the bathroom with a glass. She picked up the Mount Kenya guidebook and wandered from the guest room along a hall and into the drawing room, which happily had stopped its spinning. She hadn't been out of the guest bedroom at night since Patrick and she had temporarily moved in. Margaret was hoping that by tomorrow they would be sleeping in their own bed in the cottage.

Patrick had gently taken Margaret by the elbow and made his good nights to those assembled in the drawing room. He'd mumbled something about what a hard day it had been for his wife. She'd fallen onto the bed the minute they'd entered the bedroom, and he'd had to slide what clothes he could manage off her. When Margaret woke, she had on a slip and a blouse with complicated fastenings.

A light was on in the drawing room—a security light, she thought. She sat on the claret sofa. She knew that her notes were inadequate and that Patrick and she would have to piece the meds together from memory.

Her head ached, and her mouth was dry. Humiliating that she'd shown how little she could handle drink. Rusty nails. Never again. Margaret drained her water glass, got up, found a bowl of melted ice on the cocktail tray, and poured the contents into her glass. She drained that one as well. She went back to the couch and lay down, propping her head on a throw pillow. She reached over for the guidebook and began to read about Mount Kenya. Its history intrigued her.

The mountain, she read, was the second of the three highest peaks in Africa to be discovered by European explorers. Dr. Johann Ludwig Krapf, a German missionary, was the first to note the mountain, which he viewed from Kitui in 1849. Dr. Krapf learned that the Embu didn't climb the mountain because of the intense cold and the white matter that rolled down it with a loud noise.

In 1887 Count Sámuel Teleki of Transylvania was the first European to climb the mountain. He reached 14,270 feet on the southwestern slope.

In 1893 an expedition managed to ascend Mount Kenya as far as the glaciers. They spent several hours on Lewis Glacier, unable to traverse it.

In July of 1899 Sir Halford John Mackinder set out for Mount Kenya with six Europeans, sixty-six Swahili, two Masai guides, and ninety-six Kikuyu. They made it as far as the mountain but had difficulties with plague, famine, deserters, and thieves. Two of their party were killed by marauders.

When a relief party reached the mountain, Mackinder traversed the Lewis Glacier. They reached the summit of Batian, another peak at the top of Mount Kenya, at noon on September 13.

During the Second World War, three Italian prisoners, led by Felice Benuzzi, escaped from their POW camp in Nanyuki to climb Mount Kenya. They did it because Benuzzi longed to reach the top of the mountain he'd been staring at for months. Later, according to their original plan, they "escaped" back into the prison.

On the practice hike, they walked in tandem, Willem leading, Saartje behind him; Diana, then Arthur, following; Patrick and Margaret taking up the rear. Margaret asked Patrick to allow her to be last, since she was likely to be the slowest, but Patrick argued that it wasn't safe. Best to have a man at the head and foot of a climb, he added. Margaret thought of protesting on feminist grounds but wondered if Patrick knew something she didn't. She looked ahead and saw that no one was carrying any weapon that she could see.

Margaret discovered her limitations almost at once, the altitude making her breathe hard, causing an audible beat in her chest. The rest had all worn shorts and looked like trekkers in their high socks and weathered boots. Willem and Arthur actually sported khaki shirts and shorts. Patrick had on a well-worn T-shirt that read *McGovern*.

Despite the slight punishment to the chest, exhilaration gave Margaret determination and made her light-headed. On the way to the first knuckle, the view of the Rift was beyond anything she had been prepared for—vast and deep and seemingly endless. The temperature down in the valley would be well over a hundred degrees. It might be possible for the inhabitants down there—the Masai, now too far away to be seen—to believe they are the sole people on earth, the chosen, in charge of, if not humbled by, all that surrounds them. To come from such raw beauty would almost certainly instill a sense of superiority. Margaret knew the Nilotic Masai to be intractable in their beliefs and customs: the nomadic life, their adherence to ritual, and their diet of cows' blood and milk, an unenviable regimen that nevertheless made them enviably lean and long.

They passed grasslands like English meadows, fields of wildflowers with dozens of species, some of which no one in the party could name. The climb produced, in addition to exhilaration, a soporific haze, and sometimes Margaret wanted nothing more than to leave the trail and lie down among those flowers. It seemed reward enough. Why climb farther away from paradise? Simply to say she'd done it? She vowed that after the Mount Kenya climb, Patrick and she would return to this spot and linger.

The landscape was green and fertile and rolling, and she understood at once why the Brits had settled here. They passed remnants of old farms: foundations, stone walls, and paths that seemed made by animals. Patrick came round from behind and put his arm over Margaret's shoulder.

"How are you doing?"

"I'm loving it," she answered, aware of the breathless quality of her words.

"Stop when you want and take a rest. We can always catch up. The trail is easy to follow."

Margaret wanted to say yes, let's leave the others, experience this as a couple, but something inside her (conformity? not wanting to cause a scene? pride?) made her smile and shake her head.

"I'm fine," she said.

When they finally stopped for a picnic, Margaret felt as though she couldn't take another step. The altitude had made the steady pounding beat more insistent. She needed water, and she wanted it soon. She forgot who had the water. In her own backpack, she carried a bottle of wine and a loaf of fresh-baked bread — delicious in other circumstances, of little use to her now.

She sat down where she stood. The lovely grass was deceptive: not soft but sharp and spiny and painful. She drew her knees up and bent her head to them. It was a defeated posture that embarrassed her, but it was the best she could manage. Patrick touched her back.

"Water," she whispered.

Patrick handed Margaret a canteen, and she held it with both hands, letting the water fall into her mouth.

"Easy, Margaret," he said. "This has to last the whole hike."

She stopped and held the canteen upright. She had drunk perhaps two-thirds of the water. She reasoned that the worst was over, that they had accomplished the long hike to the top of the Ngong Hills and had conquered at least one peak. She thought about her pompous pronouncement to Arthur in the car.

I didn't come here to conquer.

Arthur and Willem, who had been carrying wider packs than the rest, produced, as if by sleight of hand, canvas stools to sit on.

"Never sit directly on the grass," Arthur said when he delivered Margaret's. He helped her to stand and then to sit. She began to forgive him his pretentious khaki outfit. He didn't tell her why she couldn't sit directly on the grass.

Several feet away, Diana and Saartje had produced a magic canvas table. Everyone was to move closer to it and deliver his or her provisions. Below the table lay a piece of blue-and-red oilcloth the size of a large quilt. No one reclined on it. Margaret moved her stool to be within the gathering, and she sat, appreciating the give of the canvas seat. Saartje and Diana spread out a picnic worthy of the best safari expeditions: four kinds of sandwiches, the crusts removed; scones with butter and blackberry jam; tea for six; fresh loaves of bread such as Margaret had pulled out from her backpack to have with cheese; several bottles of wine; and a pineapple that Arthur sliced with expertise.

Margaret chose a little of everything, relishing the slices of pineapple handed to her: juicy, succulent pieces of fruit that seemed the most delicious food she'd ever eaten. The needy beast inside her tamed a bit, and she had a delicate cucumber sandwich, a cup of tea from a thermos, and a tear of bread with a slice of crumbly cheese that someone informed her was Caerphilly. Imported, it was pointed out. The Dutch and the British opened the wine almost immediately and drank from plastic cups, roughing it. When the wine was offered to Margaret, she declined on prudent grounds. She believed everything Arthur and Willem had said about alcohol and altitude. Patrick accepted a cup of wine and handed it to Margaret for a small sip, which she took. His manners and his understanding of her body—its possibilities and its limitations—were impeccable.

"I suppose the question...well, it's always the question, isn't it...is whether or not we ought even to try to bring the Masai into the twentieth century."

Willem laid the quandary on the table for all of them to admire and perhaps nibble at.

"I happen to think the effort essential," Arthur said. "They look regal, don't they, in their robes and maridadi, but if you travel to the manyattas, as I've done, you'd be horrified. Clusters of flies the size of tennis balls hover over the infants' eyes. The smoke in the huts is suffocating. Medicine is so primitive, it does more harm than good."

Margaret wondered why Arthur had had reason to visit the manyattas. Had he been trying to sell toothpaste to the Masai?

"But they aren't confused about who they are," Patrick countered. "They have an ancient nomadic society that has been largely unbroken for centuries. They are serious about protecting what is theirs, but they are a contented people. They are not listless or lazy or bored. They have deep beliefs in their gods and rituals and ceremonies."

"They have no education!" Arthur exclaimed.

"True. But they are educated within the mores of their tribe."

"But we *live* in the twentieth century. It's not the sixteenth century, for heaven's sake. People need to adjust, adapt, in order to progress. Anyway, Patrick, yours is a very unlikely position coming from a physician."

"Well, let's take the Kikuyu," Patrick said. "They've been brought into the twentieth century—kicking and screaming, some of them. They, too, before the advent of the British, had a cohesive society. Then they had their land taken from them, were dragged into slavery—"

"Not slavery," Arthur said, having torn off a hunk of bread with his teeth. "Don't overdramatize."

"Servitude, then. As good as indentured, in my opinion. The men flocked to the cities to earn European wages, which, though pitifully small by our standards, represented progress to certain Kikuyu families. But those families, still on the shambas, no longer had fathers and brothers at home. Shantytowns built up in the cities, prostitution arrived, and some essential fabric that was Kikuyu life was torn."

"The Kikuyu run the country and are bloody corrupt," Arthur said with some vehemence.

"Are you arguing that James, for example, was better off back at the shamba, never having traveled to Nairobi at all?" Diana challenged.

Diana, by mentioning James, had effectively ended the discussion. Patrick could not respond as he might have, that James lived the bleakest of lives, cut off from his wife and children fifty-one weeks a year in order to serve another family and live in a concrete box. Such a person, Patrick might have argued, could be forgiven for wondering what the Mau Mau Rebellion had been about and what exactly *uhuru* meant. Not freedom for James, surely. Patrick sipped his wine, unwilling or unable to use another example to prove a point that the British and possibly the Dutch would never concede anyway.

"Finch Hatton is buried here somewhere," Saartje said, gesturing in a vague direction toward the grave site of Karen Blixen's lover. "We must be sure to visit the obelisk."

"Arrogant philanderer," Arthur pronounced with a moue of disdain. "Bloody awful to Tanne while she was here." He spoke as though he had personal knowledge of Karen Blixen's bloody awful treatment, even though he was a long generation removed from her.

"I, for one, would love to see the grave," Margaret said.

"Women," Arthur said. "Hopeless romantics. Well, if one goes, we all go," he said with reasonably good cheer. "Have to stay together. Can't break up the team."

"I'd like to see the spot, too," Patrick said, rising. "But I hope I'm allowed to take a leak without the team," he added, walking toward the nearest stand of trees.

"We'll send the girls to watch," Willem called, and chuckled at his own joke.

Girls, Margaret thought.

No one seemed eager to leave the picnic. When Patrick returned, he took from his backpack a kite of teal and yellow and red. He tied on the tail and let out a bit of string from a spool. He started to run sideways to give the kite a lift, and within seconds, the wind from the Rift caught it and took it aloft. It stuttered wildly as it tried to stabilize itself, but then it lifted into a different altitude and settled in with long, lazy swoops. They all watched, necks straining. Patrick returned and hitched the string to a leg of his stool.

"Marvelous," Arthur said. "The children would love it. Wouldn't they, Diana?"

"Love it," she repeated.

For fifteen minutes, perhaps twenty, Margaret photographed the kite, the landscape, the assembled. Around them, there was an easy silence. Patrick watched the kite, occasionally letting out string. Arthur sat, staring out into space, his elbows resting on his knees. Willem, who was slightly too big for his canvas chair, appeared nevertheless to be in the same trance as the rest of the group. He picked up a wine bottle and poured the dregs into his glass. Saartje, chin resting on hand, seemed to be trying to take in the Rift in one glance, which couldn't be done. Diana was simply resting, her posture loose and gentle.

A moment of perfect compatibility and ease. The last the six of them would have together.

Without warning, Diana stood. "Leave nothing. No food, no utensils, no trash."

Patrick reluctantly reeled in his kite.

"We'll do it again," Margaret said, reflecting, not for the first time, that Patrick would make a great father. He genuinely liked to play.

Margaret's backpack was considerably lighter; the bottle empty, the bread gone. She carried her own canteen now, not having realized that Patrick had carried it for her on the way up. Prior to the big climb, she vowed, she would spend the entire day drinking water. She might have to pee constantly, but she didn't ever want to experience that kind of urgent thirst again.

The oilcloth removed, Margaret stood, ready to carry on, while Willem and Arthur collapsed the stools and then tried to return them to their backpacks, an activity that proved more difficult than taking them out. As Margaret let her eyes roam over the Rift, she felt the first sting on her leg, the initial bite followed within seconds by dozens of others, as if she were being pricked hard by needles.

"Oh," she said, slapping at her jeans.

The men looked puzzled, but Diana, running in Margaret's direction, knew exactly what the problem was. "Shit!" she shouted. "Fire ants. She's standing in a nest."

Margaret swatted frantically. She looked down. A red mass was moving around her feet.

"Run!" Diana commanded. "Get your clothes off and run!"

"Oh," Margaret said, and then again. Ants had invaded her boots and her jeans and were nearing her crotch. She felt as though she were being assaulted by Africa itself, the ground rising up to sting her to death.

"I need a towel, someone!" Diana shouted.

Margaret peeled off her clothes, unbuckling her belt and slipping the jeans to her calves, while Saartje and Diana tried to get her boots off. Red welts had already risen on her legs. There were dozens of trails of the red ants, some of which Margaret could see through the nylon of her underpants. She tried to fetch them out but then realized it would take too long. She pulled the underwear down and ran away from it. After that, her blouse, her bra. Diana and Saartje brushed off every ant they could find. They inspected her hair.

"Oh God," Margaret said as they flicked ants from her back and neckline.

"Saartje," Diana said. "I have extra clothes in my pack."

Margaret wanted to levitate so that her feet no longer touched the ground. She knew that her clownlike antics would have seemed funny had the situation not been so painful. She noticed, in her nakedness, that Willem had turned away (Diana and Saartje seemed to have the situation well in hand) but that Arthur and Patrick were looking straight at her. Her husband, she understood, but what was Arthur up to? She shook the towel with a hard snap and wrapped herself in it. Arthur swiveled his head away but not before Diana saw the move.

Diana's clothes were too small on Margaret, the shorts tight, the blouse not long enough.

"What do I do about these?" Margaret asked, pointing to her clothes, strewn in a nearly straight line as she had danced away from the nest of red ants. They reminded her of garments abandoned on the way to a bed.

"Leave them where they are," Diana said. "Don't go near them. They're still full of ants."

Patrick ran and snatched the hiking boots, holding them out in front of him, shaking them, tossing away the socks. He slapped at his wrists. The boots had to be saved.

The welts on Margaret's body began to swell. She had them on her face and arms, torso, legs, and back.

"They've been known to kill people," Diana said, putting her hand to Margaret's forehead as if she expected fever already. "Good thing you weren't alone."

The image of herself alone in the Ngong Forest was one Margaret dismissed at once.

She thought about Arthur's face and wrapped the towel around her waist as if it were a khanga. She put on the hiking boots that Patrick had so painstakingly inspected. Margaret walked with care, never looking up, wary of another sting from a hiding ant. Her lips swelled, which required a stop, during which Patrick inspected them. He asked if anyone had any Benadryl, but no one did. "Add that to the list," Willem said, but all Margaret could do was nod. It was too painful to speak. Patrick let her lean on him as they made their way back to the Rover. There would be no visit to Finch Hatton's grave that day.

Diana, tight-lipped, led them off the Ngong Hills. Arthur, Margaret noticed as they made a turn, was bringing up the rear.

Later, there was talk of postponing the big climb. But Margaret was adamant. They would go. Diana insisted as well. "She'll be fine," she predicted. "Perfectly fine."

When she had returned to their own cottage, ants invaded Margaret's dreams as they would a picnic lunch: the giant brown euphorbia tree outside her bedroom window seemed to be coming through the screen and poking her from time to time. Patrick gave her pills. The welts began to itch, and then to bleed when she scratched them. Patrick covered her with bandages to keep her from scratching the welts raw. At night, she was terrified by what might be under the bed. She wore only platform shoes and watched her feet incessantly when she began to venture out of the house. She thought to herself that she wouldn't be able to see the summit of Mount Kenya because she wouldn't dare take her eyes off the ground.

On Wednesday night, when Margaret was, as Diana had predicted, perfectly fine, Patrick and she heard banging on the front door. Patrick grabbed a thick stick he kept in the closet. He told Margaret to go to the bedroom and lock the door, but she didn't. How would Patrick survive if she locked him out? Patrick called through the door, and even Margaret could hear Diana's voice. Diana stepped into the living room just as Margaret came around the corner. With Diana was Adhiambo, the children's ayah, holding a cloth over her mouth and nose, trying in vain to cover her face.

"She says she's been raped," Diana announced. One had only to look at the young African woman to know that something terrible had happened to her. Her blouse was torn, and her pink-and-red khanga had a long mud stain running from her ankle to her hip.

"She came to us for help," Diana said. "But I can't have her in the house when the children wake up. I simply can't. Not in the state she's in now. I'd like to leave her here with you, if that's all right. Well, it has to be all right. In the morning, James will walk her home and make sure her room is securely locked."

"Sure," Margaret said, reaching out her hand to beckon Adhiambo in. Margaret stopped, aware of the terror Adhiambo might feel at a stranger's touch. Or would a woman's touch be welcome?

Diana wiped her brow with the back of her arm. "Trouble comes in threes," she said.

It wasn't until Margaret had shut the door that she wondered what number Diana was on.

Adhiambo wouldn't speak. Patrick wanted to get her to a hospital, but she shook her head vehemently when he suggested it. The cloth she was using to hide her face was bloody, and Margaret noticed a swelling at her eyebrow, nearly an egg. She gave Adhiambo a glass of water. Margaret wanted to ask her what had happened, but she already knew the woman wasn't ready to talk to anyone. Patrick, frustrated, picked up the phone.

"No," Margaret told him, and he put it down.

"At least let me take a look at her."

Margaret explained to Adhiambo that Patrick was a doctor and that he just wanted to check to see if she was all right. Again, Adhiambo shook her head and headed for the door.

Margaret raced around and stood in front of her. "No one will touch you," she said. She turned and backed through the living room, encouraging Adhiambo to follow her. Margaret urged the woman into the bedroom.

"I will run you a bath," Margaret said. Adhiambo stood still. There were small bloody smears where she had walked. Margaret saw the scene: the broken window, the bits of glass underfoot.

"Before you get into the bath, please check your feet. You might have stepped on glass. Wait until the bleeding stops before you get in. If you need plasters for after, I have some in the medicine cabinet."

Margaret entered the bathroom and opened the taps in the tub. From a shelf, she took two fresh towels, which she set upon a dressing table. Before she let Adhiambo in, she found a set of clean underwear, a khanga, and a blouse. Adhiambo and

Margaret were roughly the same size. She set the clothes on the dressing table as well. She nodded, and Adhiambo entered the bathroom. For a moment, Margaret wondered about suicide. She found Patrick's razor and the pair of scissors in the cabinet and muttered something about needing them. The woman seemed too beaten down to have the energy to take her own life. Margaret left and shut the door.

She stripped the bed and made it with clean sheets. Again, she took certain personal or harmful items of Patrick's and hers from drawers and gave them to Patrick to stash elsewhere. She asked him to get out the air mattresses they had purchased for the climb and start blowing them up. Margaret sat at the edge of the bed, then nervously got off it to put her ear to the door. She heard no crying. Only the occasional swish of water. Margaret couldn't even begin to imagine what the woman was thinking.

When Adhiambo emerged in Margaret's clothes, her hair wrapped in a towel, she was carrying her own dirtied clothing in a neat ball made by her blouse. Margaret held her hands out to take them, but Adhiambo quickly moved away from her. Instead, Margaret gestured to the bed. She put her hand on its taut blanket. Adhiambo nodded, unable to demur or refuse. She was beyond all niceties now.

Before Margaret left, she turned down the bedspread, exposing the sheets. She had an image of Adhiambo lying on top of the blanket, trying to disturb the bed as little as possible. Already the woman was shivering. Margaret wanted her under the covers.

When Margaret shut the door, Patrick was finishing with the second mattress. His face was red. He pinched the nozzle and took a breath. "This is going to be a bitch at higher altitudes," he said. "Maybe this wasn't such a good idea."

Margaret's hands, always the first indication of shock, started to tremble.

"You should have let me call for help," he said.

"She wouldn't have gone."

"Maybe she's really hurt. Internally. I could have examined her."

"You saw her. She almost left. Then what state would she be in? And where would she have gone?"

"Fucking hell," Patrick said.

"We'll let her sleep. In the morning James will come, and she'll talk to him, I think. Then he'll tell us what happened. At that point, we may be able to get her to go to a clinic."

"You think so?" he asked.

"No. She'll never accuse anyone. She'd be a pariah, perhaps ostracized from her family. You saw her face."

"Shamed."

"Yes, shamed. It isn't like at home."

Patrick shook his head. "There," he said when he had finished blowing up the second mattress. He collapsed onto his back.

They unrolled the sleeping bags. They had no pillows. Patrick found their down jackets and punched them into pillows. Not a perfect arrangement, but good enough.

"I have to pee," Margaret said, "but I don't want to disturb her. She might scream, seeing someone open the door."

"A bucket, then."

"Do we have a bucket?"

"We have a cooking pot."

"I'm not using a cooking pot. I'll have to go outside."

Margaret put on sandals. The welts were ugly, but they no longer itched. She was barely off the kitchen stoop when she squatted to one side. Dozens of moths, some as big as small birds, beat at the panes of glass in the door, trying to get to the kitchen light. When Margaret finished, she ran into the kitchen as if being chased. She extinguished the lamp. With the moon to guide her, she made her way to the makeshift beds. The sleeping bag was slippery and cool.

"I meant to zip them together," Patrick said. He reached out and touched her neck. She snaked her hand up from the sleeping bag and held his.

"Diana said trouble comes in threes," Margaret told him.

"You believe that?"

"No. Yes. Maybe."

"Then what number is this?"

"From whose point of view?"

"Diana's. She's the one who said it."

"I have no idea," Margaret said. "Do the ants and Adhiambo make it two? Or does the plumbing fiasco, the ants, and Adhiambo make it three? Or does Diana have troubles I know nothing about?"

"I'd love a back rub," he said sleepily.

"I can't. You're too far away."

"I can move closer."

"Good night, Patrick."

Margaret had advised sleep but couldn't manage it herself. She no longer had fever dreams of ants and euphorbia trees, but she had wide-awake images of what Adhiambo had just gone through. She could picture the breaking of the glass, perhaps the beating down of a flimsy door. A drunken African—or had it been an Asian? a white?—had pleaded at first and then had stopped his pleading. As if he'd been refused a drink at the bar and now intended to swipe all the bottles from the shelf, he'd thrown Adhiambo to the floor. Would Adhiambo have screamed? Margaret thought not. Was she already ashamed? Would a scream be heard in the evening cacophony? Or worse, ignored?

When Margaret woke in the morning, Adhiambo was sitting at the edge of the bed, her blouse-ball tucked under one arm. The bed had been perfectly made, and Margaret couldn't tell if she had slept in it or not. For all Margaret knew, the woman had slept on the floor.

"Good morning," Margaret said, and Adhiambo nodded her head.

"Are you okay?" Margaret asked.

The woman didn't respond, but neither did she try to hide her face. The egg over her eye had swollen and blackened. Her lip was cut but was no longer bleeding. Margaret wondered how many other bruises lay beneath the clothes. She tried not to think about the ultimate bruise.

"Would you like some tea?" Margaret asked, and Adhiambo nodded.

"Good. I'll just use the bathroom a minute and put on my robe."

It occurred to Margaret that Adhiambo might be wondering about the unsightly red disks on her own arms and legs.

Margaret slipped by Adhiambo to the bathroom and closed the door. Her own clean underpants were still neatly folded on the dresser. A flash of shame shot through Margaret for having even offered them to Adhiambo. To have presumed that level of intimacy would have offended the woman. Margaret recalled that African men wouldn't touch women's underwear. Maybe the same prohibition held for African women. And then Margaret noted that the hand towel, always on a ring by the sink, was missing. The bleeding must have been so bad that Adhiambo had needed a towel to stanch it. Margaret didn't use sanitary napkins. Perhaps Patrick could get some at the duka as soon as it opened. Margaret searched the wastebasket and found three tiny shards of glass.

Adhiambo would drink tea, but nothing else Margaret offered her seemed to have any appeal. Margaret tried bread and jam, then cereal, then eggs, then fruit. Adhiambo must still be in shock, Margaret thought. She wondered where James was, why he had not been sent to the cottage first thing in the morning. Margaret sat across from Adhiambo and tried to talk to her.

Adhiambo took a great deal of sugar with her tea, and Margaret thought, *Good.* Something to allay the after-quakes of shock, something to keep her going. Margaret poured her another cup, into which Adhiambo added more sugar. Margaret glanced at the clock. Five to nine. Where the hell was James? He'd been up, as per his routine, since four thirty. Margaret heard Patrick, who had kept out of Adhiambo's sight, shut the front door behind him. He was going for the pads now.

"Adhiambo, I would really like to help you," Margaret said.

"I am just all right," Adhiambo answered in a voice barely above a whisper.

Was this, Margaret wondered, a translation of another phrase in Adhiambo's tribal language? Margaret didn't even know her tribe; she had never bothered to ask. Adhiambo had tucked her hair into the clean scarf Margaret had given her minutes ago. Her skin was dark brown, with hints of gray in the shadows. It wasn't that she looked old; it was merely the shade of her skin, just as James's was blue. Margaret wondered if the woman knew her own age or the month she was born. Many of the Africans Patrick had met at the hospital didn't know their birth dates. They took the concept of "age-mate" seriously: a man or a woman who'd been born in the same year as oneself. But the actual date? "Is there a reason to know that?" they would ask, somewhat puzzled.

"I am so sorry this happened to you," Margaret said. Adhiambo's face never moved, as if she hadn't heard her.

At nine thirty, when Margaret opened the door to James, she was angry. He apologized before she could say anything.

"The memsahib is having me make the breakfast and do the washing up. Because Adhiambo is not there to help with the children, memsahib is in a calamity."

"Never mind," Margaret said. "I'm glad you're here. Adhiambo won't talk to me. I think she's ashamed."

"Oh yes," James said, nodding. His pressed white shirt and French-blue cotton pants were impeccably clean, despite his chores. "She is very shamed."

Margaret didn't know if he meant *ashamed* or shamed by others.

"She's in the kitchen. See if you can get her to eat something."

As James walked through to the kitchen, Margaret sat in a chair by the front door in order to give them privacy. It didn't matter much anyway, since Margaret couldn't understand a word they said to each other. Was Adhiambo a Luo as well?

When James emerged from the kitchen, Margaret moved to the sofa and indicated a chair nearby. She was still in her robe; she hadn't wanted to be dressing when James arrived, worried she might miss him altogether.

"Adhiambo is saying that two men broke down her door and

demanded pombe. She didn't have the pombe. She tried to run away, but one of the men, he catches her. Both men are very drunk, and they rape her because they are angry."

"Both?"

"Yes." James shook his head, folded his hands, and let them hang between his legs.

"Is she hurt? Internally?"

James looked away, unwilling to discuss female matters. He knew, however, that Margaret wanted Adhiambo to see a doctor, so he was forced to answer her. "Not so much. She is just all right."

That maddening phrase again. *Just all right.*

"How can she be? Two men?"

James was silent for a long moment. "Adhiambo has two brothers in Kericho who will come and punish the two men. They will be well and truly beaten. They will be apologizing to her maybe this night."

"James, she can't go back."

"Where else can she go? I will go with her and fix her door. I am borrowing some good tools from Mr. Arthur. Adhiambo says there are medicines. . . ." He let his voice trail away.

"Then I am going with you," Margaret said. "I'm not letting her out of my house unless I can see for myself that she is *just all right.*"

It was an empty threat, and James knew it. Both he and Adhiambo were perfectly capable of walking out the door without her.

"No," he said.

"Then I will call the police and tell them she has been raped, and she will have to answer many questions and perhaps see a doctor. I will do this."

James looked quizzical. "Why would you do this? Punish her more than she is being punished?"

Margaret thought about the Masai and the Kikuyu and bits of Patrick's argument at the picnic in the Ngong Hills. She closed her eyes and shook her head, making it perfectly clear that she wouldn't do what she had just threatened to do.

James stood. "I am speaking to her," he said.

From the sofa, Margaret could hear a prolonged and heated argument in foreign syllables. When it was over, James came into the living room and nodded.

"I'll get dressed," Margaret said.

"First we will take a bus, and then we will walk. She is all right to walk, but it is a danger to you."

"Not in broad daylight," Margaret said, heading for the bedroom.

She heard Patrick return and speak to James for a few minutes. He came into the bedroom and put the box of sanitary napkins on the bed. He went to the doctor bag he kept under the bed and removed a tube of antibiotic cream and pills Margaret didn't recognize. He poured the pills into packets. "Give her these," he said. "The white ones are for fever, should she get one, and these yellow are for pain. One every six hours."

Margaret had on jeans and a long-sleeved blouse. She had wrapped another scarf over her head and under her chin, tossing the ends over her shoulders. She put on sneakers.

"We have to walk," Margaret explained. "I don't want a parade of little boys running after us and shouting, *'Mzungu, mzungu.'*"

"I'd rather we called a female doctor. You know Josie would come in an instant," Patrick said. Josie was a colleague at the hospital.

"I'd like to have her see a doctor, too," Margaret acknowledged. "But she won't. Patrick, she was raped by two men."

"Oh, Jesus Christ."

Margaret took the box of sanitary napkins and the medicines Patrick had given her and slipped them into her backpack. She added several hand towels.

"It makes me hate African men," Margaret said.

"You can't hate all African men," Patrick pointed out.

"I like James."

"There you go."

Patrick didn't offer to accompany them or to escort Margaret back. He knew that negotiations had been completed. "Be careful," he said.

They took a bus and then walked single file, Adhiambo in front of Margaret, James and his toolbox behind. They followed a path that began at the end of a street and wound its way through bush and forest. Progress was slow because Adhiambo could not walk fast. Margaret searched the ground for ants and snakes and wished she'd worn her hiking boots instead.

Climbing Mount Kenya. Only two days away. It seemed a remote and frivolous notion.

They walked for twenty minutes. They stepped through a forest that separated one world from another. As they approached the edges of the shantytown, Adhiambo wrapped a second scarf Margaret had given her around her face to cover her mouth and chin, a gesture that caused Margaret to do the same. Margaret watched the ground, mimicking Adhiambo, who kept her eyes lowered. James quickly moved past them and took the lead.

They entered a small slum of badly constructed rooms made

from thin wooden boards, with roofs of tin or tires. Nearly every structure Margaret passed had boards through which she could see. The footpath was smoky with the scent of cooking meat. The smell was terrible, and Margaret wondered what the natives here would think of her smell, the mzungu smell. Perhaps it was just as noxious to them. Did James work every day in an environment he could barely tolerate? They passed dozens of children, all smiling, running after them. They were a parade, after all. Margaret had imagined that with her scarf and dark glasses, she would be barely recognizable as white. What had she been thinking? James picked up the pace considerably, and Adhiambo struggled to keep up. Margaret could only imagine how much it must have hurt to walk. But James seemed eager to get to where they were going.

There were no streets, only footpaths, here and there an alley big enough for a small automobile. Margaret had been told that occasionally there would be a Mercedes squeezed into a similar alley in a similar shantytown, Mathari or Gatina. A member of the cabinet might be visiting his relatives.

Eventually, James stopped and made a *tsk* sound. If this was Adhiambo's home, it was in ruins. A broken door swung from one hinge. They entered the hut. A wooden flap that could be raised with a string from inside served as the only window. On the packed-mud floor was a mattress of pillow ticking. Adhiambo threw her scarf over it but not before Margaret had seen the stains. Glass shards were sprinkled over the marum. It looked as though they had come from a drinking glass. The room smelled of beer. On a wooden shelf was a sufuria exactly like the cooking pot Patrick and Margaret had at home, several mismatched plates, one other glass. Adhiambo's clothes were on hooks or in a pink plastic basket. There was no rug, no sink, no bathroom, and only two chairs and one table. James indicated that Adhiambo should sit. She covered her face, ashamed again. She hadn't wanted Margaret to come to her home, and now Margaret knew why.

James went next door and returned with a bowl of posho, which Adhiambo ate with her fingers. James closed the door as best he could and assessed the damage. He got to work at once, replacing hinges and a shattered board. Adhiambo waved flies away from her food. Margaret unzipped her backpack, unsure of where to put its contents.

"Adhiambo," Margaret said. "This packet is to be taken only if you have a fever. This packet is for pain. With both packets, one pill every six hours."

Adhiambo nodded. She knew what the box of pads was for, as well as the tube of antibiotic.

With the door closed, Margaret opened the wooden window to let in some light. She wanted to remove all the shards from the soil. She saw no obvious place for trash and so set them in a pile on the shelf. Where did Adhiambo get her water? Wash herself? Go to the bathroom? Margaret shifted her anger from African men to expats, who paid the most pitiful of wages. Who had probably never seen how their servants lived. To Arthur and Diana, who had felt it necessary to detain James through the breakfast hour and beyond.

James tested the door and seemed satisfied with his handiwork. He showed Adhiambo the new latch and how to work it. He told Margaret he would go outside, after which she was to close the latch. He would then try to get in. Margaret did as she was told, and James threw his body against the door. Though it seemed to give a little, it didn't open. Margaret let James back in. Adhiambo had barely said a word or moved from her place at the table. Margaret sensed that she wanted to be alone, and perhaps James sensed it, too. He walked to where she was sitting and handed her a crumpled ten-shilling note. Margaret was furious with herself for not having thought to bring more cash than she'd needed for the bus fare. James turned and nodded to Margaret, then opened the door.

"If you need anything...," Margaret said, and left it at that.

On the way home, James walked very fast. He would be late now for the noon meal.

On the morning before the climb, Margaret was taking in laundry that James had done and pinned to a clothesline. Mixed in with their own clothes were the ones that Diana had lent to Margaret. Margaret unpinned and folded them. She intended to give them to James, who would iron them to Diana's exacting standards.

As she walked toward the Big House, Margaret saw Adhiambo about to enter through the back door. Adhiambo and Margaret stood a moment, looking at each other. They were too far away to speak.

When Margaret returned to her own cottage, Patrick was in a hurry to leave.

"They've found the car in Machakos," he said. "It's been driven three hundred fifty miles."

Relegated to positions of lowest seniority, Patrick and Margaret bounced along in the back of the Land Rover. Margaret wondered if this was how they were viewed by the others, as inferior first to the Brits and then to the Dutch. The thought rankled. Or maybe it was only that Patrick and she were Americans, who were known to be good sports.

From time to time, Patrick smiled at her. His eyes would then shift away from her face to a distant image beyond the window. Already he had begun a beard, having not shaved in three days, signaling that he couldn't be bothered with shaving while on the climb. The beard was lighter than his hair and somewhat disconcerting. He had on a plaid shirt with the sleeves rolled and a down vest that he had brought with him from America. Margaret could feel the slight chill of the altitude as they ascended.

The four in the front laughed often, and when Margaret and Patrick could hear the joke, they did, too. There was, however, a muffled curtain between them and the others. It was partially a European curtain, Margaret thought, or possibly only a matter of physics.

Margaret snapped a close-up of Patrick on fast film.

"Sometimes," he said, "I think attending to a camera all the time makes you miss out on the true experience."

"Such as this drive?"

"Well, sort of."

"I could argue that the person with the camera is the best positioned to truly enter the experience."

"But so much of it is smell, touch, sound," Patrick argued.

"I can smell and hear at the same time."

"I'm pretty sure we're not going to forget this trip," he said. "Are you afraid?"

"No. Maybe. A little."

Margaret nearly hit her head on the roof. It was the first of ten speed bumps leading to the lodge. More luxurious than Margaret had imagined it to be, the main building, flanked with a sprinkling of cottages among several acres of manicured gardens, had a stone facade and many regularly spaced windows, all with leaded mullions—a common feature of middle-class African architecture, inherited from the British. Off to one side and hidden by a tall hedge was a pool with lounge chairs surrounding it.

"It used to be a lodge for hunting and fishing," Arthur explained, "back in the day when a bloke could hunt. Now it's mostly for climbers and tourists."

The six arrived just after lunch, already having had a picnic in the Rover. As Diana emerged from the driver's seat, she stretched and said she was off to play tennis. Saartje immediately asked to join her. Willem announced he was headed straight for the pool and wouldn't return until the sun went down. Arthur suggested fishing to Patrick, who, after a moment's surprise, said *yes* with enthusiasm. He turned to Margaret as if for permission, but she held a smile, not wanting to grant or deny permission to anyone, least of all to her husband. The river was stocked with trout, Arthur explained. They'd rent equipment from the lodge.

Margaret didn't mind that Patrick and the others had made plans without her. She wanted to be alone and to wander.

In their room, large windows overlooked the gardens. They had a private bath and a fireplace, and Margaret had visions of sitting with Patrick in the overstuffed chairs that flanked the hearth, a half bottle of red between them, enjoying the fire as the temperature dipped precipitously. The room was infused with a sense of *old Kenya*.

Patrick and she had packed with care the day before, consulting and rechecking lists each of them had made. Margaret was scrupulous about the meds, which she had assembled into a small carton. In the living room, Patrick had spread most of the food the six of them would need for the climb: a mix of dried soups and stews, coffee, oranges, dried fruit, dried beef, packages of crackers, cans of tuna fish and peaches, a bag of meal, and Tetra Paks of ultrapasteurized milk that didn't need refrigeration. Margaret hoped Patrick had thrown in a bag of dried banana chips, her favorite African snack.

The porter stacked the cartons in an out-of-the-way corner, for which she tipped the man generously. He had the wide face and nose of a Kikuyu, so very different from the lean profile of James. If she stayed long enough in the country, Margaret thought, she might learn to identify any number of tribes simply by sight. She wondered how many mixed marriages there were and if that was the norm or the exception. Did Luo and Kikuyu intermarry? Embu and Masai?

She drew her hair up into a knot, found a sweater in her suitcase, and settled it over her shoulders. She was eager to get outside and walk. Though the ride had been relatively short, she'd felt claustrophobic and confined during the journey.

Could she find the spot on the river where Arthur and Patrick would be fishing? Perhaps they'd hired a guide. Margaret liked the idea of Arthur and Patrick participating in an athletic activity. Their relationship so far had consisted of cool glances and verbal jousting.

Her camera slung over her shoulder, Margaret skirted the pool, not wanting to confront the Dutch burgher in his bathing suit. She followed a path that led out from the gardens. Occasionally offering the shade of a camphor tree, the path meandered through meadows. Changes in altitude produced different vegetation. In addition to the tea plantations, they'd driven through farms of coffee, banana, wheat, and maize. Along the walking path, she saw wild yellow blossoms that might have been witch hazel. Once, under the shade of a juniper, she came upon a rich half acre of orchids that stopped her. Never had she seen so many of the rare and delicate flowers in one place.

The trail broke out into tall grasses, dotted here and there with lobelia and rosewood. Not too sure when she'd left, she checked her watch. Three o'clock. She thought about heading back to the lodge when a soft snort put her on alert. She scanned the meadow ahead of her, her hand shading her eyes. When she found the impala, nearly buried beneath the height of the tall grasses, she saw only a head with lyre-shaped horns, a slight curve, and perhaps a tail. The impala faced her as a deer might, waiting for her to make her move. There was rustling in the grasses, and she saw the female and then two, three, four, five, smaller impalas making quick motions. The buck, as if a sentinel, stood guard, watching her every move, while the rest of the small herd twitched and scampered, sometimes revealing themselves but more often providing only a sensation of motion within the meadow, as if a stiff breeze disturbed the grasses.

What are you thinking? Margaret silently asked. *Can you think at all? Or are you merely waiting for a change in scent, listening for the tiniest disturbance in the air, preparing yourself for flight?* Not many years ago, Margaret might have been a member of a shooting party. They would have halted at this very point. Perhaps the kill would have been given to a woman, the prey too easy and too small for a man. Was it in the animal's DNA to watch for a flash of metal?

Margaret had a desire to take a step forward simply to see the herd in motion. She imagined the backs of the impalas rising above the grasses like dolphins from the sea. Instead, she remained still, gazing into the eyes of the buck. How did he regard Margaret, with her white sleeveless blouse and navy sweater slung over her shoulders? Would he read her hair as an indication of another species, one to be wary of?

When Margaret realized she'd been standing in the sun for too long, she remembered that she'd just passed beneath a camphor tree. She locked eyes with the buck as she slowly and reluctantly backed into the shade. Just as she reached it, which must have altered the look of her, the impala bolted and, with him, the entire herd. It was, for the brief seconds Margaret was permitted to witness this ordinary movement in an African meadow, an exhilarating sight, yet one she might keep to herself, even from Patrick, who loved the African animals but who likely would remain unimpressed by such a small event. A zebra would have provoked a raised eyebrow; a leopard, a tilt of the head and a "Really." Patrick's body might then have become alert and perhaps even alarmed, eliciting something from his own DNA. But an impala? Not fit for retelling, though wondrous to Margaret.

When she arrived on the terrace at six thirty, Margaret found Saartje and Diana in sundresses and sandals, their brown bare legs prettily crossed at the knees. Having not showered since they'd left Nairobi, Margaret had missed the cues about the dress code. She still had on her jeans, the sleeveless blouse, and the sweater. The only bare parts of her were her feet in her sandals and the V of her neck, which always got too much sun and was the first place to burn. She touched the tender skin, remembering her long vigil in the meadow.

"Sorry," she said to the two women. "Didn't realize."

"You look fine," Saartje said as one might to a teenage girl who had yet to learn how to dress like a woman. A wrist full of silver bracelets slid and tinkled as she reached for her drink, something exotic the color of salmon. Margaret thought about the prohibition against alcohol, and Diana, noting her stare, explained.

"One. To be consumed before seven o'clock. Followed by a half gallon of water. Alcohol totally out of my system by morning."

"A well-thought-out plan. I'll have one, too. How was the tennis?" Margaret asked, helping herself to a handful of macadamia nuts among an array of appetizers. "And where are the men?"

"Just saw Arthur and Patrick," Diana said. "Heading up the hill. I'm guessing they'll probably have showers and dress for dinner." A quick half glance at Margaret in her jeans. "I'm told they caught over a dozen trout that the chef will fry up."

"Really?" Margaret said, not having previously thought of Patrick as much of a fisherman. She hoped that some of the catch had been his doing.

"Willem is showering," Saartje said in her distinctive and lovely Dutch accent. "Stayed at the pool until the mosquitoes started biting."

So far, Margaret had managed to keep at bay the image of the Dutch burgher in his bathing suit lying on a plastic lounge chair, but now it flooded in.

"Do you have children?" Margaret asked Saartje.

It seemed an innocent question, though she knew at once it was a thoughtless one. Saartje raised her chin and was about to speak.

"She doesn't," Diana said quickly, with a warning in her brow.

Later that evening, out of Saartje's hearing, Diana informed Margaret that Saartje had once had a seventeen-month-old baby boy who had died of sudden infant death syndrome while the couple had been stationed in Bombay. Willem had since refused to try for another; the experience had been too awful for him. Margaret was mortified to have asked, but she did come to think of Willem as an enormously selfish man. Was it his decision to make? Unilaterally? And how strange not to want children in a country where children were so highly valued, were the basis of so many of the rituals and ceremonies of the various tribes. Did Saartje and Willem argue about it in private, or was it one of those decisions that, once pronounced, could never be brought up again? Not for the first time, Margaret reflected that it was impossible to know the truth about the marriage of another couple.

The children of Kenya were beautiful. They were also remarkably well behaved—polite, obedient, and almost always smiling or laughing. Margaret seldom saw a sad child, unless that child was ill or malnourished. She was often puzzled as to how Kenyan parents had accomplished this remarkable achievement. When she could, she watched the native mothers and their toddlers in an attempt to intuit the secret.

Margaret was almost at the point at which she might want her own children. She could feel it coming on, like a vague hunger. She was, after all, twenty-eight, and many of the married women she knew at home were pregnant or had recently had babies. Here, the rural mothers had five, six, seven, eight, children—the more, the better. African children were the future. Children were social security.

Patrick arrived, flushed and distinctly happy. He had managed a clean plaid shirt, sleeves rolled to the elbow. He was bursting with the desire for someone to ask him how the fishing went, and so Margaret obliged.

"Amazing," Patrick said, and she could see that he'd become a convert to the sport. "Arthur has the final tally. A shame we aren't able to do this on the climb itself. We'd welcome the fish, I'll tell you. As it is, Arthur gave the trout to the cook, but I doubt we'll see it on the menu this evening. Went right into the freezer, I'm guessing, or home with the help. Doesn't matter. It's the sport that counts."

Obviously eager for Arthur to emerge and repeat the glorious story, Patrick looked up toward the end of the veranda. Margaret could see this might be a topic of conversation for a considerable part of the cocktail hour. She would not disturb Patrick's moment of pride, but Diana would.

"Dodgy tennis court, but we managed, didn't we, Saartje?"

"Managed quite fine."

"How was the pool?" Saartje asked Willem, who was now looming over her, rubbing his hands together in anticipation of a

cocktail. His face was alarmingly pink. Dress shirt. Tie. Margaret
felt like asking at the lobby if there was a gift shop, since she was
pretty sure she could put together a dress from two khangas.

"So what's this?" Patrick asked, eyeing Margaret's drink.

"It's a plan. Diana can explain. One drink, followed by buck-
ets of water."

"Sounds like a clever excuse to me."

Willem immediately ordered drinks for himself and Patrick.
Apparently his previous advice had been a case of *Do as I say and
not as I do.*

Arthur appeared at the table. In addition to a white shirt and
tie, he had on a jacket.

The tally was three drinks apiece for Arthur and Willem, two
each for the rest of them. And this not counting the wine with
the meal. Dinner was a buffet: various main dishes and salads
and desserts set out on a long table. Demonstrating his dexterity,
Willem juggled full plates of the three courses. Had he grown
up in a family in which food had been scarce? Desserts even less
available? Margaret knew so little about the man who would lead
them up the mountain, who had influenced all their prepara-
tions. As she studied him, she wondered if he could even make
the climb.

All the windows were open.

"If this is any indication of how cold it will be as we climb, I'm
going to wish I'd brought another sweater," Margaret said.

Saartje, in her patterned sundress, was shivering. Diana, astonishingly, seemed impervious to the temperature.

"Lovely, the cold, don't you think?" she asked.

Margaret took this to mean that the cold was a test of character, one she had just failed. She wished Arthur would lend Saartje his jacket.

"I think Saartje could use a sweater," Margaret said.

"I'm fine," Saartje said brusquely, when *Go to hell* was what she meant. Twice now, Margaret had inadvertently irritated her. Margaret would make a point of having a conversation with Saartje in the morning. Just Saartje and Margaret. About what, she couldn't imagine. She certainly couldn't ask questions.

Patrick briefly covered Margaret's hand in her lap. She wasn't sure if this was an apology for having ignored her in his euphoria at having caught so many fish (seven, as it happened) or in the absentminded manner he normally did it. *I am suddenly thinking of you.* Or possibly he was anticipating sex in the *old Kenya* room, and this was his way of telling her. In the next instant, he removed his hand to cut his meat.

The drinks and the altitude had taken their toll (they had ascended two thousand feet during the day), and conversation was listless during dinner. Saartje shivered so violently, Margaret wanted to laugh at the absurdity of it. Even Diana began to rub her bare arms. Arthur looked distinctly under the weather, as if he were already nursing a headache. All of this seemed to make Diana cross.

"You're all very dull tonight," she said.

"The beef is as tough as shoe leather," Arthur said.

"Not properly aged," Willem agreed.

"Don't you think, Arthur," Diana insisted, "that everyone is being very dull?"

"Hadn't noticed, actually."

"Really. I'm surprised. You're normally very observant."

Did Margaret only imagine a quick glance in her direction?

"Leave it out, Diana," he said.

Had Arthur had more than three drinks?

"I was reading up on Mount Kenya last night from Gregory's *The Great Rift Valley*," Patrick offered, trying to deflect further matrimonial bickering. "Gregory has one story in which he talks about the early Europeans bringing various tribes to the mountain while on expedition. The reactions of these Africans were often those of fear and suspicion. One morning, the men came to tell Gregory that the water they had left in the cooking pots was bewitched. They said it was white and wouldn't shake, and if you hit it with a stick, the stick wouldn't go in. They begged Gregory to have a look. Gregory went to the pot. He put it on the fire and predicted that the hard white stuff would soon turn to water. The men sat around and watched. When it had melted, they were giddy. They told Gregory that the demon had been expelled. He told them that they could now use the water. But as soon as his back was turned, the men poured it out and filled the cooking pots with rushing water from a nearby brook."

"Marvelous story," Willem said with almost no enthusiasm in his voice. He had speedily moved on from his main dish of lamb (or was it goat?) and was tucking into his second pudding, a shivery, gelatinous lime. He noticed Margaret's gaze and raised his spoon. "No better way to absorb the alcohol."

Margaret had already decided that the man's advice was suspect at best.

"Did you know," Margaret asked, "that the Kikuyu built their huts with the doors facing the mountain, and that Kirinyaga, which is what they call the mountain, means *has ostriches?*"

"The feathers are the top of the mountain. Where did you learn that?" Arthur asked.

"Guidebook," Margaret said. "Also that the Embu name for Mount Kenya was Kirenia, which means *mountain of whiteness?* And I love this one: Meru songs refer to Mount Kenya as *the mountain is all speckles.*"

Diana was making good on her promise to drink half a gallon of water. Or was it a gallon now that she had had two drinks? She demanded the waiter stand and fill and refill her glass as she sipped.

Margaret, too, had a slight headache. Too early for the drinks to have done their worst; it must have been the altitude. The grounds were lit here and there, but beyond their perimeter, all was darkness, Mount Kenya outlined only by the stars, in great abundance. The mountain appeared otherworldly, a place where no man should go.

"Weather moving in," Willem declared. "Didn't want to mention it earlier. Would have ruined your afternoon. We'll have thick cloud all day."

He sat back and patted his belly while the others groaned.

"Too bad about the weather," Arthur said. "Makes a hard day grim."

Diana shot a glance at him.

"But it's only grim if we make it grim," he added. "As for me, can't wait to start the damn thing."

Margaret wanted to whisper to Patrick, *Let's get out of here.* But where would they go? Would they stay at the lodge until the others returned? Patrick would never allow it. Of all of them, he was the only one in a genuinely good mood.

Margaret summoned the waiter for another glass of water.

Patrick turned and whispered to Margaret, "Let's get out of here."

* * *

The next morning, they drove in the Rover provided by the lodge to Park Gate. There they left the car and unloaded the gear. They all had on parkas, unzipped, though soon enough gloves and hoods would appear. They were easily identified by color. Diana had on a bright-red jacket with a white fur collar. Saartje wore a high-fashion lime-green ski parka. Margaret had on a bluish-gray jacket with a hood. Willem's contours were unrecognizable beneath a white ski outfit. It was all Margaret could do not to look at Patrick, who would have been unable to contain himself. Arthur had on a beat-up Barbour jacket that looked as though it had last been worn in a stable. Patrick matched Margaret with the same bluish-gray. They had bought the jackets on sale in Boston before leaving.

They met the porters and the guide, who'd been waiting for them. The men shook hands. The guide's English was excellent, though Willem preferred Swahili, thus complicating communications for those who couldn't keep up, which may have been only Margaret.

They set out in a line, the guide at the front, the porters at the back, so that they were protected at each end in the event that a stray lion decided to attack. The Africans didn't carry guns, but they had very noticeable pangas at the ready. Earlier, Margaret had caught a glimpse of Willem's handgun. None of it was reassuring.

Margaret started out with a sense of fear mixed with exhilaration. As for the exhilaration, they were climbing Mount Kenya. This was as daring an adventure as she had ever had. She was on her way and would complete the climb, and it would be a story to tell when she came down. The fear wasn't as clear-cut.

Not entirely a physical sensation, though there was some of that, it was more a fear of the unknown. She wasn't certain what lay ahead of them, nor did she know how much of the climb she could really endure. She'd had so little training or experience.

She was afraid, too, of the dynamics of the six of them. No one, except Patrick, had left the dinner table in good spirits the night before, and some of the group were hungover when they'd gathered at breakfast. Neither Willem nor Arthur ate anything, even though Willem kept exhorting the others (and himself) to do so. Diana, as she often did, seemed to want to *get going.*

They began walking up a hill through low forest. A wind came up, and Margaret's nose ran. In front of her, she could see hoods being raised, gloves coming out of pockets. Already she was adjusting her focus to a small universe that included her feet and the ground right in front of her. She realized almost immediately that she wasn't noticing the scenery around her, and that all her effort came down to the single task of putting one foot in front of the other. Breathing was taxed.

The others were far ahead of her. From time to time, Patrick would drop back to see if Margaret was all right, but he couldn't help his own pace. Margaret grew embarrassed at her lack of speed, but attempts to catch up left her winded. She thought seriously of aborting. She hadn't gone so far as to not be able to get back on her own, but she knew that Patrick would feel that he had to go with her, despite her protests. She didn't want him to miss out. There was nothing to do but keep going.

Low cloud had descended. Margaret had been for walks in the snow in New England on gray days, the bare limbs of the winter trees outlined against the colorless background, and she had felt a kinship with the weather that seemed to drain the life out of her. Surrounded by the bleak landscape, she felt a similar kind of dread on the lower slopes of Mount Kenya. Even the parade of bright parkas ahead of her failed to lift what was rapidly beginning to be a mild depression. She began to yearn for the sun.

She was staring at her feet when she noticed an absence of sound. As she glanced up, she saw that the line had stopped. Willem had put up his right hand, mimicking the guide in front of Diana. In any language, Willem's sign meant *halt*.

A buffalo had revealed itself around a corner. Margaret could see the distinctive curving horns, the massive brown-black body, and the horizontal swagger of the head. She couldn't make out the animal's eyes, but its broad nose was pointed in their direction. Early in her stay, Margaret had been told that the buffalo was the most dangerous animal in Kenya, particularly if a trekker happened to bisect the distance between a female and her calf. The buffalo in front of them was enormous.

Margaret noted that the guide had his panga out. Willem held his handgun so that it pointed straight down. Would bullets penetrate that thick hide? Margaret watched as the line in front of her took a single slow step backward. So as not to rustle any leaves or debris, their steps were shallow and cautious. The buffalo might charge at any moment. The guide evidently felt that their best chance was to back away. Even people in cars had been charged, toppled, and killed.

It seemed that none of them was breathing. Slowly, the others made their way back to where Margaret stood, and then they all began retreating. They lost a fair amount of hard-won ground. Margaret had no idea if they would retreat all the way back to the gates, or if they would wait the animal out. There were tales of expeditions having to stand perfectly still for two or three hours until the buffalo moved on.

Eventually, the retreat came to a halt at a junction in the trail. Margaret saw the guide speak to Diana. He motioned with his arm to the porters behind Margaret that the group would be taking the other trail. They moved forward with caution, which suited Margaret's pace. No one spoke for at least a half hour. When the guide determined it was safe enough to walk at a brisker pace, the party sped up, and Margaret was again left behind.

Margaret had too many muscles that had not done any serious work in some time. She watched as Arthur stepped out of line. He waited until she had drawn even with him.

"Need a push?"

Margaret tried to laugh, but her airway hurt. "I'm sorry," she gasped. "I shouldn't have come."

"Nonsense. It's watching you that's giving me so much pleasure."

"Glad to oblige."

Instinctively, she looked for Diana, who was at the head of the line. Beside her was Willem, and behind them were Saartje and Patrick. Perhaps there was some good in these noncouple pairings. With someone not your partner, mightn't you make a better effort? She noted that she did seem to make more progress with Arthur at her side. She also seemed to be able to talk in short bursts.

"You handled the ants so well," Arthur said.

"I did not."

"Very entertaining, all the same."

Arthur put his hand at the center of her back and gave her a slight push. His hand lingered as if he might give her a second, but then he let it drop.

Margaret was still frightened by the climb and sorely tempted to let Arthur *take care of her*. She knew Arthur would be more than happy to accommodate her. Margaret's lack of speed on the climb made her vulnerable. If they'd all been wildebeests, Margaret would have been the orphan, straggling behind, ripe kill for a leopard or a lion.

"Diana seems eager to get to the bunkhouse," Margaret said. Their destination that day was Met Station.

"She's always eager."

"Surely that's a good trait."

"Of course. Marvelous trait. Useful in all sorts of endeavors."

Margaret couldn't see Arthur's face. All of them had on hoods that they'd drawn tight around their heads, obscuring eyebrows and, in some cases, lips. Arthur's breath lay listless on the damp air.

"You're actually helping us, you know," he said.

"And how's that?"

"By slowing us down. Willem and Diana and I would have competed to be the first to get to the hut. It would have been bloody awful. Possibly literally," he said.

"What about Saartje?" Margaret asked.

"Saartje."

"She's managing?"

"She's managing well. You're not doing so bad yourself."

Margaret smiled. "So I am."

"You see?" Arthur said. "You needed me."

* * *

Most of the climb was hard and grim and sometimes ugly, and it was always cold and wet. Margaret had had days in her life when the only way to the other side was through it, but seldom was that more apparent than on Mount Kenya. At a certain point, she could not turn back unless she feigned illness, which she would not do. The only way was forward and up, followed by what she hoped would be a blissful descent. She began to study the sky from time to time for breaks in the clouds. Even a modest sliver of blue would have set her up for hours. Without the sun to illuminate the scenery, the climb began to seem more and more existential. Why hike up a mountain with the almost certain knowledge that one would be able to see nothing from the summit?

They had climbed eighteen hundred feet to reach Met Station. On the other hand, they'd gained five thousand feet, part of it by Land Rover, since leaving the lodge that morning. The climb from Park Gate to Met was meant to take three hours. And had it not been for Margaret, the rest would have accomplished it easily. As it happened, it took nearly six, and they were all ravenous when they got there at three, not having eaten anything since seven, some of them not having eaten anything at all.

The building at Met Station was a banda made of wood, with a covered veranda. First making a fire, the porters set up camp. The trekkers would have a hot lunch that would in fact be dinner. To keep hunger at bay until the lunch was cooked, the group was offered tea and bananas. They sprawled on the veranda, letting their backpacks slide off their bodies. Willem had been right. Though part of an afternoon and evening stretched before them, no side expeditions were planned. No games proposed. No conversation offered. They wanted only food and a place to sit, later followed by a place to lie down, which turned out to be on the canvas cots in the banda, lined up the long way. There were ten cots. A party of three young German climbers had arrived at Met forty-five minutes after the group had. Flushed and fit, they spoke enough English to be polite. They'd intended to go straight to Mackinder's Camp, they said, but had gotten a late start. Diana explained that it was just as well they hadn't. Met was there primarily to provide an overnight at altitude so as to acclimate trekkers. The Germans smiled, and it was impossible to tell whether they were smiling because they thought Diana was funny or because they were glad to be reminded of this important point.

It was impossible also to tell if there was a view. Low cloud still surrounded them. Night fell closer to seven o'clock because of the altitude. So that they could pick out their cots and set up for the night, a lantern had been hung just inside the bunkhouse. Trips to the latrine were accompanied by a porter. A flashlight was turned off at a discreet moment, but it couldn't have been a pleasant duty for the poor African assigned the job.

Nearly everyone had lain down within an hour of sunset. Dinner had been filling. Arthur and Willem seemed exhausted, which was, Margaret thought, still a residue of hangovers. Diana, who claimed the cot closest to the door, argued with Willem for the spot. Theoretically, a man should have the cot closest to the door in case of danger. But Diana was adamant, making fun of Willem for pretending chivalry. Margaret thought, *Careful, Diana,* as she came dangerously close to insulting the man. To Margaret, the matter was simple. Diana's constant need to get going compelled her to have the cot by the door and to be the first out in the morning. In the way that one couldn't help but wonder from time to time about another's marriage, Margaret could not imagine Diana making love with any pleasure. Margaret guessed she would be brusque and quick and eager to get on to the next item on her agenda.

They lay side by side: Diana and Arthur, Saartje and Willem, Margaret and Patrick. Margaret didn't relish sleeping so close to Willem, who was uninhibited with his farts. She faced Patrick in complete darkness as soon as the lantern was snuffed out. She fell asleep listening to German and woke in precisely the same position as she'd been in the night before.

The first challenge of the second day was the treacherous vertical bog. The mud sucked at Margaret's new boots with ferocity and made her think the bog was alive. If there had been a distance between Margaret and the others during the easy part of the climb the day before, the distance increased exponentially. Margaret grew panicky with the gap, which by now was too far even to make herself heard. Though the porters never left her, she wished for a companion, someone to encourage her on as Arthur had, to make sure she didn't break an ankle. Patrick did occasionally wait for Margaret to check that she was okay, but even when she told him, "This is pure hell," he nodded in agreement and then, as if he were captive to his feet, went on ahead of her.

Perhaps the others had conversations. Margaret guessed they didn't. They all had sticks for balance, and in some sense they propelled the group upward, though Margaret thought it was more a case of holding steady so that no one fell backward. Her windpipe hurt as with the sorest of throats, simply from the effort to breathe. Mouths were wide open to capture whatever air could be found. She was sweating within ten feet of the beginning of the bog. Instead of taking off her jacket and tying it around her waist by the arms, as she should have done, she felt she couldn't spare a minute as she watched the others move farther and farther ahead. She hated the mud, hated the climb, hated everyone ahead of her, even her husband. Each effort to extract a boot from the muck dragged at her knees.

When she reached the top of the bog two hours later, the others lay on the ground as if slaughtered. Margaret began to shiver inside her wet clothes and knew she wouldn't be able to rid herself of the chill until they got to camp and she changed into clean ones. She discovered that always being last had serious drawbacks, apart from embarrassment. When she reached the point at which the others had stopped, they'd already had their rest and thus were eager to get going, ensuring no rest for the slacker. Always being last suggested the pip-squeak in gym class, as well as the one who *wasn't really trying*. There was a kind of good-natured understanding at first. But Margaret felt a subtle resentment gathering. Why had she been asked along anyway? Why was she holding them up so? Did they dare leave her behind with the porters? How exasperating Margaret was in keeping them from a meal and, even more important, from a hut with a bed. Patrick began to show a touch of impatience as well at having to wait or climb down to check on his wife. "That's it, Margaret!" he would say when she accomplished a big step, as if he were encouraging a child to learn to walk. There was an enormous irony in their impatience, which Arthur had mentioned the day before. Margaret, of all of them, was thoroughly acclimatizing herself.

Her companions, from having fallen where they stood at the top of the bog, were covered with muck from behind. Because

they'd had their rest, Margaret was given a short drink of water
and asked to keep up (with no pause for her). As they trudged
along a ridge with what might have been the glorious Teleki view,
Margaret felt as though she were following a family of troglo-
dytes. Heads down, with little appetite for the dismal and almost
nonexistent view, they seemed to be headed back to a cave. Even
Diana, in her bright-red parka, was smeared from hood to boot.

Margaret wondered how they would manage when they
reached the hut. They would have to find a stream in order to
wash the backs of their jackets. But could any of them withstand
the cold when a parka was taken off? Were they to climb into
their sleeping bags in dirty outerwear? The dilemma preoccupied her for quite a time, even though, since she had never had
the opportunity to lie down, her own jacket was relatively clean.
Later that day, she would discover just how much mud she'd
kicked up onto her jeans.

And they were all cold. Due to Margaret's stupidity, she was
shivering, but nobody was comfortable. Well, perhaps Willem
was, in his total ski outfit. Generally, though, the jackets were
inferior to the task. It felt to Margaret as if they were children,
inadequately dressed, sent out to play.

The camp they reached was a shack made with vertical boards and
covered with a tar-paper roof. Sleeping accommodations, Margaret
discovered when she went inside to change her clothes, were rudimentary. The mattresses on the ground were filthy, and Margaret
blanched to think how many unwashed bodies had lain on them.
With some gymnastics, she managed the feat of changing her clothes
without touching the putrid pillow ticking. Patrick would have to set
out the ground cloths. She was puzzled by Arthur's pronouncement

that the huts held thirty. Margaret couldn't imagine thirty bodies on the mattresses. Ten, maybe, and even that would be cozy. She wondered if they would be joined again by the Germans.

She felt better once she was dry and had had her turn by the fire. The others looked haggard, if not worse, and everyone seemed grateful that the climb was over for the day. Margaret took a stool next to Patrick.

"How are you doing?" he asked.

"Better now. You been inside yet?"

"No."

"It's hideous. I am not exaggerating."

"It's a bed," Patrick said. "It's shelter. I can't remember being so reduced to basics and appreciating them. When I saw the hut, I thought I'd cry."

"Rough on you, too."

"God, yes."

"But you kept up."

"Did my best."

"And I didn't?"

He was surprised by the question. "Of course you did."

"I feel like an idiot," she said as she poked at the dirt with a stick.

"No one minded. Everyone understood."

"You're a liar. Diana hasn't spoken to me since we got here."

Patrick shrugged.

"How were the others?" Margaret asked.

"Willem wanted to chat. Can you imagine?"

"No."

"He and Diana seemed to be jockeying for head position behind the guide. It was weird and silly."

"And Arthur?" she asked.

"He was quiet. Trying to conserve his energy, I think. We pretty much kept pace with each other."

"Saartje?"

"Right up front with her husband. She seemed the least taxed of all of us."

"Really?" Margaret said, having new respect for the woman. "Patrick, I'm not sure I can make it."

He was silent a moment. "You have to, Margaret. We can't leave you here. You wouldn't be safe, even locked inside the hut."

"I know," she said.

"Get a good rest. I'm sorry to say, the hardest part is yet to come."

Margaret groaned.

She accepted a cup of sugared tea from the cook. He passed around a tin of cookies.

"Glad we didn't run into anything bigger than a sunbird today," Willem said. "Thought we were done for yesterday."

"I'm still amazed it didn't charge," Arthur said.

"You're ponces, the lot of you," Diana announced. It was meant to be a somewhat good-natured tease, but it came out as a scold.

"We're all doing our best," Arthur insisted as he moved his stool closer to the fire.

The cook made a flurried motion, indicating that Arthur might burn his boots.

Arthur nodded. "I'll take my chances. Can't get my bloody feet warm."

"Change your socks," Diana suggested practically.

"Don't dare take my boots off."

Diana sighed. "My point exactly. You're a ponce."

"I, for one, am starved," Patrick said. He kept sniffing the air, trying to determine which stew the cook had on the boil.

"My legs are twitching," Margaret said as sparks ignited the muscles along her thighs.

"You really haven't done any climbing, have you?" Saartje asked.

Margaret didn't think this was the moment to mention Monadnock. "Not really. And I'd just like to say to all of you that I'm sorry for being so slow. I shouldn't have come. I'm slowing you all down."

Diana looked away, a brief turn of red hood and white fur.

"Nonsense," Willem said. "We'll make a climber out of you yet. You'll do better tomorrow."

"But I thought tomorrow was the worst part. The scree and the glacier and all that."

"The glacier requires no strength, just nerve."

"You'll be fine," Patrick said. "Just do as the guide says."

Diana was having none of it, and she sighed pointedly. So loud in fact that Patrick looked sharply over at her. Diana was undoubtedly sorry that she and Arthur had asked Patrick and Margaret to come along, but even she wouldn't suggest leaving Margaret at the hut.

"Bloody long time to get here," Diana said, in case anyone had missed the point.

The cook ladled out in tin cups what looked to be a beef stew. A hunk of bread went with it. Margaret asked for water.

Her legs continued to twitch all through the evening as if tiny electrodes had been implanted in the muscles. When the meal was over, people shifted and changed positions as various needs were seen to. Margaret had already been to the latrine, a ditch dug far enough away from the camp so as not to be troublesome. Managing the latrine required deft moves, a shovel, and courage. Who knew what was out there?

They had had precise instructions from Willem. "When there's no toilet, bury your feces in a fifteen-centimeter hole." Margaret tried quickly to convert to inches. "At higher altitudes, soil lacks the organisms to break down the feces, so leave them in the open where UV rays from the sun can break them down. Spreading it facilitates the process. Always carry your own toilet paper."

Margaret sat next to Arthur.

"What I wouldn't give for a stiff drink right now," he said.

"What I wouldn't give for a clean toilet."

Arthur glanced at the porters. "Can't imagine doing this every day."

"Their lungs must be as big as inner tubes."

Arthur had a candy bar in his pocket and offered Margaret half.

"Diana is a good climber," Margaret said.

"Has to be first. At everything. She'd be leading the guide if she thought she could get away with it."

Margaret let the chocolate melt and sink into all the spaces in her mouth. It felt like a rare and exotic treat.

"Sun's going to set in fifteen minutes," he said. "You'd better get all your gear together, claim a cot."

"There aren't any cots. It's all mattresses."

"We're going to the mattresses?"

An exhausted Arthur making a joke. Margaret smiled in appreciation.

Patrick, who had a wonderful voice, began to sing, partly to entertain himself and partly for the rest of them. Margaret had heard him sing a hundred times, and she'd never tired of it. He had a clarion tenor and might have sung professionally had he not gone into medicine. Margaret watched the expressions on the faces of the rest of the climbers. Each was surprised and then pleased. One didn't expect a serenade on a cold and grim mountain. Margaret could scarcely believe that fewer than two days before, she'd been standing in the hot sun.

Patrick sang "If You Leave Me Now" and "Fifty Ways to Leave Your Lover" and "Imagine," because everyone else wanted to join in. When even Patrick's Irish repertoire started to wear thin, the guide and the porters started up with their African songs. Margaret could understand none of the words, but they must have been humorous in nature. Periodically, the Africans would be overcome with laughter midsong and fall apart from one another, infecting even her with the giggles, though no one had any idea why the Africans were laughing. Margaret imagined the songs being about stupid wazungu trying to climb a tall mountain in Africa.

One by one, they made their way into the banda. Another party, not the Germans, was supposed to have joined them, but the guide said they would be a day behind. Margaret laid her gear on a mattress that was at the outside of a string of three. At her head was another group of three mattresses, those set perpendicular to the first three. The two to Margaret's left had towels on them, which suggested occupancy, so Patrick took the mattress at her head. But because Saartje and Willem had already laid out their bedding with their heads at the other end, Patrick did as well. Margaret thought he must have assumed that she wouldn't mind his feet as much as someone else.

Earlier in the evening, one of the porters had washed the backs of their jackets as they had sat in them. The jackets had dried off as they'd huddled by the fire. None of the party was entirely clean, but they weren't covered with muck. Margaret had already changed clothes and so slept in what she had on, but several of the others changed outside or awkwardly inside their sleeping bags. Patrick sat at the foot of his bag as Margaret slithered into hers. She propped herself on her elbows as she and Patrick chatted. Then he gave her a kiss, as he had done every night they had been married. Even if he was angry with Margaret, he never failed to kiss her. Eventually he turned and slid into his bag.

Arthur and Diana were still outside.

Margaret didn't know if they were changing clothes or if Arthur was leading Diana to the latrine. A porter stood by the lantern just inside the door, eager to turn it out. He and the other Africans would sleep by the fire. It seemed wrong when they had extra beds, but Margaret had already learned that there was no talking a porter out of his routine. She'd tried convincing the guide to take the extra mattresses, but he'd made it clear it was his job to stay outside and guard the fire and the banda. She knew that as long as they tipped well at the end of the climb, he would be fine.

Margaret heard voices at the entrance to the hut. The porter turned off the lantern and shut the door just after Diana and Arthur entered the banda. Margaret couldn't make out their faces or even their bodies. There was a rustle of movement as they sought their beds, an exchange of murmurs back and forth, and the distinct sound of them sliding into separate sleeping bags. Margaret thought Willem might already be asleep because she could hear male snoring, and it didn't have the rhythm or pitch of Patrick's. She imagined Saartje on her back, staring at the ceiling. As the wind buffeted the hut, Margaret could hear the African voices from outside.

She didn't know if she had Diana or Arthur next to her. She turned onto her side away from them, facing the wall. The smell of the smoke from the fire had permeated the hut and was helping to make her sleepy. There were slight rustlings, which she took to be restless climbers trying to find a good position. She drifted off.

Margaret yelped and snatched her hand from where it dangled off the mattress's edge. She rolled over and faced away from the wall. Too afraid even to bring the sleeping bag over her head, she wanted to wake Patrick. If only she could find the courage to reach out a hand and wiggle his feet.

Instead, a hand reached out and found hers.

"They're rats," Arthur whispered.

"They're rats?" she whispered back.

"Yes."

"I felt it run over my other hand."

"I can feel them running over my feet from time to time. Of course, my feet are in the bag."

"Oh God," Margaret said.

"They're a special feature of the huts at altitude."

"Very funny."

"Sometimes you get them, sometimes you don't. We seem to have gotten lucky."

"Oh God."

Her body was sweaty. "I have to get out of here," she said.

"And go where?"

The answer was obvious.

"Will all the huts be like this?" she asked.

"Who knows?"

"Will they bite?"

"The rats? Probably not."

Arthur's grasp was not so hard it hurt but firm enough that she couldn't easily slip her hand from his. He held it the way you might catch the hand of a child who was stumbling forward.

Arthur's hand was warm and solid, a man's hand. Not calloused but firm. It was a human gesture, one creature trying to calm another. Or it was not. Either way, Margaret wouldn't be the one to let go. She lay awake, her face turned toward Arthur, whom she couldn't see. She felt only his hand, which was all she needed or wanted. She inched her face closer to their clasped hands. It seemed that she was safe within a certain radius of that grip.

Margaret knew nothing about what was in Arthur's mind, though she might have guessed. When she brought her face closer to their hands, the movement felt similar to crawling toward the warmth of a fire. Not toward the fire itself but simply toward the warmth. She wondered what Patrick would have done in similar circumstances. Would he have taken Saartje's hand, tried to calm her down, thought nothing of it? As Margaret would discover in the morning, Patrick was not next to Saartje but rather Willem. Poor man.

It was possible that Arthur moved his face closer to his hand as well. Margaret didn't know. Nor did she know the moment when Arthur fell asleep.

Having been told to get up by Patrick, Margaret woke to the sound of muffled and angry voices. She hustled to pack up her belongings in the meager light of the lantern. She identified the voices as belonging to Diana and Arthur. Margaret had brought Dentyne gum along with her in case the cleaning of teeth wasn't on the agenda. It was three a.m. on the day of the scree and the glacier.

The cook presented the climbers with hot coffee and cookies. A proper breakfast would be had at Top Hut once they'd managed the glacier. People blew on their fists to keep warm, or held their mugs with both hands. Lanterns had been lit, since it was still dark and would be until sunrise at six thirty. Margaret saw Arthur sitting on a stool near the blaze. Diana, at the opposite end of the circle of warmth and safety made by the fire, was in conversation with the guide. Margaret searched for Patrick and found him ten feet behind her, just at the edge of the circle, sipping his coffee.

His jacket was unzipped.

"Aren't you freezing?" she asked.

"Margaret, what's going on?"

"What?"

"With Arthur?" Patrick's breath was rank.

"With Arthur what?"

"When I woke up this morning and leaned over to wake you, you and he were holding hands."

Margaret was surprised. Arthur and she had held hands all night?

"There were rats," she said quickly.

"What about the rats?"

"A rat ran over my hand. I woke up and must have cried out. Arthur explained that there were rats in the hut. I was terrified, Patrick. He clasped my hand to calm me."

Patrick was tight-lipped.

"It wasn't like that. It was what you'd do with a child who was scared."

"Can you honestly say you haven't noticed his interest in you?"

At first Margaret was silent. "That doesn't mean I have a thing for him," she said finally.

"Margaret, where's your head? You let him hold your hand. How do you think Diana felt when she woke and saw your hands clasped together?"

Margaret tossed the dregs of the coffee onto the ground.

"You should have woken me up," Patrick said. "I'm your fucking husband."

"You're not my fucking husband," Margaret said. "You're my beloved husband."

"Christ." Patrick shook his head as if there were nothing to discuss.

Margaret might have pursued the matter, but the guide called them to gather round. She wondered who else had seen her hand in Arthur's, and if that explained the angry voices outside the banda when she'd woken.

The porters gave them flashlights so that they could make their way. Diana appeared beside Margaret.

"Do try to keep up today," Diana said icily. "Make an effort, will you?"

Negotiating the scree was a case of three slow steps up, followed by an inevitable two-step slide backward. While the body did the work to accomplish three, the reward was only one. The trek was Sisyphean.

If Margaret looked up, she could see small blots of light dotting the steep scree, but the bodies themselves were in darkness. The going was torturous. Her legs screamed; her throat screamed. She thought of Diana's admonition and knew that keeping up was out of the question. Margaret would have to endure Diana's condescension once again. But Diana was the least of her problems. Margaret wanted to stop. She had the porters behind her, and from time to time one or another would come up and ask her if she was all right. One gave her a cup of purified water, for which she nearly wept. She could barely speak to thank him.

She wondered why she had signed on for the expedition at all. Theirs was meant to be the fastest and steepest and yet the easiest path to Point Lenana, but that fact was relative, she realized, and directed at experienced climbers. At the very least she should have been in better physical condition. She remembered the nearly criminal nonchalance she'd felt at the thought of climbing the mountain. She recalled the moment Patrick had come into the guest room and said, *We're climbing Mount Kenya.* Margaret might so easily have said, *Not me.*

There was a short period of rest at the top of the scree. The other climbers accommodated Margaret by allowing her to catch her breath, always in short supply. She was given water, and they were permitted another small meal: two oatmeal biscuits.

"The worst is over," Patrick said. "I'm afraid we have to keep going, though. The guide wants to get us to the glacier before the sun comes up."

"Why does it matter?" Margaret asked. "There won't be any sunshine."

"I assume they have their reasons. They've done this a hundred times."

"Can you imagine?"

"Frankly? No."

In the dark, Margaret couldn't make out the faces of the others, which was a blessing. They'd been asked to turn off the flashlights during the rest period in order to conserve batteries. Patrick put his arm around Margaret and gave her a squeeze, which she accepted as a peace offering. Had she had the energy, she would have hugged him back.

They were asked to turn the flashlights on and to line up. The route ahead was fairly flat; they'd reached a kind of plateau. Margaret began to yearn for the sun to come up, even if all they were to see was cloud. The dark was eerie. On the scree, she hadn't worried about animals. What animal, no matter how wild, would go near the scree? But now, in the open, they might smell the humans. Or had the party reached the point at which the larger animals no longer roamed?

When the sun rose, the immediate past erased itself. As soon as it was daybreak, they knew that the cloud cover had broken. Though they couldn't actually see the rising sun, Margaret's spirits lifted. Here and there, the light hit the flat planes of the rocks above them. What they'd done, she soon realized, was to climb above the clouds. There wasn't much view, but the landscape ahead grew clearer and clearer, and for the first time, they could make out the smaller peaks that would lead to the summit. The light, rosy and soft, was a photographer's dream. Margaret stopped Patrick and took her camera from his backpack. She snapped a dozen pictures in all directions. She held her face to the sun. She wanted every ray to penetrate whatever skin was showing. She now believed they would make it to the top. Willem and Saartje began chatting. Arthur popped his head round from time to time to say something to Willem. Only Diana remained silent, seemingly unmoved by the sight of the land come alive. The grim grays and browns were gone, replaced with the saturated blue of the sky, the sparkling gray of the rocks, and, in the distance, the menacing white of the glacier.

At the beginning of the glacier, the guide addressed the climbers. The glacier was a serious matter, he said. First, he demanded that everyone who had not already done so put on sunglasses, explaining that snow blindness was real and crippling and dangerous. Second, he wanted them to take a good look at the slope of the ice. Margaret's legs began to tremble, and she guessed she was not alone. The guide continued to explain that they would, in fact, all be safe if they followed his lead. He would cut footholds into the ice; the climbers would be clamped into a guide rope, with the guide at the front and porters with pickaxes interspersed among them; all they had to do was put one foot in front of the other and pay attention. They would be able to hear him, the guide reassured the group, even those at the back. They would be across the glacier in no time.

The guide came along then and put them in order. He would be first, then Diana. Clearly, he had recognized Diana's restlessness and knew she would want to be first among the trekkers. Arthur was next, then a porter. He put Margaret after that, followed by Patrick and another porter. Saartje and Willem, the last of the trekkers, led the rest of the porters. The guide gave Willem a pickax and told him he would alert him if and when it was needed.

Margaret felt reassured by her position. Arthur and a porter ahead of her, Patrick behind. She was no longer last. For the first time on the climb, Margaret felt confident, despite the continued trembling in her legs. The only requirement was nerve, and she believed she could manage that. All she had to do was think about the scree to realize how easy the glacier might be if she just followed instructions.

The guide carefully clipped them to the rope at appropriate intervals. Once he had fastened himself in, he raised his hand high to signal one step forward. They were to practice this for the twenty feet or so to the beginning of the ice to get the rhythm of walking in tandem. Once they reached the glacier, Margaret could hear the guide digging in with his pickax. The climbers were following prior footsteps, but they had to be sharpened up, cleared of any ice that may have melted in the interim. Except for the wind, the only sound was that of the guide with his ax. They moved a step forward. This procedure continued until five footholds had been carved, and Margaret moved out onto the ice for the first time. The steps sloped slightly into the ice — not enough to make one tilt toward the upper glacier, yet enough so that a minor slip wouldn't topple the entire group.

Margaret took a peek down the glacier and realized she couldn't even see its end. She snapped her head up. She didn't want to view the slope above her either. Margaret stared straight at the feet of the porter in front of her, watching his every move. When he moved forward, so did she. When he halted, so did she. She assumed Patrick was watching her feet in a similar manner.

The going was slow. The footholds had to be carved or recarved. Each step was a sculpture dependent upon the skills of the guide. Margaret hadn't before realized how very much they would need to trust the man. One false move on his part, and the entire party might slip off its footholds and wind up clinging to the glacier by a rope with a hold at either end. Margaret found these thoughts nonproductive and began to count instead. She did this often when bored on a walk. It helped to pass the time. *One, two, three, four*—a kind of military beat. Her arms were extended for balance, a clear prerequisite. In a vivid way, each of them held the others' safety.

It took maybe twenty minutes for the guide to reach the center of the glacier. Margaret knew what lay below her. She took heart from the loose posture of the porter ahead of her. He had done this dozens of times, if not more. If it wasn't safe, would he have come along?

For him, the traverse was only tedious. She longed to be on the other side, which was becoming more and more desirable with each step.

"What the hell is she doing?" Patrick called out.

Margaret looked up. She saw a flurry of red. The guide raised his voice. Diana seemed to be on a different path just above the rest of them. Her posture, bent forward, showed an impatience with the guide's slow progress. Margaret realized that Diana had unclipped herself from the guide rope.

"Diana, stop!" Arthur cried. "Get back here!"

The guide shouted. Above them, Diana was carving her own footsteps into the glacier without benefit of ax or rope.

"Diana!" Arthur yelled again.

Margaret watched as Diana dug into the ice with either her instep or the side of her boot, depending on which foot she was trying to secure. Margaret could see that Diana was now above and just forward of the guide, who was trying to keep step with her. The group moved as well. The ice had softened some, so that Diana was able to make a rudimentary shelf with each step.

"Stop her!" Patrick cried. "Someone! Anyone!"

Diana had been impatient to get going. Possibly, the altitude had finally gotten to her and had impaired her judgment. She had her arms out, but Margaret could see that the force of kicking in new steps was producing a counterforce that was pushing her body outward, requiring more balance than had been needed before. As if the sheer volume of his voice alone would make her obey, Arthur pleaded with her.

But, as they all knew, Diana obeyed no one.

Suddenly, Diana was on the ground, knees up, and sliding past the guide. Margaret couldn't believe what she was seeing. The guide reached forward to catch the white fur of Diana's hood. She turned and tried to grab hold of his hand. She missed it and tore off a mitten to get at the ice with her fingernails. She hit a bump, which she tried to cling to, but gravity and velocity defeated her. The last Margaret saw of Diana, as she plummeted into the deep ravine, was a patch of red, spiraling out of control toward the bottom.

It was a horror such as Margaret had never imagined.

Arthur fell to his knees, howling Diana's name. He reached out toward her as if, even as she was sliding fifty, a hundred, two hundred feet away from him, he might still snag her jacket with his hand. When Arthur went down, they all went down—crouching or on their knees. Saartje was the first, after Arthur, to cry out, but her cries quickly became sobs. Margaret said nothing, frozen in place. She couldn't see Patrick behind her, but the porter in front of her was on high alert. Arthur was losing it, bent toward the ravine, reaching out toward his wife. The guide scooted backward and took hold of him. He had one hand on the collar of Arthur's jacket, the other on his own pickax, which he sank deep into the ice. Arthur's cries became guttural, awful to listen to. Margaret bent her head to her knees.

It had happened in the space of an instant. In a few minutes they would have been across the glacier, Diana exulting, no longer impatient, celebrating like the rest of them. They wouldn't have reached the summit yet, but they'd have conquered the worst the mountain had to offer. Margaret wanted to step in and undo the moment of Diana unclipping herself from the guide rope. Over and over and over, she tried this. Arthur was bellowing and beating the ice. He swayed from side to side in his keening, and their bodies swayed with him. The last porter in the line was dispatched down the mountain to assemble a rescue team. They could hear the guide speaking into his radio. There was a squawk of a reply. The guide summoned the rangers from Top Hut. Then he covered Arthur with his own body, speaking to him in an intimate and calm voice. The guide had but one task—to get Arthur and the rest of them across the ice to safety.

They stayed as they were for what seemed a long time. A minute felt like twenty. Margaret thought of Diana with her dogs and with her children. Of her sudden, dazzling smile. Of the way she had helped Margaret on the Ngong Hills. It was essential now to get Arthur to the other side in one piece. His children needed him. Margaret could not imagine the man's grief, what lay ahead of him.

She wanted to crawl across the glacier, but they were told to stand. Each of them had to figure out how to rise simultaneously with their feet in awkward positions, all the while maintaining perfect balance. Each of them had to take steps away from the site of the accident. Each of them, including Arthur, had to leave Diana in the ravine. Arthur was crazed with shock and grief, but everybody else understood that safety now was paramount. Though the guide was outwardly calm, Margaret could see his concern. Any rash movement, and they would all be dead. The greatest danger was a deranged Arthur, an Arthur who, in a frenzy to find his wife, might at any minute jump off the ledge made by the footprints. The pickaxes could not withstand the sudden torque of a lurch like that.

The group became eerily quiet. They walked as slowly and as carefully as possible. Though Margaret was not an especially religious woman, she repeated the Lord's Prayer over and over as a kind of ritualistic chant. If she kept saying it without mistakes, she thought, they would make it to the other side.

It wasn't until they were ten steps away from solid ground that Patrick, behind her, in a voice that was meant to reach the top of the mountain itself, cried out an unintelligible sound—a summons that echoed off the rocks there and there and there, a sound that scuttled her bones. The cry was meant for Diana and Arthur. Later, Margaret would learn that the rest was meant for Patrick and her.

At the far side of the glacier, Arthur unclipped himself. He took off down the mountain, as if he might get ahead of Diana and break her fall. Willem realized the folly of this—one couldn't get down the mountain on that side of the glacier—and started racing after him, surprising Margaret with his agility and speed. The guide stayed close to both men. Saartje lay prostrate on the ground, and Margaret knelt beside her.

Patrick sat, maybe twenty feet away, knees raised, head in his hands. Margaret knew better than to go to him. Saartje, momentarily coming up for air, turned her head to find Margaret's face. "Get off me," she blurted.

Margaret wasn't on her, but she stood anyway. Willem yelled, "Arthur!" Margaret could hear distant shouting while Willem sought to subdue the grief-deranged husband. When the scuffle was over, the two men sat. Together they stared into the place where Diana had gone. In deference, the guide stood fifteen feet away. Ready for whatever might happen next.

"Could she still be alive?" Margaret asked Patrick.

He didn't answer. He wouldn't look at her. He wouldn't come to where she stood.

Saartje got up and brushed her pants and jacket off.

"You know what Diana and Arthur were arguing about this morning?" she asked Margaret.

Margaret's skin went hot inside her jacket. She shook her head. (Though she knew, didn't she?)

"God, why did you even come?" Saartje asked, and walked away.

Margaret had her hands in her pockets as she stared at her feet. She couldn't look down the mountain. She didn't want to glance at Patrick, who wouldn't return her gaze. She avoided the glacier, which they would soon have to recross, an almost unthinkable endeavor. How would Arthur be able to handle that? How would any of them manage? Was there another way around the glacier? The guide would know. Maybe if they went up and over? *Over what?* Margaret wondered, as she surveyed the peaks above them. Would Arthur have the strength to climb farther?

It was as though Diana had disappeared into the earth, to reappear in a hundred years or maybe never. She had gone somewhere none of them could follow. Margaret prayed that Diana had died early in her slide, perhaps whacking her head on the ice, the spiraling Margaret had seen indicating unconsciousness. What Margaret couldn't bear was the thought of Diana alive and knowing her fate, even for an instant. But, then again, wouldn't Diana have believed in hope, in rescue, right up until the last minute? Or would she have seen the bottom of the ravine coming at her and panicked, as Margaret imagined people who jumped off buildings did as they saw the earth rushing to meet them? No, Margaret decided then and there. Diana had been struck unconscious early on. Margaret tried to imagine Arthur's frustration as Diana had slid past him and out of his reach. To want to save her and to have to remain still would have been an excruciating torment.

The cook came around with hot soup. Each of them accepted the broth, but none of them could drink it. After a time, Patrick rose to his feet and walked to where Margaret stood. Neither of them spoke. The words they had in their heads could not be said aloud. Not there. Not in front of others.

Arthur and Willem began the climb back up. Margaret hoped Willem had prepared Arthur for the need to recross the glacier.

As the two drew closer, Arthur's face stunned Margaret. It wasn't Arthur. Though the man wore Arthur's Barbour jacket, he was no one she recognized. He gasped for breath like a fish, and his eyes were so swollen they were nearly shut. Despair, Margaret saw firsthand, rearranged the features.

Saartje went to Arthur and held on to him. He laid his head on her shoulder and scrunched his eyes, but he didn't sob or cry out. The grief was already beginning to go beyond the tears to a place that had no outlet except to worm its ugly way into the center of his body.

Margaret wished to evaporate. She didn't want Arthur to have to look up and see her face. Did he blame her, as the others clearly did? Was she responsible for worrying Diana about her husband's small attentions to her? Had that caused Diana's anger and her impatience? Or had Margaret caused it by being impossibly slow and making everyone in the climbing party wait? How many hours had been lost to Margaret's tardiness? Or was it simply the glimpse of the clasped hands when Diana woke that had filled her head with fury?

Margaret wondered how Arthur would have played that scene outside the door. Margaret had been terrified and had reached for his hand? Margaret wouldn't let go? He was so tired he gave up and just went to sleep? Or might there have been enough

lantern light from outside for Diana to have seen the position of
the hands, Arthur's over Margaret's? Would Diana have added
that to the litany of perceived slights that had accrued over time:
finding Margaret, a strange woman, drink in hand, in her drawing room one day; watching as Arthur put his hand on Margaret's
shoulder when he got up to get her a whiskey; noting that her
husband was staring at Margaret while she was naked on the
Ngong Hills (when Willem had had the good sense to turn away);
observing the way her husband dropped back to give Margaret a
push or the way he had shared his chocolate bar with her just the
night before? Had Diana seen that?

Only Willem seemed without accusation. He was preoccupied, as was she, with the image of Arthur losing it on the glacier,
yanking the guide rope in such a way as to endanger the safety
of the rest of them. Willem would stay near Arthur, Margaret
guessed. The guide first, Arthur second, Willem third. Willem
would have an ax and would dig it hard into the ice if Arthur
wobbled or fell, thus keeping the line steady for the rest of them.

The rangers arrived from Top Hut.

The crossing was made without mishap, though the pace was
slow. Each minute on the glacier increased the chance that
Arthur might fling himself toward Diana, to the place where
he imagined his wife lay. When finally they reached the other
side, the guide went ahead. The two rangers led Arthur down the
mountain, each occasionally taking an arm. Patrick and Willem
followed close behind. They didn't run; the guide forced them to
walk slowly, which seemed nearly impossible on the scree, where
one was tempted to sit and slide the entire length of it. (Willem
had warned that "a skinned ass" would be the consequence.) The

bog was almost as miserable going down as it had been going up. Margaret had developed severe cramps along the way and had to retreat often to the bushes with burning diarrhea. Was this AMS in reverse? Or had the shock unnerved her system, too? She felt sick and shaky and at times not sure that she could take another step. She unpacked the meds and took a teaspoon of Imodium. After she had stumbled a couple of times, she noticed that the cook, whose name she didn't know *(whose name she didn't know!)*, stood near her in case she fell badly. After the bog, Arthur shook the two rangers off and walked by himself to Park Gate. He seemed to have regained some of his emotional strength and now wanted to mount a rescue mission. Patrick tipped the guide handsomely, but the man wouldn't take the money.

At the lodge, Arthur was told that there was little hope of rescue, and that they likely would recover only a body. He collapsed into a chair. A half hour later, Arthur was on his feet, throwing his weight around in an unpleasant way—rudely, condescendingly—though one could hardly blame him. He made phone calls: to the police, to a friend of his in Langata, to James. Perhaps he also made one to Adhiambo, who had the children. Arthur faced another sickening task: having to tell the children that their mother was gone.

There would be a memorial service to prepare for.

There was some talk of spending another night at the lodge. But a more rational Arthur realized that he must get to his children, that he had responsibilities—unasked for, unimagined. They had only the one vehicle. Patrick quietly tried to rent another so that Arthur could return with Saartje and Willem only. But there were no vehicles available unless Patrick and Margaret wanted to wait until the next day and take the local bus. Patrick shook his head. They would return as they had come.

The ride back to Langata was ghastly. Willem drove in what would have been Diana's seat. Arthur sat beside him, holding Diana's belongings. Saartje and Margaret had the middle seats, while Patrick took the back, more than willing, Margaret knew, to be away from the rest of them. Saartje had her body turned away from Margaret the entire journey, and Margaret thought the woman must have arrived in Langata with a crick in her neck. From time to time, Margaret had to look between the men so that she wouldn't become motion-sick. Once, she humiliated herself by having to ask them to pull over so that she could find rudimentary shelter for another pit stop. The cramps had not abated. Margaret wanted only to fall asleep and wake a month later.

From time to time, Arthur smacked his head against the back of his seat. The scene on the ice, Margaret imagined, would freshly occur to him, again and again, in all its horror. Sometimes he would cry out; at other times, he would simply bend his head forward and weep.

After they'd arrived in Langata, Saartje and Willem went immediately into the Big House, to be there for Arthur when he told his children, perhaps to be there for the children. It was something Margaret dearly wanted to do as well, to help in some way. She watched them walk off, but Patrick steered Margaret in the direction of their cottage. He would get the gear later, he said. He was insistent that Margaret lie down.

Patrick wouldn't say what he wanted to say. The words that had been in their heads on the mountain would not be spoken while they were both too shaken. That conversation would happen in the morning.

* * *

Sleepless that night in bed, Margaret couldn't believe that the tragedy had really happened. Diana was there, making footsteps above them, and then she was gone. Just like that. Gone.

And Margaret was to blame.

Was a woman, Margaret wondered, who allowed attentions from a man permitted to accept his touch even though she had no thought of reciprocating? Was she implicitly making a bargain she had no intention of keeping?

Wasn't Margaret guilty, since she could see clearly that any exchanges between Arthur and her were causing Diana irritation or pain? And Margaret did see that, she was sure of it. She certainly intuited it. She believed that Diana would have been annoyed at Margaret's pace up the mountain even if Diana had never met Margaret before. And Margaret remembered that Diana was a person who needed always to get going. But Margaret couldn't see Diana unclipping herself, knowing how dangerous it was, if those two factors were her only motivation. (And, oddly, Margaret had had nothing to do with the slow trek across the glacier. That had been the guide's decision.)

Margaret *could* imagine, however, the angry white noise inside Diana's head and the passionate desire to escape the thing that was hurting her, a thing she considered beneath her in the first place (was that why she had needed to be above them?), which would have exaggerated the pain. That, combined with an almost desperate need to get somewhere faster, made sense to Margaret as the real reason Diana undertook the most risky venture of her life. No one in her right mind would have unclipped herself had the white noise not drowned out rational thought. Diana hadn't climbed Mount Kenya before, so it wasn't as though she knew the terrain well and had felt confident on the glacier. She was as much a neophyte as the rest of them. Or had she so believed in her invincibility and her capabilities that she thought even if she tried that insane act, she would be victorious?

And what exactly did Diana imagine she would accomplish? She would have reached the far side of the glacier six minutes before the rest of them. What would Diana have done with those six minutes? Sit down and rest, a smile on her face? Climb up onto a small ridge to be able to look down on the others as they finished the trek? Or was the gesture meant to be a major *fuck you* to Margaret and Arthur?

Margaret suspected that a little of everything — pride, hurt, annoyance, an urgent need for speed, anger — combined in a single reckless moment to make Diana unclip herself.

"We're going to talk about this once," Patrick said when he came out of the bedroom the next morning. Margaret had risen early and made him a breakfast of eggs and bacon, mango slices and pawpaw juice. The smell of the bacon would have woken him. "And then never again."

In a short-sleeved shirt and jeans, he sat down to breakfast. He toyed with the yolk of an egg.

Margaret was relieved that he wanted to talk. She hoped this would clear the air. She believed that by talking about what had happened the day before, they would better understand it. That the talking itself would defuse the tension.

"There was nothing between us," Margaret began.

Patrick brushed his chin with his knuckle. "Yes, there was, Margaret."

She was momentarily taken aback. "I was aware that Arthur was occasionally flirting with me, but I believed it was harmless."

Patrick picked up his coffee cup and then set it down. "Harmless to whom?"

"If you noticed anything, and you thought it was causing harm, why didn't you say something? To me, anyway?" Margaret asked.

Patrick picked up a spoon. "Because it didn't seem enough to make a fuss about. I've always believed in your fidelity, your integrity. I didn't like watching Arthur flirt with you, but I was pretty sure it would end soon. I suppose I snapped at the sight of the two of you holding hands. Even if he had reached for your hand, I trusted you to extricate yourself, however awkward that would have been." Patrick began to rap the spoon against the tablecloth. "But you didn't. So what did that mean exactly? I had to ask myself. I didn't want the question. I didn't want the worry. What I wanted to do was wake you up and shake your arms out of their sockets."

The rapping of the spoon grew more rapid. "So I can pretty much imagine what Diana would have thought when she woke," he added. "She was up before me, and I'm certain that she saw. Otherwise there would have been no fight outside the door of the banda. She believed that something was going on. I know she did."

"And because of that, you think me responsible for her accident and her death."

The accusation sounded harsh in the sunny room with the cooked breakfast. Margaret hoped that Patrick would immediately say no, that he didn't, that Diana and only Diana was responsible for what she had done.

Patrick laid down the spoon, leaned over the table, and put his fingers to his forehead. "I don't know what I think, Margaret. I wish to God I had some clarity, but I don't. If you and Arthur hadn't been holding hands and sleeping so close to each other, Diana wouldn't have had the anger to do what she did. I guess I believe that."

Margaret was still.

"I'm sorry, Margaret. You asked."

She shook her head back and forth. Did he mean to punish her for causing him doubt? For making him have to alter the portrait of his wife? For knowing that he faced a future in which he might never be able to trust that wife again?

"I've explained to you what happened," Margaret said in her defense.

He looked up at her. "So you have."

"And you don't believe me?"

"Oh, I believe you, all right. And had Diana not died in an icy crevasse, we'd probably be jubilant about having reached the top of Mount Kenya and would be crowing about that accomplishment. But she did die, and that changes everything."

"Why?" Margaret asked.

"Because before, the consequences of your actions were irrelevant. Now they aren't."

"You can't separate the actions from unintended consequences?"

"I don't know."

"Patrick, it's me you're talking to—your wife."

"I'm very aware of that."

"This isn't happening," Margaret said, standing. "How can you stay in a marriage in which you believe I was responsible for Diana's death? How can you possibly love me?"

"Well, I do love you," he said, picking up the spoon again and beating it against the lip of the table. "That's the point." He looked up at her. "I lay awake last night asking myself the same question. Does this change what I think about Margaret? Do I still love her? And, oddly enough, it didn't change anything. Not really. I love you and want to stay married to you."

"You made a cost-benefit analysis?"

"Don't be crude. That's why I said we would have this discussion once and then never again."

"But why have it at all?" Margaret asked. "Why was it necessary to tell me I'm guilty if you intend to stay with me? If you love me, as you say."

Was Patrick simply being honest with her, or was there a hint of jealousy of his own?

"First, you asked," Patrick said. "And second, it had to be said. This thing would have festered had we not tried to talk about it. I believe you think yourself guilty, too. I don't mean you believe you directly caused her death. Not that. I just think that you know that had you and Arthur not been holding hands yesterday morning, the day would have gone very differently."

Margaret's legs were beginning to twitch.

"And third," he continued, "in case you're not aware of this, I never lie to you."

"You kept from me the fact of the students in the mass grave."

"That's different. That was to protect you. And besides, I'm still not sure it's true."

"Patrick, how do you expect me to continue to love you, knowing you think as you do?"

"I'm more worried about you loving yourself."

"You arrogant son of a bitch," Margaret said in a deadly quiet tone. She reached over and grabbed the annoying spoon from Patrick's hand and threw it, watching it ding the wall.

"That's what rage does," Patrick pointed out calmly. "You're not a person who throws silverware across a room."

"This is an object lesson?"

"I'm just trying to get you to understand why Diana might have done what she did."

Margaret sat down and put her head on the tablecloth. She pictured Diana at the bottom of a ravine. She imagined Arthur next door, waking to the knowledge that his wife was dead and having to live through the shock of it. Or would his children be in the bed with him, softening the shock but intensifying the ache?

Margaret kept her head on the tablecloth. She heard Patrick push the chair back and stand. She expected to feel his hand at the back of her neck.

"We're going to have to move," he said matter-of-factly. "We'd better start looking for places."

He was farther away, not closer. So he wouldn't touch her. He was going to leave her at the table to digest what had been said. He wasn't going to massage the strife away.

The memorial service was a quiet affair at a chapel attached to a large Catholic church. Margaret hadn't known that Diana was Catholic. Patrick and Margaret sat near the back, not wanting to intrude in any way upon Arthur's moment with his children. The sight of the children—hair shiny and brushed, chins trembling—made Margaret cry. She searched for Adhiambo, who should have been sitting close to them. Had she been fired already? They knew that Arthur was taking his family back to

London, that Edward and Philippa were to be raised by Arthur with help from his sister.

Many of Arthur's colleagues attended the service, as did a large contingent of Diana's friends. Women's faces were obscured by large hats, and it was difficult to spot anyone Margaret knew. She searched for Willem's oversize body but couldn't find it. Had he and Saartje gone away? The service was surprisingly formal and lasted nearly an hour. When they all emerged from the darkened church into the blast of the noonday sun, many of the mourners fled to their cars. There was to be a reception back at the Big House, one that Patrick and Margaret would not attend. Instead, they would be packing. They'd found, through a friend of a friend, a house-sitting job in Karen, another suburb of Nairobi. They owned very little, and the packing would be easy.

Margaret wouldn't leave, however, without saying good-bye to Arthur. They waited just off the steps of the church, holding their hands to their foreheads to ward off the sunlight. When Arthur finally appeared, he stood alone. The children had gone ahead with a woman Margaret didn't recognize. Patrick approached Arthur, and Margaret followed. Patrick held out his hand and said how sorry he was. Arthur was in mourning clothes, a dark silk handkerchief in his pocket. His mud-brown hair had been slicked back, as though he'd put pomade in it but hadn't actually washed it. Patrick said he would leave the keys to the cottage on the table. Arthur nodded and then glanced over Patrick's shoulder at Margaret. There was a moment—a distinct and unambiguous moment—when their eyes met.

There was no mistaking the complicity and guilt Margaret read there.

Part Two

"You're sure you're okay with this."

"Absolutely."

"Some of it will be hard to look at," Patrick warned.

"I know."

"I just thought you might like to see what it is I do."

"I want to. I'm glad you invited me."

They emerged from the Peugeot onto the tarmac of Mathari Hospital, formerly called Mathari Mental Hospital. It was still a psychiatric hospital, though the unpleasant stigma had been removed. The government was thinking of changing the name yet again to the Muthaiga Hospital to further sanitize the facility. Mathari suggested squalor, whereas Muthaiga had classier connotations: a playground for the rich, white expatriates of an earlier generation.

Margaret could feel the heat of the tarmac through the soles of her shoes. She carried her camera; Patrick, his doctor bag. He had recently gotten a short haircut. His skin was white in the places where his hair had been removed, giving him a strangely boyish look.

The visit to Mathari Hospital marked the first time Patrick had asked Margaret along on one of his academic research projects. She thought perhaps that he was "making an effort" to save a marriage that had plateaued the morning after the fight about what had happened on Mount Kenya. Three months had passed, and their relationship hadn't worsened, but neither had it improved. Margaret didn't have a lot of experience with marriage, but she sensed that a plateau wasn't an especially good place to be, particularly if that plain did not feel comfortable for either of them.

They had moved to the house-sit in Karen, unnerved at first by its size: something between the Big House, which had been sold to the Kenyan minister of transportation, and their cottage. The new home was furnished with antiques and Orientals and came with a house servant named Moses. Moses did for Patrick and Margaret what James had done for Diana and Arthur, and it had been made clear to Patrick and Margaret that there was no *not* having Moses. The owners, a couple from Australia, considered him a fixture in their lives and wanted to ensure that he would be there when they returned in six months' time.

Moses was a good cook and would greet Margaret each morning with a list for the day's shopping for her to approve: garam masala, king prawns, ghee, Kiwi Kleen Bowl. He had an extensive repertoire of main dishes, and she hadn't yet come up with a meal he couldn't figure out how to make. He had an easy disposition as well and smiled often; Margaret liked him. But whenever she was with him, she couldn't shake the sensation that she was a fraud, living a life she hadn't been bred to and hadn't earned. Giving instructions to Moses, she was an actor in a play someone British had written for a previous generation.

Apart from his convivial presence, which lent the household a positive ambience, Moses served as a kind of buffer between

Patrick and Margaret. Knowing that Moses was just around the corner kept their dialogue civil, even pleasant. Most of all, it kept them talking. The perception that they ate their meals in silence was one neither of them wanted to convey. It was as though they rose to their best behavior when Moses was in the house. Still, Margaret was hard put to treat the man as a servant. She wanted to invite him to sit with them at dinner. This was an entirely American idea, Patrick explained.

Periodically, either Patrick or Margaret would "make an effort" to break through the clot that was thickening just below the surface of their civility and pleasantries. In February, a month after the climb, Margaret had had Moses prepare an extravagant dinner, with champagne cocktails to be had first in the drawing room. Moses had lit the fire and retired to the kitchen, and Margaret had placed candles on the mantel and side tables. When Patrick came through the front door, doctor bag in one hand, briefcase in the other, and she called to him, she could see his surprise in his raised eyebrows. She had bought another surprise she intended to reveal later: a white silk nightgown.

"What's this about?" he asked.

"Nothing," Margaret said. "Just us. Thought we needed a lift." She was wearing a long blue dashiki with a V-neck and slits at the sides of the skirt.

At first Patrick sat on the sofa as if he might not be staying.

"You don't like this?" she asked.

"No, it's just that...I don't know..."

"Should we still be in mourning?"

"I don't know. I guess not. I never thought about it, really."

"It's just a drink and dinner."

"Just a drink and dinner with caviar and champagne?"

Margaret turned away and looked steadily into the fireplace, and Patrick must have sensed he'd gone one comment too far. He touched her arm and signaled to her to snuggle up against him. He opened the champagne and poured them each a glass. They didn't toast; nothing seemed suitable. They drank the champagne and ate the caviar and laughed, something they hadn't done since before the Mount Kenya climb. When they left the drawing room, having polished off the champagne, there was at least a hint of real intimacy between them.

But something happened in the dining room — with its perfect place settings, candles lit, Moses serving — that flattened whatever brief stab of happiness they'd managed to create just moments earlier. Too late, Margaret realized they'd have been better off eating on trays by the fire. Or sending Moses home early after he had cooked the meal, with promises that they would do the washing up. By the time dinner was over, any joy they'd managed to produce had evaporated like the champagne bubbles they'd had earlier. Patrick rose to go to the study to review papers about equatorial medicine. Margaret went upstairs and removed the white nightgown from its impudent toss across the bed.

"You brought your camera?" Patrick asked Margaret on the tarmac.

"Thought I'd give it a whirl. If they insist, I'll take it back to the car."

Just then, the stench hit her, assaulting her nose and throat and stomach. "Patrick," she gasped.

In the car, Patrick had been civil, even animated, trying to prepare Margaret for the hospital. As they had passed the slums of Mathari, she'd glimpsed cardboard roofs covering the shanties.

The huts had seemed piled one upon the other until all the ground was swallowed up.

"This was cleaned out during Mau Mau," Patrick began. "It was thought to be a hotbed of rebellion. After independence, the people returned and built houses, if you can call them that, of thin wood or of mud. They make their income hiring out rooms or brewing a maize beer called bazaa to sell to customers, mostly men, who flood the slums in the evenings and on weekends."

"Have you ever tried it?" Margaret asked. "The bazaa?"

"Awful stuff. Really."

Below them, she could see no roads, merely miles and miles of cardboard and tin rooftops.

"No water, no electricity, no drains, no way of disposing of garbage," Patrick continued. "Every once in a while, the police come along and bulldoze a hundred or so huts. I'm all for it. Diseases spread fast in the slums. Cholera. Typhoid. Tuberculosis."

"What happens to the people whose houses are destroyed?" she asked, thinking of Adhiambo.

"They move in with relatives. Eventually everything the government has bulldozed grows back. Like a weed."

On the tarmac, Margaret felt blinded. When her eyes adjusted, she could see masses of hot-pink and orange blossoms covering blue and white buildings. Several men in green cotton uniforms were working on cars under a corrugated tin roof. An attendant in a white coat walked slowly with a woman in a green shift. The scene struck Margaret as a normal one. It was only seconds later, when she saw that the woman's head had been shaved; that an adolescent boy, flailing in the hot sun, was strapped into a high chair; and that every window in the long string of buildings was barred, that she understood that the men working on the cars were really very sick.

"The place is woefully understaffed," Patrick said as they walked to the entrance. "All I'm doing here is trying to separate out the organic diseases, which would require different treatment, from the strictly psychiatric diseases. In return for being allowed into the hospital to do my research, I run a clinic whenever I come."

Margaret brought her straw hat farther down on her brow to ward off the glare. Short of wearing a mask, there was nothing she could do about the smell.

"There are seventeen hundred patients, eight hundred of which are incarcerated," Patrick explained. "For those eight hundred, there are eight doctors. You do the math. Everyone here has been brought by family or police because his or her behavior was deemed either criminal or suicidal. The men's wards are on the other side of that fence. We'll just see the women's wards today."

Margaret saw women lying on the paved courtyard, some alone, some in pairs. She felt bludgeoned by the sun and couldn't imagine how hot and uncomfortable the tarmac must have been for them. As Margaret and Patrick passed, they caused a commotion. The women ran to Patrick and chattered in languages Margaret couldn't identify. He talked encouragingly in Swahili to them, scolded others. Margaret knew enough Swahili to understand some of Patrick's admonitions. Eat well. Drink a lot of water. Drink the milk they offer you. Take the medicine. Rest in the shade if you can. He turned and introduced Margaret. The women touched her, and she knew not to shrink away. The women's hands were filthy, and, up close, the stench made

Margaret's eyes water. The women especially wanted to touch her hair, with its sun-bleached streaks. With their fingers, they reached out toward her head and then hissed, as if their fingers had been singed.

"Everyone here is thought to be psychotic," Patrick explained.

"Are they not allowed baths?" Margaret asked.

"The overall stench is because of the plumbing," Patrick said.

They were greeted by the senior nursing officer, Mr. Jesani, an Asian with a thick beard that covered the bottom half of his round face, a heavy head of black hair, and thick glasses. He would be the tour guide. Margaret asked if she could use her camera. He said no. Then maybe. Then that he would signal her when a picture could be taken. Margaret took four that day. One was taken through bars to an outdoor courtyard where the women, in cotton dresses, milled around one another. A second was of a woman with a shaved head, lying on the dirt next to a wire fence, a picture she managed to snap without permission. Another was of a similar woman, her new hair growth gray, making a basket with a long piece of straw. A fourth, staged for Margaret, was of a female nurse in starched white, teaching a group of women gathered at a table how to read.

A wire fence surrounded one ward. Yellow doors and yellow bars, along with the green shifts of the women, provided a touch of color in an otherwise bleak scene. For the most part, the women were in courtyards, some alone, some huddled in pairs, some contentedly weaving baskets. In the center of the first courtyard, a woman named Wanjui, six months pregnant, was drinking a Tetra Pak of milk, her extra ration. When her baby was born, Mr. Jesani said, it would go to Dr. Bernard's Home, an orphanage. Mathari Hospital, it was explained, was no place for babies.

Wanjui's child to come would be her second. The first was staying with her husband's family while she was in the hospital. It was doubtful that Wanjui would be allowed to care for either child again. Her parents had always regarded Wanjui as a strange girl, given to long, sullen crying spells and fits of bad temper. When she married, the parents felt better, for she immediately became pregnant, had a baby, and began to care for that child in a way they deemed appropriate. One day, however, her husband arrived home and found Wanjui trying to drown her baby in a tub of water. Wanjui could not explain what she was doing. Sometimes she couldn't even remember the incident. Sometimes she wasn't able to remember that she had a child at all.

"Psychotic," Mr. Jesani pronounced.

Many of the women suffered from hallucinations and delusions, while others could not control their bodies. The latter were the patients Patrick was interested in. *Why* couldn't they control their bodies? Patrick was convinced that some of these women, if correctly diagnosed, could be treated with conventional medicines and sent on their way.

On the grass were women lying so motionless that the flies didn't even bother to buzz around them; they simply rested on the brown flesh. From a long corridor Margaret could hear a woman moaning. Mr. Jesani explained that she had had to be locked in her room because she "couldn't control herself," again a loose reference to what might or might not be an organic disease. In a corner by a fence, an older woman cradled a younger woman in her arms as a mother would a baby. A gregarious patient followed

Margaret, asking questions she couldn't understand, continually touching her and wanting to be touched back.

"Don't," Patrick whispered to Margaret.

They moved from ward to ward until they came to the final locked door. There was some discussion as to whether or not Margaret should be allowed in. Mr. Jesani was worried about the chaos that might ensue if there was an upset in routine. White women seldom visited, Margaret was told. She argued that if there was a problem, she would leave at once. The nurse unlocked the door to the female criminal ward.

Tall, thick stone walls surrounded the women. The building was damp and airless, the smell terrible, the atmosphere gloomy. The women approached Patrick and Margaret aggressively. They demanded her bracelet. They wanted money. They pulled her hair. When bananas were served in the dark courtyard, they fought for their share. They laughed at Margaret and pursued her relentlessly down the long corridor of locked doors, behind which lay women in solitary confinement. At times it was so dark in the criminal ward, Margaret couldn't see her hands. Mr. Jesani communicated with the patients, chiding and scolding if necessary. From time to time, Patrick would ask to examine a patient. On their way out, they passed by an open door. Inside sat a lovely elderly Masai woman, in regal splendor, finishing an enormous basket, ten feet in diameter. The fact that she had become incontinent and incapable of caring for herself did not diminish the grace with which she came to the bars in her window and held out her hand in greeting.

"*Karibu,*" the woman said. *Welcome.*

"You have seen the worst," Mr. Jesani said.

*   *   *

Margaret couldn't drink the tea that was served to them in the director's office. Patrick had two cups and two sandwiches to match. He glanced at Margaret from time to time. At one point, she thought he was trying to tell her, "It could be a long afternoon. You might want to eat something."

After lunch, she followed Patrick to the place where he was to hold his clinic, a damp stone corridor with a window just behind him to enhance the light from the single bulb overhead. He asked Margaret to give the waiting women cups of water and the tray of biscuits the director had held out to them when they'd left his office. Margaret thought that the promise of the biscuits may have been the draw of the clinic; that, or the handsome young doctor who waited to treat the women. When she had distributed the water and the food, she sat in a chair in the corner and observed her husband.

He resembled the Patrick she'd known before the climb: focused, but quick with a joke; searching for the problem, but not immune to a sudden hug; pulling a young woman who was crying to his shoulder. He palpated glands, looked down throats, felt for lumps that had been shyly pointed to. He gave orders to an attending nurse in a calm voice that clearly communicated urgency. He dispensed pills. He wrote notes the entire time in a shorthand only he could read. When the clinic was over, Margaret knew, he would meet with the top physician at the compound and review the records of the eighty patients he was following for his research. She watched him, his dark hair haloed by the bright midday light beyond the window, his face backlit.

"Patrick, Patrick, Patrick," she said silently to herself.

* * *

Shortly after the day at Mathari Hospital, a colleague of Patrick's named Munira and his wife, Naomi, invited Patrick and Margaret to visit Munira's family shamba in Limuru, a village north of Nairobi in Kikuyu territory. Munira drove. While still in the car on the way to Limuru, Margaret was overtaken by a soporific lassitude, one brought on by the seemingly endless panoramas of red dirt and carved green terraces, of mango trees and banana plantations, of seas of red coffee beans. She thought it must be the saturated color, too many bright hues overwhelming the senses. Or perhaps it was the fact that Naomi and Munira spoke English with a musical and mesmerizing Kikuyu lilt.

When the four arrived in the town, Munira announced that he and Naomi first had to pay their respects to Naomi's father, who was an advocate and had an office there. Patrick and Margaret took cups of tea they'd ordered at a tea shop to an outdoor terrace. Below them lay a maze of red and green, punctuated by grass huts.

"This is too beautiful," Margaret said. "It makes me feel alive and yet dreamy at the same time. I just want to close my eyes."

"It's the altitude."

"You don't think it's beautiful?"

"I do. But it's the altitude."

"Okay."

"Did you know Munira's grandfather fought during Mau Mau?" Patrick asked.

"Where?"

"Right here."

"You mean right here, in this town?" Margaret asked, taking another sip of the sweet tea.

"And in the countryside. It's like sitting at the site of a Civil War battle twenty years after it happened." He paused and then asked, "Are you okay?"

Margaret met his eyes. "I'm trying," she said.

Anger begets anger, she wanted to say. Distrust begets distrust.

They could hear their friends and Naomi's father approaching.

"My father-in-law wants to give you a drink from the bar of his friend," Munira said.

Margaret checked her watch. It was eleven in the morning.

"We'd love a drink," Patrick answered. He smiled and shook hands with Naomi's father.

They followed the man to a cement box of a bar, where they were greeted with much enthusiasm by Naomi's father's friends, all Kikuyu men of varying ages and builds, all with a distinct Bantu likeness. They were ushered into a back room, where Patrick was offered chang'aa. Not far from the bar was the actual grave site of Munira's grandfather, which they visited. While Margaret snapped pictures of Munira, Naomi, the grave site, and the surrounding countryside, Munira spoke about his grandfather's sacrifice.

"He was a very brave man," he said. "He killed eight of the British troops with his panga alone."

"How did he die?" Patrick asked.

"He was executed," Munira said. "A bullet to the back of the head."

Margaret tried to imagine the beautiful terraces as a bloody battleground. The prize had been freedom, as flawed and as difficult as that had turned out to be.

"I think it is time we are eating," Munira said.

He drove Patrick and Margaret to his family's shamba, a mud-

and-wattle hut with a grass roof—Munira's home when he was a boy. From that hut, he had gone to grammar school, high school, university in the UK, and then medical school in Nairobi. Now he worked as a physician at Nairobi Hospital. Naomi was a banker. She had on an electric-blue suit that hugged every curve of her body. From time to time, she settled her hands on her belly and sighed with contentment. Munira announced that Naomi was pregnant.

Was this the real Africa? Margaret wondered as she was beckoned into the darkened hut to sit awhile. She chatted with Munira's female relatives in her best, if rudimentary, Swahili. There were many smiles on both sides. Margaret examined the pictures that hung on the walls. One was a portrait of Jomo Kenyatta. The others were pages that had been ripped out of magazines and taped to the wall: pictures of the countryside, one of Mombasa, and one of a particularly difficult hairstyle of complicated braids. Margaret admired a red-and-yellow handwoven rug in the center of the room. Munira's sister said she had made it, and Margaret complimented her. The cooking was done in a separate hut, one of the women explained, the hut that had a hole cut into the roof.

Patrick and Margaret were plied with irio, a Kikuyu dish of mashed potatoes, maize, and peas, while outside, chickens ran in the dust. A goat was slaughtered in their honor, and Patrick and she were given the "delicacies" in a ceremonial manner. Margaret stared down at her tin plate. Biological forms she couldn't identify sat in a pool of what she could only assume was blood. Patrick took a bite, which he swallowed nearly whole. Margaret summoned her courage and did the same, allowing only a hint of taste and texture as it went down. Refusing the delicacies would have been rude, a notion Margaret had intuited as soon as the plate had been put in her lap—the irony being that all of Munira's family, at least a dozen siblings and cousins sitting at their feet, longed for the offal that had been given to Patrick and Margaret.

They were offered pombe, a milder beer, which helped with the organs. As they were leaving the shamba, there were many handshakes and pleas to return. Margaret invited the family to visit them in Karen, a suggestion that was greeted with mild enthusiasm. (Patrick and Margaret had Munira's extended family over for a typical American meal on the Fourth of July. They served hamburgers, potato salad, coleslaw, and strawberry shortcake for dessert. The Africans barely touched their plates. They would not pick up the hamburgers despite the fact that Patrick and Margaret demonstrated how to do so. They poked at the coleslaw, ate the potato salad—though they said it had a sour taste—and had only a bite of the strawberry shortcake. Too sweet, they proclaimed.)

As Margaret and Patrick were about to climb back into Munira's car to go home, Munira's sister gave Margaret a basket of pawpaw and the rug Margaret had much admired when she'd entered the hut. Margaret was horrified by the gift of the family's only rug and protested that she couldn't possibly accept it, that their dirt floor would be bare without it. In the end, the rug was slipped through the back window and onto their laps. Though Margaret was embarrassed, she thanked them profusely for the generous gift. There would be other trips to other family shambas, but Margaret would never again make the mistake of admiring anything another woman owned.

Once, Margaret went on a trip without Patrick. Aarya and Karim, a Pakistani couple who worked with UNICEF and who lived next door to Margaret and Patrick in Karen, had been given permission to view a Masai ceremony, one that took place only once every twenty years. Aarya asked Margaret if she wanted to tag along. It might be possible for her to take a picture or two, which would help Aarya and Karim document the siku kuu.

They drove along a treacherous and winding route to the floor of the Rift Valley, where it was dusty and hot. It was easy to spot where the ceremony would take place: two hundred fifty manyattas formed a perfect circle a half mile across. Margaret felt as though they were journeying back in time to an ancient archaeological site. When they parked near the opening of the circle, they climbed atop the VW Kombi that Aarya had borrowed from UNICEF. A wind came up and stuck the dust to Margaret's sweaty face. She had brought a hat and sunglasses, which were essential. Without them, she almost certainly would have gotten heatstroke.

The ceremony they were to witness that day atop the Kombi was for women. A separate ceremony for men had taken place just two days before. Then, a group of young men had made the transition from warriors to junior elders.

The purpose of this ceremony was to ensure fertility for each of the women who attended the ritual. Two thousand Masai participated, having come from as far as Kajiado. The event lasted the entire day.

Close to five hundred women gathered at the center of the circle and began to sing and dance. They were magnificent, each a queen in her brightly beaded maridadi and red blankets. Every woman's head had been shaved, while heavy jewelry (sometimes film canisters) hung from large and drooping ear holes. Occasionally, several of the women would throw themselves to the ground, wailing and beating their breasts.

"These are the women who have not borne children," Aarya,

who was sitting with Margaret on the roof of the Kombi, explained.

The dancing culminated in a four-step ritual. One by one, each Masai woman stepped to a small bath of honey beer made in a trough of dung. She touched her hand to the liquid and rubbed it on the insides of her thighs. She then went to another pot of honey beer in an animal skin and knelt down to sip from the beer or to be lightly slapped by the men with a branch of leaves dipped in the liquid. Her own marital and family status determined her treatment. From there, she walked to a group of men who sat with shallow dishes of white paint. The woman was painted on her face, back, or between her breasts, according to her fertility status.

From there, the woman joined a growing semicircle of other women, who also began to sing and dance. A contingent of men, by now quite drunk, passed before each of them, spitting and spraying honey beer first onto the woman's arm and then between her breasts, which she exposed. The woman was expected to stop singing and then to sit down once the men had blessed her in this way. Gradually all the music stopped. The symbolism was blatant.

Early in the ceremony, Margaret had taken out her camera and snapped a couple of shots. She and Aarya hadn't asked permission to photograph the event, and Margaret was reluctant to reveal the camera. Still, she wanted to capture the essence of the ceremony, the interactions between the men and the women. After perhaps fifteen minutes of quick, nervous shooting, Margaret felt a tug at her sleeve. Aarya pointed to a dozen Masai elders surrounding the Kombi. Margaret set the camera down on the metal roof, as if the innocent mechanism were a weapon.

An elder who spoke rapid Swahili, which Aarya then translated to Margaret, asked for money. He pointed out that if he went into Nairobi to have a picture taken, it would cost him thirty shillings. "When you pay us this money," he said, "that money can be gone in a day. It is so easy to spend. But if you have your photographs, they will be good for a hundred years."

While Margaret was trying to listen to the translation, a boy climbed up the Kombi behind her and snatched the camera. She was frightened, and although she wanted her camera back, she could not imagine getting off the bus and confronting what had now become forty or fifty elders attending to the matter. Each carried a spear or a panga. Karim, who'd been watching the ceremony from within the enclosure, jogged to the Kombi and spoke to the elders at length. He then turned his head up to Margaret and explained that unless she surrendered the film, she was liable for a three-thousand-shilling fine. Margaret nodded and said yes, she would give them the film. She simply wanted the camera back. But after a quick consultation, the Masai elders informed Karim of another decision they had made. They would no longer discuss the matter with Margaret, an elder explained, because she was a woman. And as women can have no possessions, the camera, in the eyes of the elders, did not belong to Margaret but to her husband. Did she have a husband? Margaret said that she did. In that case, she was told, she must send her husband back the next day and the matter would be discussed with him.

"But it's mine," Margaret protested. "My husband had nothing to do with it. I own that camera."

"You cannot tell that to these men," Karim, who had climbed to the roof of the Kombi, said. "They won't pay any attention to you."

"Do what they say," Aarya whispered beside Margaret.

* * *

The next morning, Patrick and Karim drove to the circle of man-yattas. Patrick asked to speak to an elder. He apologized pro-fusely for his wife's behavior, paid a small fine, and was given the camera back.

When he returned to the house in Karen, camera in hand, he seemed slightly amused by the entire encounter, amused enough not to have minded the long ride to the Rift and back.

Margaret, however, was furious. "Can't you see how demean-ing this is to me? To women?"

"Of course it's demeaning. That's the point."

"Doesn't that bother you?" she asked as she stared at the tainted camera on the hall table.

"Not really," he said.

"How can you say that?" she asked, her voice rising.

"You and I don't live in that culture, Margaret. We don't feel that way. The Masai have a separate culture with very different rules of behavior. The two cultures briefly intersected, *on their territory,* and a camera was confiscated. We got it back."

"But at what cost?"

"What's more important, your pride or the camera?"

Margaret couldn't answer him, because she didn't know the answer. She was glad to have the Nikon back, but she was seething at the thought of having been demoted to the status of a child. Or would a male child have had more authority than she? It was days before Margaret could bring herself to pick up the camera again.

Margaret was finding it increasingly difficult to fully absorb Africa when the very thing that had brought her to the coun-try—her marriage to Patrick—was troubling her. In theory, the lingering tension between them seemed like such an easy thing to fix. In reality, it was not. Patrick handled it better, Margaret thought, because he was engaged by his work. She was fascinated with photography, but to what purpose? It had not been imperative for Margaret to have a job in Kenya—Patrick's income supported them—but she had been feeling increasingly fraudulent. In June, Margaret determined to do something about that.

After a particularly grim and rainy weekend of no social engagements and no excursions, she drove to Nairobi with a portfolio she had assembled the previous day. She parked the car on a side street off Kenyatta and walked into the offices of the *Kenya Morning Tribune.*

"But maybe these are not so nice."

Solomon Obok sat across from Margaret at a metal desk so cluttered with papers that he'd had to lay her portfolio on top. He'd apologized for the mess, saying that he knew where everything was, but Margaret found that hard to believe. He'd begun with pictures she had taken of the countryside and portraits of men, women, and children (African, Asian, and white) she had done since arriving in the country. Those, he had admired, or at least Margaret had assumed he'd admired them, since he'd examined each slowly and nodded. Now, however, he was studying the clips she had brought from the Boston alternative paper, the pictures small and grainy and not at all as compelling as those he had just seen. How could a photograph of a meeting at the state-house compare with small black bodies emerging from the dust of a truck that had recently passed their way?

"You have improved since coming to this country," he said.

"Yes."

He removed his glasses and pinched the bridge of his nose. He had the blackest skin Margaret had ever seen on a human being. His face was oblique and long and handsome. When she had entered Mr. Obok's office, he'd risen from his desk and had shaken her hand, immediately sitting again, as if he had only a minute or two to spare on her. In that time, she'd noticed his tall, slim frame and the grace with which he moved. His fingers, elegant and tapered, were smudged with pencil graphite.

He set aside the newspaper photos and once again examined the portraits Margaret had taken.

"This I like very much," he said, referring to a shot of the mother on Kimathi Street whom Margaret had passed so often, the one who sat on the sidewalk with her children.

"It is all here," Mr. Obok said, lifting the photo and tapping it lightly with the backs of his fingers. "This is exactly what a good picture should be. It must tell the story at once. That and a headline should be able to stand alone. Of course, we wish to lead the reader to the text. We are a newspaper, so we cannot be as artful as we would like. But that does not mean that strictly reportorial photography cannot be art. If we have a great photograph, we will work a story around it. I am already thinking this would be a picture to illustrate an article on beggars. We might keep it for when the need to write such a piece comes round again."

"Thank you," Margaret said.

"I see that being a woman is perhaps advantageous for a photographer," he said, reviewing the picture of the beggar and her children again. "The woman here might have pulled her head scarf over her face had the photographer been a man."

Margaret thought, but didn't say, that if the man had put enough shillings in her tin cup, the woman would have let him take all the photos he wanted.

Mr. Obok leaned back against his wooden swivel chair and for the first time actually looked at Margaret. She'd been surprised at how claustrophobic the office of the *Kenya Morning Tribune* was. Only Mr. Obok had his own separate space. Several chairs were scattered around the room — for editorial meetings, she guessed. From the front door, she'd been shown the way through a larger room of metal desks, each occupied by a reporter or a secretary or an advertising salesperson. Hardly anyone had glanced up at her as she'd made her way to Mr. Obok's office. Putting together a newspaper, Margaret knew, required intense focus. The reporters searched for hot leads; the advertising executives, for great ad buys. Each of the desks had on it a manual typewriter and a telephone. Margaret had noted that there were no windows, which lent the place an air of the sweatshop.

"You worked for this newspaper in Boston for how long?"

"I had the job straight from college."

"You were lucky, then."

"Do I hear an American accent?" Margaret ventured.

"I was educated at a college in Indiana."

Margaret couldn't imagine Mr. Obok in Indiana. "Really? Where?"

"A small Quaker college named Earlham. I was raised as a Quaker."

Margaret had guessed Mr. Obok, because of his name in addition to his looks, to be a Luo, or from a Nilotic tribe similar to the Luo. But she had to stretch her imagination to picture the Quakers moving into his parents' village, converting the inhabitants there.

"How did you manage the Hoosier winters?" Margaret asked.

Mr. Obok smiled broadly — purple-black lips, white teeth tinged mauve near the gum line — and then he laughed. "My first year, I thought I would perish. The snow, it is like fire on the face, no?"

"It is," Margaret said, thinking of a Boston blizzard or, worse, an ice storm.

"You are here for how long?" he asked.

"We've been here eight months. We plan to stay for three years," Margaret said, though she didn't really know. She doubted anyone would give her a job if she said she was staying only a year.

"You are married?"

"Yes."

"What does your husband do?"

"He's attached to Nairobi Hospital. He's researching equatorial diseases. In return, he gives free clinics around the country when asked."

"And he is staying here three years?"

Margaret realized this was a fact that could be checked. "We believe we will be," she said, sure that Obok could see the uncertainty on her face.

"You do not have a work permit?"

She shook her head.

"So that is all right. I will hire you on a freelance basis. Almost all of the photographers I use work under those conditions. Either I will give you an assignment to photograph or I will buy shots from you that I might need in the future. I would, for example, purchase four of these." He indicated the portfolio. Margaret was elated. "We cannot pay much here," he added.

Margaret had anticipated this. She'd almost said, but hadn't, that she would work for him for nothing.

"Three good photographs from an assignment will net you one hundred fifty shillings."

About twenty dollars, Margaret calculated.

"Not much, according to American standards," he added, "but I can offer you quite a lot of work. We are shorthanded here." He smiled. "You might, on a good week, have as many as ten assignments."

Two hundred dollars a week. And more for the odd shot Mr. Obok would buy from her own collection. Margaret would be adventurous, she decided. She would take shots like the ones of the beggar woman and her children. Two hundred a week would be a good addition to Patrick's modest stipend. He couldn't help but be pleased by that.

"That would be fine," Margaret said, trying not to sound too eager.

Mr. Obok had a captivating smile. "I am not averse to hiring expatriates," he said, "as are some of my colleagues. I hire the best people I can find, regardless of tribe. Out in the newsroom, you will find Luo, Kikuyu, Nandi, Ugandans, Turkana, and Asians. I am a Luo. The expatriates tend to work freelance, as you will do. But you will find that even in the office, there will be some who will give you a cold welcome. You may find yourself journeying out to Tsavo, for example, with a reporter who feels that all jobs should be given to Kenyans. By the way, do you have transportation?"

"Yes," she said, "most days."

"Reliable?"

Margaret shrugged her shoulders. "Pretty reliable," she said.

"Good enough." Mr. Obok picked up the four photographs he wanted from her portfolio. "I will pay you one hundred shillings for each. Please give Lily outside all your information. Do you have your passport and visa information with you?"

"Yes."

"Very fine," he said, rising. "We give out checks on Thursdays. You can arrange to come in here, or we can send them to you."

Margaret's post office box was at the hospital, which meant that Patrick would pick up the mail and bring it home, as he always did. She wanted to collect her own paycheck.

"I'll come in to get them," Margaret said.

Mr. Obok put the portfolio back together and handed it to her. "We will see how you do on assignments," he added, suggesting that until he reviewed the results of two or three assignments, he would reserve judgment as to whether she would find a warm welcome from him. They shook hands.

"Thank you," she said.

At the door, she gave a quick glance back at the editor's desk. Mr. Obok already had his pencil out.

As soon as Patrick arrived home that evening, Margaret told him her news.

"It's with the *Tribune*," she added casually.

For the first time, she'd noticed that morning a half dozen new wrinkles around Patrick's eyes. He was often outside for his work, and the weathering was beginning to show. She imagined he thought the same of her.

"The *Kenya Morning Tribune*?" he asked.

She was chewing gum from a pack she'd bought in Nairobi. She never chewed gum. She nodded.

"Really," he said, setting his briefcase and doctor bag on the floor by the hall table.

"Really."

"Jesus, Margaret."

"I'm sorry?"

"Of all the publications in Kenya, you pick the most controversial?"

"It's a good paper," she answered. "Very respectable. It's only photos, anyway. I could make as much as fifteen hundred shillings a week, plus more for the odd shot the editor buys without having assigned it."

"And that editor would be Solomon Obok?"

"You know him?"

Patrick moved into the living room with his hands on his hips. Moses had set out a bouquet of pink and white lilies on the coffee table.

"Everybody knows him," Patrick said. "Did he call you?"

Margaret laughed and inadvertently swallowed her gum. "No," she said. "How would he possibly know me? I just showed up with my portfolio." She was aware that her tone was a little too offhand.

"Why?" Patrick asked.

"Why?"

He paced behind the couch.

"I'm going mad here, Patrick. I need a job. You have one. I had one before I came here. I can't dabble anymore."

"Well, I guess I'm glad for you, then," he said without enthusiasm.

"Mr. Obok thought the stuff from Boston routine," she said, "but he liked the African photos."

"Good."

She waited.

"That's all?" she asked. "Good?"

"I can't say I'm thrilled, Margaret. I'll worry for you. I can't pretend that I won't."

"Why is it necessary to worry about me?"

"Have you read the paper? It's run by Luo, and they have an agenda, and the tribe that runs the country is Kikuyu, in case you hadn't noticed."

"There are half a dozen expats who work there and at least as many Asians."

"And?"

"And nothing. There's nothing nefarious about it."

Patrick nodded slowly in the way that people do when they're not buying any of it.

"If he asks me to do something I think is risky, I won't do it," Margaret said.

"We'll see."

It was all she was going to get, and it would have to be enough. Besides, she reminded herself, she wasn't doing this for Patrick's approval. Or was she?

"Oh, and there's one other thing," Margaret said. "I might be needing the car more now. Mr. Obok expects me to be able to drive to some of the assignments. You and I can work it out. I can take you in in the morning and use the car and then pick you up when you're done."

"You just be careful, Margaret," he said.

"I'll be making some money, so maybe we could save and go on a real vacation. To Mombasa. To a resort. Just lie in the sun and swim. We need that."

Patrick took a deep breath and exhaled. "We sure as hell do," he said.

Margaret sensed that some of the reporters wrote better English than they spoke. Her first assignment was with a man named

Jagdish Shah, a reporter who had been with the *Tribune* more than a decade. He was that day to report on an event honoring the marketing manager of East African Airlines.

"You are living in Karen?" Jagdish asked with a distinctly Asian lilt. Margaret wondered if she'd been assigned the story simply for the transportation. The luncheon at Utalii Hotel wasn't far from the *Tribune,* but the journey required a car all the same. She had bought a second camera for her job, a Leica M3, which lay in its case in the backseat. Jagdish sat stiffly forward. He had a full mustache and beard that were trying to hide a bad complexion. Dressed in a white shirt, jacket, and tie, he wore large, thick glasses that made his eyes pop. Because the car didn't have air-conditioning, Margaret drove with the windows down, which seemed to bother the man. He smelled heavily of cologne.

"I am third of three boys," he said before they'd even reached the city limits. "My father is giving his business to his first son. To his second, he arranges to buy for him a motorcycle-distribution business. But me, I am expected to go out and work for someone else."

At first, Margaret didn't know what to say. It seemed a startling revelation from someone she'd known less than five minutes.

"This bothers you," she said.

"Oh yes," he answered, looking out the window. "It is bothering me all my life. My wife, she is at me always: *Tell your father this. . . . Tell your father that. . . .* She tries to charm him, which is horrible to watch."

"Perhaps you could find a job you like better than this," Margaret suggested.

"No, I am not finding anything else. There is nothing in Nairobi for me to be my own boss."

Jagdish lapsed into a depressed silence. He sighed. Margaret wondered if she would be attached to him for all of his stories. She hoped not.

Jagdish wasn't any more charming with the marketing manager of EAA than he'd been with Margaret. Her task, Mr. Obok had told her, was to get the principals — the marketing manager, the minister of tourism, and the head of Utalii — in a three-way handshake, each looking at the others, but somehow revealing all their faces. The most interesting part of the dull photo was the mix of black and white hands (four black, two white) at the moment of the handshake, but though Margaret took a number of shots of that alone, she knew that Mr. Obok wouldn't use them.

(The following day, Margaret examined the photograph in the newspaper and then read the text below it. There was no photo credit or byline on either the photograph or the very short piece.

EAA has had a good year — more of that on page 34 — and one
of the people responsible for this is Mt. Kevin Britt, who was
the airline's Marketing Manager on a 2-Year secondment from
Eastern Airlines which has just ended.

The entire story had only two more sentences, but much was revealed in just the first sentence, not least of which was the awkwardness of the writing. Was the reader to think that Eastern Airlines had just ended? Margaret noted the capitalization of *Marketing Manager* and the suggestion that the reader turn to page thirty-four for a fuller story about EAA. She deduced that EAA must have made a terrific ad buy to merit two stories. Referring to Kevin Britt as a mountain, she guessed, would have been a copyeditor's mistake.)

Jagdish and she left the hotel and drove back to the *Tribune* office. Along the way, Margaret heard the sorry tale of his elder son, who was fat and doing poorly in school. He was about to start on his daughter when they pulled into a spot in front of the *Tribune*. They went upstairs, Margaret to surrender the film, Jagdish to type up his story. But as they entered the *Tribune* office, they could see Mr. Obok, who was speaking animatedly to someone on the telephone, through his open door. He beckoned to them.

"Plane crash," he said when he put down the phone. "Thika Road. Fifteen miles out of town. Flying Doctor Service."

He pointed to Margaret. "You, too," he said, and tossed his head in the direction of the door.

Jagdish turned and started jogging, and Margaret followed him. She gave the film of the marketing manager to the receptionist on the way out. When they got to the Peugeot, Jagdish stood at the driver's side and asked for the keys. He seemed to have come alive.

"Shouldn't I drive?" Margaret asked.

"I know the way," he said, sliding into the seat.

Margaret held on to the dashboard as Jagdish took the Thika Road like a rally driver. More than once they passed a full matatu on the wrong side, catching the ditch as they did so. Mud splattered over the windshield, over the side window. Margaret didn't ask Jagdish to slow down. He was a shrewd driver, despite the speed and a few near misses. She didn't need to be told that getting there first was paramount.

Margaret had never seen a plane crash, not in real life.

On the way, she had fifteen minutes to prepare herself for the scene that awaited them. When Mr. Obok had said the Thika

Road, she'd imagined that the plane could be seen from the highway. What she hadn't envisioned was that the plane had crashed directly onto the tarmac, suggesting a botched emergency landing. Traffic had begun to thicken. Jagdish took to the ditch again, swerving the Peugeot back onto the road as close as he could get to the plane before stopping. He slid out of the car and began running. Margaret grabbed her camera and followed.

Onlookers stood about fifty feet away. Local askaris guarded the plane. No help had yet arrived.

The plane had taken most of the impact in the nose. A wing had been torn off. The pilot would have had to make a crucial decision to land in the scrub or on the tarmac. The scrub, though softer, was rife with obstacles. The road might have promised a better landing, except for the oncoming traffic. It looked as though the pilot had picked a moment when there hadn't been any vehicles nearby. Margaret saw no other wreckage. Perhaps the pilot had run out of fuel or the landing gear had not descended.

Margaret could see a torso in the plane itself. White shirt and blue tie. A second body, shrouded in a sheet, lay half in and half out of the wreckage. A third body had been tossed twenty feet away.

She stood immobile as Jagdish hurriedly spoke to the askaris and showed his credentials. He signaled to Margaret with impatience. He wanted pictures of the crash at once.

"Shouldn't we see if anyone needs help?" Margaret asked. "One of them could still be alive."

"They're all dead," Jagdish said. "Don't think, just shoot."

When Margaret hesitated yet again, he came forward as if to wrest the camera out of her hand.

She moved closer to the plane. When she peered in, she could see the torso, as she had before. She could even see the legs. It took a few seconds for her brain to register what the eyes clearly saw, that the pilot had been beheaded.

Numbly, she shot from many angles, Jagdish pointing there and there and there. After a dozen shots, she put the camera down. She couldn't take any more pictures; she was certain she was going to be sick. It wasn't obvious what had sheared the man's head off. She coughed and bent over. Jagdish was at her side, holding her elbow. "This is your first body?" he asked.

"No," she said. "It's just..."

"Shoot," he said. "In minutes they will take away the bodies. Come with me."

He dragged Margaret to the body that lay on the tarmac twenty feet from the crumpled plane. Overhead, buzzards circled. A group of Africans in Western dress surrounded the corpse. Beyond them was a flat, bleak plain of dust and scrub. In the distance, Margaret could see a wooden building with a red sign out front. She couldn't read the writing on the sign.

Jagdish pushed his way through the gawkers and knelt over the body. He never stopped writing.

"Here," he said, rocking back on his heels. "This one. Do it now." He fanned the onlookers away. Margaret took the shots she was asked to take. She bent to the body. It was an African woman, and she wore the insignia of the Flying Doctor Service. Her neck was twisted in such a way that it was clear she was dead. The body in the sheet would have been the patient, then.

Why had help not arrived yet? Margaret marveled that she and Jagdish had been permitted such ghoulish access. In the States, she reflected, first the police and then aviation officials would have locked up such a scene at once. A reporter's access would have been limited to the remarks a spokesman made.

Margaret's hands began to tremble, and she couldn't hold the camera steady.

Jagdish, jacket gone, shirt in disarray, came to her side.

"You are going to be sick?" he asked.

"No," she said. "My hands are shaking."

Margaret wondered if Jagdish would report this fact to Mr. Obok.

"You will get used to it," he said. He reached into his pocket and removed a vial of small white pills. "Take one," he insisted. "They'll make the hands stop shaking."

Margaret had no idea what the pill contained, but she didn't hesitate. She swallowed it dry.

"Give it one minute," he said. "Then go back to the plane and shoot from the other side." He looked up. In the distance, they could hear the faint wail of a siren. "No, go now!" he urged.

A special edition of the paper was printed in the evening, the front page covered with Margaret's photographs. They were gruesome, and she was glad that no credits had been awarded.

Still, she had some pride in her work. The quality of the photographs was sharp, the composition alone revealing the story. No one offered her a compliment, not even Mr. Obok, who'd been able to print a separate edition only because of her pictures. The story of the crash without the photos would not have merited the rushed edition. The *Tribune Extra* hit the streets an hour earlier than the *Evening Standard*. There were handshakes all around.

Margaret had the relevant pages of the special edition folded and tucked into the bottom of her camera case. The pill that had made her hands steady had begun to wear off. She tried to wipe the slickness from her palms onto the skirt of her dress. As she drove to Nairobi Hospital to pick up Patrick, she thought about the three dead bodies she had seen. The pilot, the patient, the doctor. The story, of course, had been sensational but then had taken an unusual turn at the end. Margaret had thought that the message would be one of people perishing while trying to perform a heroic service. But her photographs had been used to illustrate the need for more oversight of the Flying Doctor Service. She could hear Patrick's cynicism already.

As she entered the road to the hospital, she remembered that the Peugeot was covered with great splashes of mud.

A month after the plane crash (and Margaret was to see many dead bodies during her time at the *Tribune:* six dead at the East African Safari Classic; seventeen dead when a matatu overturned; an Asian family macheted to death while sleeping), Patrick made an announcement. He would be away for two weeks. He had to visit the coast, specifically the medical facilities in Mombasa and Malindi. There would be a conference in Lamu. Patrick and Margaret had not yet been to the coast, though she remembered their earlier wistful exchange. She wanted to go with him but couldn't because of a job that was growing busier and busier.

"We've never been apart this long," Margaret said, moving toward him.

He wrapped his arms around her. "You'll be okay," he said. "And besides, we can work it out so that I'll be on Lamu during a long weekend. You can join me there."

Margaret noted that his tone was similar to the one she'd employed while telling him about her new job. He was selling her on this trip.

"We'll spend a night or two in town at Petley's," he said, "and then we'll stay at the beach at Shela. We'll take a trip on a dhow," he added, referring to the ancient sailing vessels the Swahili of Lamu had been making their living from for eons.

"When do you leave?" Margaret asked.

"In two days."

She lifted her head from his chest. "That soon?" she said.

"The project got moved forward. It's something I have to do. I've spoken to Moses, and he'll take good care of you."

It meant nothing to Patrick, but the echo of the phrase Arthur had used so often was unsettling.

That night, when Patrick and she made love, she sensed repair and apology. There was also, she was certain, the electric current of a future adventure.

Patrick left two days later by train. Margaret stood at the station with him. He had bought her ticket to Lamu, he said. She would fly because a train would take too long. There was a small airport on Manda; she would leave from Wilson. He had given her directions and cash. He had had Moses stock the fridge and the cupboards. He had taken the Peugeot in for a tune-up and had filled it with gas. He had done all of the things a loving husband would do for a wife except hide from her his tremendous impatience to get going.

Margaret often thought about Diana. She replayed the scene in her head a thousand times. Sometimes she could see the moment the guide missed the fur of Diana's hood; at other times, Margaret could feel the way they'd all gone down, right there on the ice, all hooked to the rope. Margaret could hear Arthur in her dreams, his howl waking her. Had he gone to London as planned? Were he and his children living with his sister? Did he have a job with Colgate-Palmolive UK? Margaret wanted to talk to him, to reassure herself that he was all right, though she knew that no one could be all right after such a horrific accident. She remembered the moment they had locked eyes outside the church. Margaret thought of the terrible conversation Patrick and she had had after the accident.

As time went on, Margaret began to hope for a letter from Arthur. It might be addressed to Patrick, and that would be fine. Even more, she wanted to see Arthur and speak to him. There was much she had to say. It wouldn't help Arthur at all, but it might help her.

After a few phone calls, Margaret learned that Diana's body had been located after all and sent to London for a proper burial. Margaret thought that Diana wouldn't have liked that, that she'd have preferred to be buried in Kenya, the country of her birth. Diana had hated London, and Margaret could not imagine that she would rest easy there. Margaret wished that Diana's ashes had been scattered on a field where her dogs had run free, or on one of the knuckles of the Ngong Hills.

The task was to photograph a teacher. Margaret expected Jagdish as she chatted with Lily, the receptionist, a woman with an acerbic wit worth hanging around for. Margaret was taken by surprise when a tall Asian man stood in front of her, held out his hand, and introduced himself.

"Rafiq Hameed," he said.

Margaret said nothing.

"And you are Margaret," he said.

"Yes. Sorry. I was expecting . . . No, this is good," she babbled.

"And we are to interview a teacher."

"Yes."

He smiled, whether at her sudden awkwardness or simply because he was looking forward to his interview, Margaret couldn't tell.

"Well," she said.

Though Rafiq's skin was the light brown of the Indian or Pakistani and his hair the thick black Margaret had become familiar with (Rafiq had neither mustache nor beard, however), his features were distinctly European.

Rafiq checked his watch. "We should get going. We'll take my car. It's just outside."

Rafiq had a car. This would make a pleasant change.

Margaret said good-bye to Lily while Rafiq held the door, an unexpected gesture. Jagdish more often than not had barreled through a door, leaving it to shut in Margaret's face. He was either a thoroughly evolved male or simply rude. Margaret had decided on the latter.

"This interview is part of a larger piece I've been working on for a few weeks about the state of education in Kenya," Rafiq explained as they jogged down the three flights of stairs. "Apparently, the Ministry has been eager for the *Tribune* to do such a piece, since it's the one thing the government offers that actually works. A hundred problems, of course, but all children want to go to school."

"I'm surprised I haven't seen you before," Margaret said.

"Well, I've seen you," Rafiq said with a tilt of his head. "Hard to miss a young white woman in a sea of brown and black."

Margaret was about to protest that there were several (well, two) white women who contributed to the paper besides her, but she let it go.

"What is this?" she asked about his car when she was inside.

"Citroën," he said, pulling out of the parking space. "A stranger vehicle was never invented. Did Obok talk to you about what he wants?"

"Portraits," she said.

"We're headed to Parklands. I imagine he wants some children in the shots, but maybe not."

"I'll do a little of both," Margaret said.

Rafiq had on the uniform of the respectable journalist—jacket, tie, and white shirt—but it looked less rumpled and ill-fitting than Jagdish's had. Margaret tried to guess Rafiq's age but couldn't. The jacket and tie probably made him seem older than he actually was. Margaret wasn't any better with Asian ages than she was with African ones.

"So you are here from America?" he asked.

"Boston. Massachusetts."

"And that is on the coast."

"The northeast coast. Frigid in the winter."

"Yes. And what led you to Kenya?"

"My husband is a physician and is completing work on equatorial diseases."

"Important work."

"It is."

She thought of Patrick, who was on the Kenyan coast, and tried to imagine what he was doing. Was he vaccinating impoverished children or was he sitting on a white beach, contemplating a swim? No, that wasn't fair; Patrick was nothing if not hardworking. Still, she'd like to be on that beach with him.

"What about you?" Margaret asked. "How long have you been in Kenya?"

"Since nineteen seventy-two, when the Asians were chased out of Uganda. I'm actually Ugandan."

"During the purges?"

"Sixty thousand of us," he said without bitterness. "The Asians ran the economy. Idi Amin wanted us out so he could give the businesses and jobs to Africans. Gave them all our land as well."

"That must have been brutal," Margaret said, trying to imagine what it would be like to be stripped of everything and forced to move from one's home, one's country. She thought of her parents in the suburban home they'd lived in all their marriage. Unthinkable.

"It was very bad for an entire people, certainly," Rafiq said. "I think for my family, it was a jolt to the spine. Made them realize they really wanted to return to Pakistan."

"Your parents are Pakistani?"

"My father is. My mother is Welsh."

Margaret twisted her head and looked directly at him. "Really?" she said. "You don't have anything like a Welsh accent."

He laughed. "No, I was educated in the UK. London tends to take the edge off whatever you were before."

The Citroën was tiny. Rafiq's knees hit the dashboard.

"What were you doing when you were expelled?"

"Studying law at Makerere. I thought I would continue my studies here, but my father lost all his fortune. Hence this job. Saving up for the fees. I've been at the *Tribune* for only six months. Before that, I was with my uncle in his typewriter business, but I discovered I'm an abysmal salesman."

"Do you mind being a reporter?"

"No, I don't, funnily enough. Great way to learn a country."

Parklands, a suburb of Nairobi, was home to white-collar Asians and Africans, as well as a scattering of whites. They drove through residential roads, on which the houses and maisonettes were much the same: stone, stucco, red-tiled roofs. The area bore a striking resemblance to a suburb of London—one with a better climate.

When they arrived at the school (stone with multipaned casement windows; Margaret might have mistaken it for a residence), they were met by the headmaster, who in turn introduced them to his staff. In Kenya, any occasion was reason for ceremony. As Margaret looked around, she thought about the difference between this school and the one she'd attended in the States.

Where there had been concrete parking lots in Massachusetts, at Parklands there was a large garden with many flowers: carnations, lavender, orange lilies, and roses. The football fields of home became cricket pitches and soccer fields at Parklands. Tea was served at eleven each morning to teachers and students alike. Even in the schools, there were servants.

As Margaret took pictures, she listened to Rafiq's interview with the teacher he'd come to talk to. She was a pretty, westernized African who wore a dress Margaret had admired in Jax, a shop that catered to European women looking for a blend of African and European style. She had an Afro and a beaded necklace. In the photograph that would be used for the paper, she looked at schoolwork with an Asian boy with a bowl haircut. While she appeared to be trying to explain something to the boy, he stared wide-eyed at her.

In Kenya, teachers were revered, even regarded with awe. They held a respected place in any society of parents and children. Margaret hadn't seen in Africa the unruliness that she associated with schoolchildren in the States. Children in Kenya wore uniforms to class and paid hefty school fees, often a strain on a family's budget. One incidence of bad behavior could lead to expulsion.

Between photographs, Margaret watched Rafiq at work. Nimble, he wandered among the children, squatting to be at their level. Whereas Jagdish had been a no-nonsense reporter, leaving an interview as soon as he had the facts he needed and often conveying some of the deep depression that was always with him (which tended to deflate the interviewee as well, not to mention the photographer), Rafiq's manner put the subject at ease. He often lapsed into a patois of Swahili and English, keeping the questions light.

After the interview, Rafiq and Margaret had tea with the teacher and the headmaster. With the teacher, Rafiq had used a small portable tape recorder, which now sat on the headmaster's desk. The discussion in the headmaster's suite centered on the school itself. He spoke passionately about overcrowding and the necessity for better supplies; of a much-needed release of funds marked for more classrooms. They shook hands politely all around, and Rafiq and Margaret left and headed for the Citroën.

"Would you mind," Margaret asked, "if we took a walk in the garden? I hate to leave these beautiful flowers so soon."

"Of course."

Rafiq found a wrought-iron gate that opened to the garden. It was a bright day, the temperature in the midseventies.

"How do you think that went?" Margaret asked as they strolled along a pathway. She noted that Rafiq was a good six inches taller than she. He walked with his hands in the pockets of his trousers.

"Fine," he said, "though I could have written the piece without even coming here."

"How do you mean?"

"She was a sincere and lovely woman, but I could have predicted much of what she said. And though one can't predict what children will say, I certainly knew ahead of time the tenor of the comments. I prefer to do pieces I can sink my teeth into, pieces in which I don't know the answers before I ask the questions. I was thinking this morning of getting inside Mathari and taking a hard look at the conditions there, at what the people are thinking, perhaps a 'Hope Among the Slums' kind of thing. The *Tribune* has done pieces on Mathari before—I've checked the archives—but recently they've been centered around the bulldozing, with commentary from the government officials who ordered it. I have something else in mind. The trick, of course, is to get someone's confidence. To find the right person who will open up to an Asian. Africans, as a rule, tend to mistrust Asians."

"I would like to go with you when you do that piece," Margaret said.

"Yes," he said, glancing at her. "Of course."

They walked through the maze of flowers. The lush garden was a common bit of paradise in Kenya. Margaret thought about what she would say next.

"I might know someone," she said.

Rafiq looked at her with interest.

"The slum isn't Mathari, but it might as well be. I know a woman who might talk to you. Are you allowed to pay for interviews?"

"In some cases, yes. Usually, it's the wrong end of the stick, though. The paper pays the ministers for interviews. Those who need the money least."

"How much?" Margaret asked. "For the woman I'm thinking of?"

He thought a minute. "I might be able to get five hundred shillings. Are you sure about this story?"

A little more than sixty dollars, Margaret calculated. It might well be worth it to the woman she had in mind.

"I don't know whether she will talk to you, but I'm sure that if she does, the story will be good."

"I'm intrigued," Rafiq said. "When can you arrange this?"

"It might take a few days."

In their excitement, their pace had picked up.

"I want a rose," Margaret said suddenly. "One stolen rose can hardly matter to the school, do you think?"

"Kenyan roses have the straightest stems in the world," Rafiq said. "Did you know that?"

"No, I didn't."

"It's because of being on the equator and the altitude. Good growing conditions and a straight shot to the sun."

A jackknife snapped open, startling Margaret. Rafiq cut a two-foot stem. He had picked a lemon-yellow blossom with many petals. He handed it to her, and she thanked him.

"That's quite a knife you have there."

"I never go anywhere without it."

When they reached the *Tribune* office, Margaret realized she didn't want to get out of the car.

Margaret walked to a shop on Kimathi Street and bought a map of Nairobi and its environs. She had a similar map at home, but she didn't want to waste the time it would take to drive there. Over a quick lunch, she studied the city's geography. She easily found the area in which Adhiambo lived, but she couldn't figure out, even from the fairly detailed map, exactly where Adhiambo was located. Then Margaret remembered that Adhiambo didn't actually live on a road but rather on a makeshift path. Margaret would have to get in touch with James, which would be difficult enough. He, too, had left the Big House when Arthur had, and Margaret didn't know his whereabouts. Still, she thought Arthur and Diana's former house the best place to start.

A thick wave of nostalgia hit Margaret when she turned onto the old road in Langata. She hadn't been back to the town since they'd left. Its soporific beauty and intoxicating scent were so familiar to Margaret that she felt as though she were returning to her true home. A series of images appeared: their small table covered with the vermilion-and-yellow khanga; the drawing room at the Big House with its seventeen patterns; James standing at the doorway to the kitchen, waiting patiently for the diners to get up from the table; Adhiambo at Margaret's door, face covered by a cloth; Diana exasperated and eager to leave her with them.

Margaret knew the Big House was now owned by the minister of transportation. She had never met a minister in person, but she'd unfairly developed a stereotype: overweight, arrogant, and powerful. She pulled up to the gates and studied the askari who came to speak to her. Margaret wasn't positive about his identity, but it was worth a try.

She rolled down the window. The askari in his greatcoat bent toward her and asked her name. His demeanor was stern, even menacing.

"Do you remember me?" Margaret asked.

At first he thought she was being flippant, and he seemed about to start in on a warning. But then he tilted his head and judged her sideways, and he nodded. "You are living in the banda."

She smiled. "I'm not anymore, but I used to. I think you worked here just before I left."

"Yes, that is so. I am coming here with James."

"Actually, I'm trying to get in touch with James." Margaret was embarrassed that she didn't know his last name.

"He is not working here now," the askari said, straightening a bit and relaxing his face. She was certain the askari was a Masai.

"I know that," she said. "I wondered if you knew where he lived."

"He is working for the Germans now."

"What?"

"He is cook for Germans," the askari said as if there could be no other possibility. Margaret supposed he thought the same true of himself—that he would be an askari until he died, not an unreasonable expectation. There was some pride in being an askari, a domestic soldier, battle-ready.

"Can you tell me the name of the people he works for?" Margaret asked. "I could try to find him."

"I am thinking," the askari said, standing perfectly still and closing his eyes. He bent one leg and rested it on the opposite knee. He remained that way for so long that Margaret thought he'd gone into a trance.

"You must ask Isaac, who goes to the duka in the mornings," the askari said finally. "Do you know Isaac?"

Margaret shook her head.

"Go to the duka and ask for Isaac. He is cousin to James."

Margaret got out her wallet and came up with a twenty-shilling note, which she gave to the askari.

"*Asante sana,*" he said, bowing to her.

It was a short drive back to the duka, a store she'd been to many times. She braced herself for the smell of meat, but once she got inside, she found the familiar products on their stocked shelves comforting. She went to the counter and asked Juma, whom she knew well, if he could tell her where a man named Isaac was.

"And you are Miss Margaret? You are not greeting me? It has been a long time since you are here."

"Oh, I'm so sorry," she said with heartfelt apology. Where had her Kenyan manners gone? "How are you, Juma? And your family?"

"We are well," he said. "And you?"

"I moved away," Margaret said. "To Karen."

"Yes, I know. I am sorry, sorry about Miss Diana. A tragedy, that is sure. She was English, but she was generous."

Margaret wondered what he meant by that. Should she have tipped Juma all the times she'd been in his store?

"In what way was Diana generous?" she asked.

"She is always giving us the clothes. To my wife. Many clothes. For the children, too."

Margaret was surprised by the notion of a generous Diana.

"Isaac is gone now," he said, "but he will be here in the morning."

"Do you know what time?"

"Always at six thirty. To buy the meat."

"Yes," she said. "Thank you." She didn't tip the man, but she did buy provisions. She hadn't looked to see what Moses, on Patrick's instructions, had gotten, but she selected items that appealed to her: a pineapple, a packet of Aroma coffee, two bottles of Tusker, and, though she didn't need it, a tube of Colgate toothpaste—in Arthur's memory, she supposed.

"I will be here in the morning," she said.

"And I am always here," Juma said.

In the morning, Margaret spoke with Isaac, who told her that James was doing well and that he liked his new job, mainly because it came with a small house. James was thinking of bringing his family with him from Kitale, but the German couple, whose names Isaac didn't know, weren't certain they liked the idea. Isaac also knew James's address—not by a street or a number but by the markers he had used to walk there himself from the bus stop. After giving Margaret the location of the stop, he explained that further directions involved a light that was broken, a garden of white roses, a Z in the road, and six houses beyond that. She wondered how she would find a broken light while in the car, but Isaac said she couldn't miss it. The light was a tall lantern in which the glass had been shattered.

Margaret drove to Lavington, a suburb not dissimilar to Langata in that many expatriates had settled there, both in the past and more recently. Because Lavington was closer to Nairobi, the gates around the houses were more ubiquitous; taller and thicker as well. Margaret noted that in some cases, outer gates opened onto inner gates. Platoons of askaris manned these fortresses. The people inside could come and go with ease, but it felt as though an entire population was under siege. Did they lie awake listening for strange noises in the night?

Margaret found the tall streetlight Isaac spoke of with the shattered glass. She drove until she came upon the garden of white roses, after which the Z began. When she finished the sharp curves, she counted six houses. She arrived at the front gate and waited for the askari to question her.

"You are here to see the memsahib?"

"No," she said. "I just wanted to say a few words to James, their cook. Do you know James? Does he work here?"

The askari's demeanor changed. Asking for a servant was a different matter from asking for the mistress of the house. He stood, pondering the circumstances. It might have been the first time a white woman in a car had come calling for James.

"You must visit the memsahib first," the askari decided. "To ask permission. James is her boy."

For a moment, Margaret was confused. But in the next instant, she understood. In the askari's eyes, James was the woman's property.

Margaret took out a ten-shilling note. "I just need to speak to James," she said. "There's no need to bother the memsahib."

Every askari understood the language of the ten-shilling note.

"I must wait for my replacement," he said.

"I'll guard the gates while you are gone. Simply lock them, and I'll tell anyone who comes that you will be right back."

The askari nodded, and Margaret hoped the mistress of the house would not be one of those looking for entry to her own home.

She was watching two dogs playing in the street and wondering if they were the *Mbwa Kali* of the warning signs at all of the gates — they looked pretty harmless to her — when there was a sudden knock at her window.

"James," she said, getting out of the car.

"How are you, Miss Margaret?"

His face lit up with a broad smile. She wanted to hug the man, but the gesture would only have embarrassed him.

"I am fine," she said. "We miss you, Patrick and I. How are you doing with your new employers?"

"They have a great many parties," he said, miming the expression of *ooooff*. "Much work. But I have a small house, which makes me very glad."

"And you are well?"

"Oh yes," he said, dismissing the question. "Always well."

"And how is Adhiambo?"

"Better," he said. "Better."

According to African manners, this pleasant banter could have gone on for fifteen minutes or even a half hour. But Margaret knew that James had been called from work and might be needed at any moment. Perhaps he, too, was afraid of seeing the mistress's car.

"Well, it's Adhiambo I've come to talk to you about."

James misunderstood. "She is finding temporary jobs, but not a job with a family, which she must have. I go there every week to check on her door."

Margaret smiled. "You're a good friend."

"Her brothers in Kericho, they are not so good. They come to her house that night, but not to find the men who did Adhiambo harm and punish them. Instead, they find her little cloth of coins under her bed and steal them."

"Oh my God," Margaret said.

"It is very bad luck to have such brothers," James said, shaking his head.

"James, listen. That's sort of why I've come. I know someone who wants to write a story for a newspaper about how hard it is for women—and men—to live in a place like she does."

"A slum," James said.

"Well, yes. The newspaper will pay five hundred shillings just to talk to her."

James tilted his head, the money registering. "She is using her own name?" he asked, already thinking of reprisals.

"I'm not sure about that," Margaret said. "But I will ask if she can have another name, just for the purpose of the story. But she has to tell the truth. You would have to impress that upon her."

"Oh yes. Adhiambo is always telling the truth."

"And the reporter is Asian," Margaret said. "I would take the photographs. The reporter is a very nice man. I can vouch for him."

James pursed his lips. He was silent for a long time. Margaret wondered if either "Asian" or "photographs" would be a deal breaker.

"So will you talk to her?" she asked finally.

"I will talk to her tonight." He paused. "How will I give you the answer?"

"I have a telephone," she began, but James shook his head. She thought a minute. "I'll be right here, tomorrow," Margaret said. "At this same time. You can just run out and tell me. I'll need a date and time for the interview and some directions." Margaret knew she wouldn't be able to find Adhiambo's shack on her own.

"No, is not good you wait here." James pointed back down the street where the Z had ended. "You are seeing that tall house?"

Margaret nodded.

"Wait there. The people, they are away now. Do not be early."

Margaret laughed. "I doubt anyone has ever said that to me before."

"I must go," he said. "I am hoping for the luck."

"James," Margaret said as he began to run up the long driveway, "what is your last name?"

He broke into a broad smile. "Ogollo," he called.

Margaret got into the Peugeot and turned the car around. She would have to persuade Rafiq not to use Adhiambo's real name and to get the full five hundred shillings.

The next day, Margaret pulled up to the tall house at the appointed time. James must have been watching from his gates because he walked briskly in her direction. She rolled down the window. James had on a hand-knit sweater with short sleeves and a pair of cotton pants. His shoes were burnished to a high gloss.

"I am free in the morning," he said. "I will take you there. You must be here at nine o'clock."

"Thank you, James." Margaret shook his hand through the window.

"I must be telling you. If she is using her real name or if you do not have the shillings, she will not speak to you."

"Everything you ask will be taken care of," Margaret said, promising herself that she would supply the shillings if Rafiq couldn't wrest them from the *Tribune*. She had set up expectations, and she would have to fulfill them.

At the very least, she was looking forward to seeing Adhiambo again.

"Do you know where Rafiq is?" she asked Lily at the front desk of the *Tribune*. Lily missed nothing and narrowed her eyes at Margaret. "I need to find him for a story," Margaret explained.

"Sure, sure," Lily said. She consulted a log-in sheet. "He was here, but he has left to interview the old mzee Mr. Kamante, the man who was once a servant to Karen Blixen. They are meeting . . . at the café next to the theater."

"Kamante, the man who cooked for Karen Blixen? The boy with the wound in his leg?"

Lily chuckled. "Yes, the little boy."

"How long ago did Rafiq leave?"

Lily consulted her watch. "I am thinking . . . mmmm . . . twelve minutes."

Margaret knew where the theater was because Patrick, she, and their friends had gone there to see *Sleuth*. She ran down the stairs and sprinted to her car. Who knew where Rafiq might go after the interview?

Margaret could have run to the theater from the *Tribune,* but the car had the advantage of perhaps three minutes. She entered the small Indian café. As she did, Rafiq looked up at Margaret with surprise. On the table between him and the mzee was a tea tray and its accoutrements. She walked directly to the table.

"Hello, Rafiq," she said. "I'm very sorry to bother you."

He stood. The old man did not. "Margaret, this is Kamante, a respected and famous fellow."

Margaret and the old man shook hands. "I have read about you," she said. "I am honored to meet you." Margaret could hardly believe she was with the man who was once the slight, limping Kikuyu boy of *Out of Africa.* He was now heavier and white-haired. He wore an orange V-neck and a short-sleeved cotton shirt.

She turned to Rafiq. "I shouldn't have interrupted you. I'm sorry. I can wait and come back."

"This interview may last awhile. Excuse us," he said to Kamante. "This won't take a minute. I'll be right back."

Rafiq and Margaret walked as far as the door. "I have someone who has gotten in touch with the woman we mentioned," Margaret began. "In fact, we have an appointment to speak to her. Tomorrow morning at nine we'll meet my friend in Lavington, and he'll take us to her. Rafiq, I went ahead and promised the woman friend that she could use a false name. She is, quite understandably, afraid of reprisals. And you must have five hundred shillings with you."

Rafiq whistled. "That's a tall order. The paper doesn't like using pseudonyms. But sometimes it's necessary. It's just a question as to what Solomon will say, but I'll do my best. Let me phone you when I have the answer." He took a notebook and a pen from his pocket. Margaret gave him her number in Karen.

"I don't want to keep you from your interview. Just let me know."

"I will," he said. "Thank you. This is a big thing you have done for me."

"For me, too," she replied.

When she slid into the passenger seat of the Peugeot, she realized she hadn't thought about Patrick the entire morning.

That evening, when the phone rang, Margaret thought it would be Patrick. He called every other day. The domestic routine had changed a bit since Patrick had left. When Margaret ate alone, she never asked Moses for a three-course meal. At best, she would have a salad, or salad and soup, or just guacamole with celery sticks. Moses, who believed a woman should keep a few extra pounds on her, worried over her diet and tried to tempt her (successfully) with pastries he'd made for breakfast and for tea.

But it wasn't Patrick on the other end of the line.

"I've got the anonymity and the five hundred," Rafiq said. "It wasn't easy. I am to try to continue on with the interviews and use accurate names with those. So you are not to make that offer to anyone else."

Margaret felt vaguely chastised, but before she could work up a head of steam, Rafiq said immediately, "We were both amazed at how quickly you managed to arrange this. Solomon said I should hire you as an assistant, until I pointed out he would lose you as a photographer. So I am set for tomorrow."

There was nothing more to be said, but Margaret could sense that Rafiq didn't want to hang up. Nor did she.

"How is your piece on education going?" she asked.

"It's coming along. I was hoping to be able to add a slightly different angle after tomorrow. I want to see if those children get any kind of education at all."

"This might be kind of rough. When I went to Adhiambo's house, if you can call it that, I was pretty shaken."

"That's her name?"

"Yes."

"Believe me, I've seen plenty of rough."

The telephone had been placed on a high pedestal table in the hallway with no seating within the wire's radius. Margaret thought the reason must have been to keep conversations short and therefore less expensive. She was longing to sit down.

"And your husband?" Rafiq asked. "He is well?"

"He's traveling."

"Yes, you said."

"I thought it might be he when I answered the phone."

"I'm sorry to have disappointed you."

"You're not disappointing me at all. If it had been Patrick, he would have told me about the doctors he'd met or the patients in the clinics, all the while trying not to mention the glorious beach outside his window and the tiki bar at the pool beneath his room."

"You are jealous," Rafiq said.

"A little. Maybe. Not really. To be jealous would mean that I didn't like my job, and that wouldn't be accurate. I could use a vacation, though."

"So soon?"

"I've been in the country nine months. And some of those months have been a strain." Margaret didn't elaborate.

At the other end of the line, Rafiq was quiet.

"So I should go," she said.

"Yes, absolutely. Who is driving?"

"I think I should," she said. "James will feel more familiar in my car, and I'm pretty sure your Citroën wouldn't be that comfortable."

He laughed. "So you will collect me? No, I will meet you in front of the *Tribune* office."

"Okay," she said.

Rafiq and Margaret discussed the time she should pick him up if they were to make it to James's street by nine.

"Well, good night," Rafiq said.

"See you tomorrow," Margaret said.

After Margaret hung up, she hadn't walked a dozen steps before the phone rang again.

"Who were you talking to?" Patrick asked at once.

James walked in front of Margaret, Rafiq behind. Margaret had noticed, when she picked Rafiq up, that he had on a suit. Though he had been deep in conversation with James as they drove, he grew silent as they stepped out of the car. He took notes as they walked.

Margaret had put the camera in a straw basket such as a woman might take to market. She didn't want to advertise her intent.

James went into Adhiambo's hut first while they stood in the pathway outside her door. Margaret watched as Rafiq looked around and took notes. She saw that Adhiambo's wooden window was gone, replaced by a canvas shade that rolled up and down. How on earth did she have any security?

Rafiq and Margaret stood silently side by side, trying not to attract attention. Margaret was counting the seconds until James emerged.

"She will see you now. But first I must present the money to her, and you must tell me now what name you are using. In the story."

"Teresa," Rafiq said without hesitation, as if he'd prepared for this. He pulled the five hundred shillings from his breast pocket.

James nodded and went inside again.

"That's an African name?" Margaret whispered to Rafiq as they remained outside.

"As much as James is an African name."

James opened the door. The interior was so dark that at first Margaret couldn't find Adhiambo's face. The only light was filtered through the canvas at the window. When she could see, she walked toward Adhiambo. "How are you?" she asked.

Adhiambo nodded.

"You're okay with this?" Margaret noted that the money had already been tucked away. She hoped Adhiambo hadn't put it under her mattress.

Adhiambo nodded again.

Margaret saw that she had cleaned up for the interview. A newish quilt lay over her bed. She had borrowed three chairs and set them around her table. On the wall next to it, she had a hanging Margaret hadn't noticed before. Margaret saw another one by the bed. She was certain the wall hangings had not been there before. Adhiambo wore a colorful head scarf and a plain, shapeless dress.

"Thank you for agreeing," Margaret said. "This is Rafiq Hameed, the man who will ask you questions."

Rafiq extended his hand, and Adhiambo shook it. Even this small gesture seemed like a victory of sorts.

"Do you want me to sit here or to wait outside?" James asked.

"No, no," said Rafiq. "We should all sit around the table and just think of this as a conversation. James, you should feel free to add anything you want."

Adhiambo studied Rafiq, as though judging whether or not she could trust the man. Even James had tilted his head. Margaret could smell smoke and the scent of meat cooking, probably from the hut next door. She looked to see if Adhiambo had replaced the drinking glass that had been broken. She had.

James suddenly grinned. "Adhiambo, she is making these," he said, pointing to the hanging on the wall near the table. Margaret examined the cloth. In the gloom, she could just make out a batikish sort of print, studded with brass and black beads.

"They are very nice," she said. "When we are done, may I take them outside to see them properly?"

"You will love them," James said.

"Your name is Teresa," Rafiq began.

Margaret had decided not to take any pictures until the interview was finished. She tried to frame the shots. She knew that nothing inside would work because of the lack of light, but she might be able to get Adhiambo standing at the threshold of her door. Either that or get her face through the window opening.

Margaret learned that Adhiambo was twenty-four, that she had left her three children with her mother in Kericho so that she could travel to Nairobi and make money for her children's school fees. She said that she had had a good job where she made 360 shillings a month with a family, but the family had gone away. Of that 360 shillings, she had sent 160 back to her mother. She paid 90 shillings for her single room, which was without electricity or running water. She also had to pay for the pots of water she used for bathing and cooking from a common tap. She had a simple diet of posho and vegetables. She made only one reference to the rape: she often worried at night, she told Rafiq, because drunken men from nearby bars tried to force her door. Shortly after that, Margaret heard her say, "I'm just all right. I have no bad luck." Margaret was certain the phrase would make it into Rafiq's piece.

An hour turned into two hours, which turned into three. Adhiambo boiled water on the stove as she talked and then served them tea. Margaret took from her basket a packet of shortbread cookies she'd brought to prevent hunger pangs in the event that the day went on longer than was expected. For a few minutes, around the table, Margaret forgot her surroundings. The chatter was convivial, and she could have been at any friend's home having tea. Rafiq scrupulously addressed Adhiambo as Teresa, so much so that Margaret wanted to call her Teresa, too. The woman seemed a happier person as Teresa than she had as Adhiambo. Perhaps all the talking about her troubles or the attention paid to her had lifted her burden somewhat.

James spoke at length as well—about his life before he finally got work as a cook with a family. In the thirteen years he had lived in Nairobi, he had held a series of jobs ranging from dishwasher in a hotel to a guitar player in a band. His wife and four children tended a six-acre shamba back home in Kitale, and because of the demands of that work, they visited him only once a year for a week, a fact Margaret had known but one that still staggered her.

When the interview was over, Margaret asked Adhiambo if she could take a couple of pictures of her.

"You must not show my face," she said.

Margaret thought.

"I can shoot you doing an activity that shows you but not your face."

Adhiambo smiled. Her bottom teeth were crooked, and there was a gap between the two front teeth, but when she smiled, she was beautiful.

Outside, a group of children, all about five or six years old, had gathered around James, who had squatted to tell them a story. Three of the children held babies. Margaret called to James and asked if she could take his picture with the children. He said yes and told the kids, and Margaret adjusted the lens to get them all in the shot. Though they had been laughing and giggling a second earlier, they immediately turned somber when Margaret aimed the camera at them. She noted, as she continued to shoot, that Rafiq was scribbling on his pad. *Careful, Rafiq,* she was thinking. When an adult passed by, Margaret lowered the camera and pretended to be in conversation with James. She asked Adhiambo to bring out her wall hangings so that she could see them better, which Adhiambo did. Adhiambo laid them on the top of a bush in front of her hut. In the light, they were something entirely different. "You put the beads on this cloth?" Margaret asked her.

She nodded.

"And you bought the cloth?"

"No, no," she said, waving her hands. "I am making the cloth."

Margaret was impressed. The cloth was not a batik, she discovered, but rather hand-painted. With broad but strategically placed lines, Adhiambo had painted scenes of women cooking and of children tending other children. At first the eye thought the lines abstract. The positioning of the brass and black beads further confused the viewer. All of which made the surprise of the figures more exciting. "You learned this where?" Margaret asked.

"I think I am inventing it," she said.

"These are terrific."

Margaret took several shots of each, and two with Adhiambo holding the larger of the wall hangings in front of her. In the pictures, her face was turned away, but one could still make out her profile.

Margaret was reluctant to have Adhiambo take the cloths back inside the hut.

"Hang on a second," Margaret called.

Adhiambo stopped.

"I'd like to buy one if I could."

Adhiambo seemed bewildered and looked to James for guidance.

James grinned. "She is selling them for one hundred shillings each," he said.

Twelve dollars. A bargain. Margaret reached into her basket and retrieved the notes. She had brought five hundred shillings with her in case Rafiq had been unable to get the money from the *Tribune*. If only there were a place outside the hut for Adhiambo to display her work for all to see. James leaned closer and said, "We must go now."

"Have you told Rafiq?" Margaret asked.

"Yes."

They said elaborate good-byes to Adhiambo. Margaret wished she had had Moses cook some meat to bring to her. They all bowed and turned back on the path.

"The askaris who live here are coming home soon," James said. "They will not like our presence here."

Once again, they walked on the path, this time Rafiq ahead of Margaret, with James behind. Rafiq had removed his suit jacket;

his shirt was soaked to the skin in the back. They had stood in the noonday sun for at least an hour while James told stories and Margaret took pictures. Rafiq, during that time, had interviewed a neighbor who had walked him to the pump from which Adhiambo got her water and then had given Rafiq directions to the latrine. It was almost three o'clock, and James reminded them that three was the time when the day shift of askaris returned home and the evening shift went out.

"Those hours aren't so bad," Margaret said. "What? Seven to three? Eight-hour shifts?"

"No, no," James explained. "There are only the two shifts. The askaris are working twelve hours."

Margaret drove James home first, because he said he had to prepare the evening meal. Then Rafiq and she headed to the *Tribune,* where Rafiq had left his car.

"That was wretched," Rafiq said when they were alone. "Ghastly."

Until that moment, Margaret hadn't seen him express intense emotion of any kind. Even when he'd been chronicling his ouster from Uganda, he'd been calm.

"You've never seen conditions like those before?" she asked.

"I have, but from a distance. Never this...intimate."

"Your piece should be good," she said, "if you feel this way."

"Yes, I'm eager to get at it. It will take some work, though, to make that place as real to the reader as it is to me."

"Some of the people who live in such conditions will read your piece," Margaret said. "James, before he ever got hooked up with a family as a cook, had eight years of school and spoke English very well. I often saw him with a newspaper when I was living on the same grounds as he."

"And where was that?"

"Langata."

"Really?" Rafiq seemed surprised.

"Long story," she said. "We lived in a small one-bedroom cottage on the property of a larger house. We used to get invited to dinner a lot at what we called the Big House. There was an incident during which James and I got to know each other better."

"What incident?"

Margaret was sorry she'd brought up James. "It's something you can't write about, even though you're going to want to."

"Now I'm completely intrigued."

"Promise?"

"I promise."

"Adhiambo was raped by two men. She was brought to our cottage to spend the night. In the morning, James came to collect her, and we all walked back to the place you saw today. She'd been beaten, too, and was deeply ashamed."

Rafiq nodded his head slowly. "I wondered about that. Her reference to men trying to get through her door..."

"Even if you'd pursued it, she never would have told you."

Rafiq sat back in his seat for the rest of the way to town. Margaret wondered if he was composing sentences or thinking of Adhiambo and the rape.

"I can't thank you enough," he said, putting his hand on hers for just a moment. Even his palm was hot.

"Someone in my debt," Margaret said. "A novel sensation."

The following Friday, Margaret flew to Lamu. She'd been given precise instructions. Drive herself to Wilson Airport, collect her tickets from the agent, and then she'd be told which aircraft to board. When she arrived on Manda, she'd be led to a dhow that would ferry her to Lamu, a brief journey. Patrick would be waiting for her at the town landing.

Margaret had seen small planes at air shows and on television, but never had she seen one with the intention of actually flying in it. There were three passenger seats—two behind the pilot and one beside him. She didn't know the make of the aircraft, but she did note the propellers. She sat behind the pilot, who had on a mod suit—gray, slim-fitting, short-sleeved, Nehru collar. The two other passengers were a South African couple with thick accents. The man was deeply tanned and had stiff blond hair, as if he'd done a lot of swimming in a chlorinated pool. The woman was a petite brunette. "Hi. I'm Kathleen Krueger. This is my husband, Gary."

They asked Margaret why she was headed to Lamu, and she told them she was meeting her husband, who'd gone ahead of her. Margaret asked them the reason for their journey. They were in the start-up phase of a jewelry business and wanted to meet with a pair of brothers who made extraordinary silver bracelets. "You'll love Lamu," Kathleen said with assurance. "Everybody does. Where are you staying?"

Margaret answered Petley's.

"Good hotel," Kathleen said. "Don't drink the water—even the ice cubes in the drinks."

"Oh God," her husband said, obviously remembering an unpleasant event.

The pilot turned on the engine. Several instruments lit up. He spoke to a pilot in another plane that they could see. Apparently they were to follow the first plane to Lamu. Margaret wondered if Kenyan aircraft routinely flew in pairs. To be able to instantly call in the site of a crash?

Margaret had always been a white-knuckle flier until she got bored enough to relax. On the flight to Lamu, however, she never relaxed.

Had she not been so frightened, she might have said the liftoff was thrilling. The South African couple kept up a steady chatter and pointed out what seemed to be important moments of their personal history.

"Remember, darling, when we were returning from Mombasa in Drew's truck during the rains, and the road had washed out?"

"We almost died that night. I don't know how Drew managed to come to a stop where he did."

"We spent the entire night there, didn't we? Until it got light enough to figure out how to avoid falling to our death?"

"I'll never forget it."

"No, me neither."

Immediately, the city fell away to endless plains. Hadn't Finch Hatton crashed his plane over Tsavo, a town they would soon fly over? Margaret tried then to just think of Patrick, of his arms around her and the feel of her face against his chest. Before the trip to Mount Kenya, that would have done the trick, but now it only made Margaret anxious. She had no idea what she would find when she arrived. Would they be as they once were, or would they fall again into that murky no-man's-land, the aftermath of a disastrous expedition?

Manda Airport was smaller than Wilson. A thick forest of mangrove surrounded them on all four sides. She followed the others to a narrow path. Gary offered to carry her suitcase. Normally, she'd have said no, but she let him. When they emerged on the other side of the thick forest, they found dozens of other people clamoring to get on one of the dhows that were approaching shore. The

South African couple turned out to be valuable, announcing they had diplomatic credentials and needed to make their way to the landing at once. Margaret had no choice but to follow, since Gary had her bag. They pushed forward to the front of the throng.

"We'll get on now," he said, handing Margaret her suitcase.

"Thank you," she said.

They were among the first to board the small dhow. Margaret thought she should feel guilty, but she didn't. She just wanted to get to Lamu. She grew somewhat alarmed, however, when she saw how many people the dhow's captain, a sinewy man in a loincloth, was letting on. Even the South African couple sighed heavily as yet another family climbed aboard.

She felt the push-off and then the gentle glide. All around her was chatter.

"Jesus Christ, Gary," Kathleen said to her husband. "We've only got an inch of freeboard."

"At least nobody's shooting at us," Gary replied.

Patrick waved and blew a kiss, and Margaret would have done so back if it weren't for having to keep her balance on the rocking dhow with her suitcase in her hand. First one on meant last one off.

When she finally reached the pier, Patrick swept her up in his arms. His spirits were high, and Margaret felt her spirits rise as well. "I'm so happy to see you," she said, burying her face in his shoulder.

The trip had broken the ice jam. They would be all right together.

Patrick took Margaret's suitcase, and they walked the length of the dock.

* * *

What was it that Margaret noticed first? That there was a person going the wrong way along the dock? That, oddly, that person seemed to be stopping directly in front of Patrick? That before the woman spoke, in her appealing Italian accent, Margaret couldn't help but notice that she was beautiful in a way that Margaret would never be? How fast that thought was formed. The slim body, the long, flowing skirt that fell from narrow hips, the sunglasses pushed up over the mass of long, dark curls caught up in pins, the wide, dark eyes, the prominent jaw, the mouth, the self-confidence that was evident in every gesture.

"Elena, this is my wife, Margaret," Patrick said by way of introduction. "Margaret, this is Elena, an ophthalmologist who is working with our team."

Elena, her wrist covered in gold bangles, held out her hands. In them she held a thin black shawl. "You'll be needing this," she said.

Behind Elena, Margaret could see an ancient city of small white buildings dotted with several mosques and their round domes. There were no roads to speak of, only narrow cobblestoned streets better suited to pedestrians than to vehicles. All paths led upward to the heart of the city. Patrick carried her bag while she held the translucent shawl over her shoulders for modesty.

"How was your flight?" Elena asked.

"Fine."

"I hate to fly. I try to put myself to sleep."

"What work are you and Patrick doing together?"

"We're part of a team that was sent out as a kind of medical think tank. We treat patients, we talk about them and their lives, the conditions in which they live, and then we have roundtable discussions among ourselves to try to find solutions. Theoretically, the idea is to direct charitable organizations to the places that need the most help."

"Where are the others? How many are on your team?"

"Much of the collaborative work was done in Malindi. Two others are joining us tomorrow."

"And you got to Lamu when?"

"Yesterday afternoon. There was no other way to do it and still be here in time to collect you."

Margaret followed her husband up a steep set of steps. The men passing them wore kaffiyehs on their heads and white kanzus. They glanced at Elena and Margaret but didn't speak and weren't in the least rude.

"We're all at Petley's," Elena said. "You and Patrick have a rooftop room with wonderful views. I am just off the lobby."

Margaret continued to move forward, but it was as though she'd been pricked by thorns. Why the deliberate mention of how far apart the rooms were? How did Elena know that Patrick's room had a wonderful view? Was that a feature he'd have mentioned to a colleague who hadn't been lucky enough to get such a view? Or had he invited Elena up just to see the Indian Ocean, as one might do for a friend? Would they have had a quick drink together, watching that magnificent low skyline against an indigo blue? And what happened after that?

Margaret's mind wouldn't go there; it had never been necessary to do so. All of the above could be explained away. She was being too suspicious. Unfair to Elena, whose only crime was that she was beautiful. Had Elena been a dumpy woman with dull hair and pimples, would any of this have occurred to Margaret at all?

Margaret wanted and yet didn't want to have a discussion about this with Patrick. Either way, she thought, she would lose. Patrick might be genuinely shocked, and then angry she'd even thought to ask such a question. Margaret would lose. Or he might use that moment to tell her that, yes, he and Elena had been having an affair and had planned the coastal trip with that in mind. Margaret would lose. Or he might employ the former tactic simply to blow smoke in her face, so that she wouldn't ask another question on the subject. She would lose. For a moment, she was furious with Patrick for having put her in that position. Why ask her to join him in Lamu (risking her life, she might add) for what was supposed to be a private weekend only to introduce another woman into the mix? And, come to think of it, why hadn't he prepared Margaret on the telephone for Elena? He wasn't a stupid man.

Halfway up a narrow street, they stopped at a small coffeehouse with elaborate metal chairs outside. Inside, Margaret could see low wood furniture with many white cushions. She was glad to be able to sit in the shadow of the building across the street. In that building, she saw a vendor standing in his doorway, chatting with a second man. In the window was a display of handcrafted jewelry, most in silver: long cuffs, necklaces that looked more like art than jewelry, and earrings that would fall to the chin line.

"Have you been in that store?" Margaret asked Elena.

"I haven't had time. When we got here, we walked around, but all the shops were closed. They reopen later in the day, but I gather that it's hard to know the schedule until you've been here a couple of days. Why? Are you admiring the jewelry in that window?"

"Do you know how to bargain?" Margaret asked her.

Americans were notoriously bad at bargaining. They lacked either the subtlety or the patience for the way the game was played. Some "negotiations" could take as long as a half hour, with both sides smiling at the end. The elaborate games were always entertaining to watch.

"Sometimes," Elena said.

Coffee arrived and, with it, cubes of sugar.

"I suspect you're dehydrated," Elena said. "Patrick, can you get her a bottle of water?"

There was something wrong with the request. How could Elena so easily order Patrick around?

"He is nice, your husband," Elena said when Patrick had gone. "Highly competent but kind as well."

The muezzin began the call to prayers. Margaret sat back and closed her eyes and let the minor notes, which she'd always loved, wash over her. She opened her eyes when Patrick returned with the water.

"Thank you," she whispered.

Margaret could see the feet and ankles of the two men who had been talking earlier outside the shop. Now they were inside on prayer rugs laid upon the stone.

At Petley's, they split up to go to their separate rooms, with plans to meet for dinner at the rooftop restaurant. Once inside, Margaret went to wash her hands. When she came out, Patrick was sitting on the bed, waiting for her.

"I thought this was going to be a weekend for just the two of us," Margaret said.

"You mean Elena?" he asked. "She wanted to come ahead early to set up meetings with the people who run the clinic here. But the way I see things, our weekend begins here," he said as he patted the bedspread.

Margaret had to go to her husband, who was already unbuttoning his shirt. She had no choice. But the walk from the bathroom to the bed felt among the most arduous of her life.

It's impossible to have sex with a man you love, Margaret thought, and not relax into his arms. From the bed, she heard the sounds of commerce and men talking. Through the window, a sharp blue hurt her eyes. From Patrick's genuine passion, it was difficult to conclude that he and Elena were anything more than colleagues. Margaret would not ask questions about Elena. She was not a jealous woman.

Margaret wore her best dress, an off-the-shoulder, slim-fitting black. With it, she chose an ivory necklace with brass and black beads that she'd bought on Kimathi Street. She remembered Elena's admonition and slipped the thin shawl over her shoulders.

Elena sat alone at the table when they entered the restaurant. Her curly black hair had been released from whatever had been holding it back. She had on a black strapless dress with matching shawl and no jewelry apart from the diamonds at her ears. The Italian woman was nothing if not elegant.

Patrick and Margaret crossed the restaurant holding hands. When they reached Elena, Patrick bent over and gave her a kiss on each cheek. Because everyone in the restaurant appeared to be a tourist or a visitor, Margaret allowed her shawl to slip a bit when she sat down. A moist, warm air moved along her bare back. The foreign voices at the other tables and the particular smell of Lamu — a scent of sea and incense, of smoke from cooking fires and even a faint whiff of drains—was unique, one she was certain she would never forget. Patrick put his arm around her, and Elena stared. Margaret thought the stare odd. Wouldn't a normal person politely look away or take a sip of wine? Maybe Elena was lonely.

"Are you married?" Margaret asked.

"No, but I have a boyfriend who is growing very angry with me. I have stayed too long here, and he wants me to come home."

"Your boyfriend should be angry at Todd, who convinced you to stay on for this project, " Patrick said. "And good for him, or we'd have gotten nowhere."

"He's a man who will go far," Elena pointed out. "His own research, I thought, was weak, but he is very good at putting people together and making work happen."

"I gather you're talking of a colleague," Margaret said.

"Sorry, hon," Patrick said, and Margaret's skin pricked as it had done earlier. Her husband had never called her "hon" before. And why was it, Margaret wondered, that Patrick hadn't chosen to come to the landing alone? Why had it been necessary to bring Elena along? Wouldn't he have known how much that might rattle Margaret?

She took a sip of chilled white wine.

Elena gave Margaret a quick glance. "How is your own work going?" she asked. "I have heard so much about you from Patrick."

"My work is going very well," Margaret said. "I'm being assigned to more and more complex stories. And I've partnered up with a far more appealing reporter than I began with."

"And who is that?" Patrick asked, accepting a menu from the waiter.

"His name is Rafiq Hameed. He was kicked out of Uganda in seventy-two with all the other Asians. He's quite educated— schooled in London, continued with his studies at Makerere. Then the purge. He's in his late twenties, I'd say. Drives a Citroën that makes his knees bump up against the dashboard. He's tall."

She was about to add "and handsome," but she thought that might be taking it too far.

Two could play at this game.

After the meal, Elena said good night. Patrick walked Margaret to a quiet corner of the roof deck. From Petley's Inn, the other buildings of Lamu village appeared to be topless boxes, two to three stories tall, with large courtyards inside. Every rooftop in the village was visible, and Margaret was surprised to see how many of them had gardens. Some even had beds surrounded by mosquito netting.

"The coolest place in many of these buildings is the rooftop," Patrick said. "From there, you can catch the sea breezes."

"What if it rains?" Margaret asked.

"It hardly ever rains."

"It's so lovely. So exotic."

"I don't have to worry about you, do I?" Patrick whispered.

"About what?"

"This tall, educated reporter by your side daily?"

"You must be joking," she said. "And from you, of all people?"

"What do you mean?"

"You and Elena? Can you tell me what that's about?"

"We're colleagues."

"Who spent the night together in the same hotel, who both found it necessary to greet me at the landing?"

"Elena and I had a working breakfast, and it seemed rude not to invite her along to meet you."

"We need a chaperone now?"

"Don't be ridiculous."

Margaret's words made her ill, even as she continued to utter them. "And you can't possibly deny that she's incredibly beautiful."

"Margaret, listen to yourself."

"I'd rather listen to you."

"I have nothing to say."

His body stiffened.

"Are we together?" she asked. "Together as we were before the climb? Or did that cause us irreparable harm?"

Patrick closed his eyes. "I'm not going to talk about this. Your obsession with the climb is eating away at you. I've been watching it for months. Until you deal with that, I guess we're not as together as we once were. No. How could we be?"

"I'm not obsessed with the climb," Margaret protested. "I'm obsessed with our marriage."

"I think we should go in," he said.

Margaret had a sudden change of heart. She felt a fierce desire to physically hold on to her husband. "Oh, I'm sorry," Margaret said as she snatched his sleeve. "Patrick, don't go. I didn't come all the way to Lamu for this. I just wanted to have a nice weekend with you that would brush away all the cobwebs. Please stay."

He stood next to her. "No more talk about the marriage."

"No more talk about the marriage."

The next morning, Patrick and Elena went to a meeting while Margaret had the day free. The man at the front desk suggested a walking tour, but Margaret found herself off the trail almost as soon as she'd started. Side alleys beckoned: the eighteenth-century houses of coral covered with layers of ancient plaster beguiled her. She noticed the carved wooden shutters and doors, and, from time to time, when one of them opened, she caught a glimpse of courtyards with fountains and carved niches and low white sofas. She wanted to be invited into one of those courtyards with its hint of jasmine.

Everywhere she walked, she saw Rafiq. Each man she passed might have been his cousin. All the native women wore the bui-bui. Had Rafiq ever been to Lamu?

On the cobblestones, donkeys and cats roamed freely, and occasionally, on what seemed to be a narrow passageway, Margaret found a store: one that sold silver jewelry; one that sold itos, round painted eyes from Swahili dhows; another that offered kikois, patterned wraps worn by Swahili men. She'd discovered that the prices on Lamu were extravagant. A beer at Petley's the night before had been nearly a hundred shillings. Of course, it all had to do with the difficulty of importing foreign goods to the island, but even the locally crafted silver jewelry was dear. Margaret bought a kikoi for Patrick and an ito for the household. She half wondered what Patrick would think of this talisman meant to ward off the evil eye. The other half wondered if it would work.

She returned to the hotel in time for lunch and found Elena and Patrick waiting for her. They were still in that animated state of two people fresh from a meeting, whereas Margaret had just returned from another century, one with a much slower pace. Sensing Margaret's near stupor, Patrick ordered for her.

"You okay?" he asked as he cocked his head.

Margaret tried to open her eyes to a normal size. "I'm perfect," she said, meaning it. "Can we live here?"

"And she hasn't even been to the beach yet," Elena said. "You positively won't be able to leave if you spend any time at Peponi's."

A man, a hotel employee, stopped at their table. "Mr. McCoglan?" he asked.

"That's me," Patrick said.

"I have for you this message."

"Thank you," Patrick said, tipping the man.

Patrick opened the envelope and read the note inside. He laid it on the table and slowly rolled his head back as far as it would go. He closed his eyes. Elena looked at Margaret, who picked up the piece of paper.

Dear Bwana Patrick,
The house is empty. Bandits came and took everything except from your bedroom, which is still locked. The police came. Please return soon.
Your friend, Moses

Margaret imagined Moses dictating the note over the phone to the man at the front desk, who might, in writing down the message, have corrected Moses's grammar. Margaret turned to look at her still-immobile husband.

All his research.

She held the note out to Elena.

"I'm so sorry," Elena said when she read it. "Everything?"

Elena arranged for Patrick and Margaret to fly out of Manda that afternoon. Lamu left Margaret as if it had been only a dream.

The scene when they arrived at the Karen house was as alien

as any Margaret had ever witnessed. When Moses said "everything," he meant it. The drapes had been hacked from the windows, all the telephones and wires taken. The sconces over the fireplace had been dug out of the walls. One bathroom was without a toilet. Margaret thought about the dinners they had had in the dining room, the phone calls at the hall table, the cocktails she and Patrick had had on the sofa in the living room. All vanished. That the avocado and lime trees should still be out back struck her as surreal.

She stood with Patrick when he entered the study. All his research, all his books—gone. His notes, the family photographs from home—gone. Patrick leaned against the doorjamb. There was nothing Margaret could say to him. There was no reassuring him that the papers would be found; no consolation available in the hope that there must be copies somewhere. Had he used carbon paper for everything? She didn't think so. And what about all the handwritten notes, the ones he hadn't typed up yet? Irreplaceable.

Margaret was relieved that she'd taken her cameras with her, but there were other things she would deeply miss: funny illustrated letters from Timmy, the photos that weren't on file at the *Tribune,* the cloth Adhiambo had made.

"I'm so sorry," she said.

"We're cursed," he answered quietly. "The other thefts, the climb, then this."

"We are not cursed," Margaret countered, wanting to dispel that notion. She thought of the ito, the good-luck charm she had in her suitcase. When was that supposed to kick in? she wondered.

"Excuse me."

Margaret turned to see a Kenyan policeman in civilian clothes.

"I need to speak with you both, if you please. I am Inspector Wambui," he said, showing them his badge.

They followed the man into the foyer of the house. Three large stones, each a little bit smaller than a bowling ball, lay on the wooden floor near where the hallway table used to be. Margaret wondered if the thieves had contemplated ripping up the expensive parquet.

"Are these yours?" the inspector asked.

"Those rocks?" Patrick answered in disbelief.

"I didn't think so. Then these are what the thieves were going to kill you with, had you been in the house."

Margaret was speechless.

"Do you know who is doing this to you?" the inspector asked.

"No, no one," Patrick answered.

"Do you have any enemies?"

"I don't think so," Margaret said. "Really, I can't think of anyone who wishes us harm."

"We have examined the house. There is a broken window in the kitchen. We have interrogated your house servant and the neighborhood askaris, as procedure dictates. I do not think it was the house servant. He was sleeping at the time, and he is as distressed as you. He is afraid of what his employers will say. Do I understand that you were renting the house?"

"Not actually," Margaret said. "We were house-sitting. Our job was to make sure nothing happened here."

The inspector raised an eyebrow. Patrick ran his hand through his hair.

"We will be needing the address and telephone number of the owner," the inspector said.

"I know their name, but Moses has all the contact information. I hope he kept it in his own house and not here."

A consultation was had with Moses. The contact information was found, and it was agreed that Patrick should make the call. Moses, clearly, was terrified.

"How do I tell a couple that everything they once owned is now gone?" Patrick asked.

The violation felt personal. Nothing was left—not a spoon, not a toothpick, not a glass to fill with water. It had to have been a gang, Margaret thought. A normal move would have been arduous; this would have been a gargantuan task. She thought of the owners' heavy sideboards and their sofa. She remembered rooms filled with furniture.

Margaret turned to the inspector. "How could this have happened without someone seeing or hearing it?" she asked. "There had to have been a vehicle involved."

"The thieves, they are very quiet. Always. They carry the goods to a waiting car, sometimes parked in the woods. They cannot be stopped. Unless you have the askaris or the gates. Still, it sometimes happens then, too. Usually when the owners are away. Often these things are random. Can you tell me who knew about your trip?"

"Moses," she said. "Some people at the newspaper where I contribute photographs from time to time. On a freelance basis only," she added, realizing she was talking to a government official. "It was to be such a short trip—two nights only—that I don't think I bothered even to tell our friends."

"Are you sure?"

"I'm pretty sure."

"Someone who could have overheard you speaking of the trip?"

"I suppose any number of people might have overheard me speak of it or later learned of it at the newspaper. But, honestly, I'm sure no one there would do this." Margaret tried to think. Had she told anyone but Moses and Rafiq and Solomon Obok? "The people at the airport would have known," she added, thinking. "You might check the personnel at Wilson."

"We have done that. You were a woman traveling alone. If an agent there was a thief, he might have assumed that there was a man who remained at the house."

Patrick had to go next door to make the phone call.

Margaret walked upstairs and unlocked their bedroom door. It was exactly as she had left it the day before: towels slung on doorknobs, one of the pillows knocked askew.

She sat heavily on the bed, no longer able to stand.

"We are not cursed," she said aloud. "There's no such thing as a curse. I've never believed it before, and I'm not going to start now."

Patrick entered the room and sat beside Margaret. "This looks like a movie set in a vast empty studio."

"How was it?" she asked.

"It was horrible, just as you'd expect."

"They're mad."

"Furious. They seemed to think we were supposed to be in the house at all times. When I told them we were in Lamu when it happened, they went insane. They never asked about our personal losses. Then they asked to speak to Moses. I felt sorry for the guy." He smoothed the covers. "Well, at least we can sleep here."

Margaret leaped from the bed. "Are you crazy? And lie awake all night waiting for the thieves to come and empty out this room as well? With us in it? Didn't you see those three rocks? We're packing up our stuff and getting out of here."

"And going where?" Patrick asked. "I suppose Karim and Aarya would take us in. We could sleep on their floor."

"Maybe," Margaret said, "but I have a better idea. Let's just head for the Norfolk."

"It'll cost a fortune."

"I don't much care at this point," she said. She sat again on the bed beside her husband.

"We'll have to rent a place now," he said. "I don't think we're going to get a house-sitting reference."

"I'll start looking for places tomorrow," Margaret offered.

"Some of the research is at the hospital. The most recent, in my briefcase. I'll try to patch it together as best I can. I was almost always working with someone else."

They lay back together and stared at the ceiling.

"I'm not leaving," Patrick said.

"I'm not leaving," Margaret said.

Patrick and Margaret found a flat not too far from the hospital. A physician, vacating it to return to Delhi, had posted a handwritten *For Let* notice on the bulletin board. They'd spent two nights at the Norfolk and knew they couldn't afford many more.

The flat was in a large stone house that had once been stately, and as they drove up along the walled driveway, Margaret grew mildly intrigued. Shaded by tall jacaranda and eucalyptus, and surrounded by overgrown gardens, the house seemed like one an early settler might have had and then, down on his luck, abandoned.

Inside, Patrick and Margaret were surprised to find both an askari in a uniform and an elevator in the lobby. An elevator! As the askari used the telephone to call the owner, Margaret reflected that a doorman was an askari without the machete. The owner, a Sikh, took them up to the third floor. Selecting a key from an enormous ring, he opened the door to 3F.

Margaret was reassured to find casement windows that opened outward to the untended garden, and they were both surprised to discover that the flat had two bedrooms, one of which Patrick could use for a study. (The next morning, Patrick called for a locksmith to install a double lock for the study door.) There was a fireplace for the cold nights, a dining table of decent size in the space shared by the living room, and a kitchen with all the "mod cons," as the turbaned owner was quick to point out. The mismatched furniture reminded Margaret of grad-student housing in the States, and she wondered if they could survive the vile green sofa. With a little work, she thought, Patrick and she could make a go of it. They'd wanted a flat in a building with other tenants, since they no longer wished to be isolated. They thought that a flat on the third floor would present a challenge to the usual thief.

"Thick walls," the owner said, patting the plaster. He had brought the paperwork and a pen.

Patrick settled into his routine of going to the hospital every weekday and often traveling on weekends as part of his promise to visit clinics all over the country. Margaret went with him on the excursions when she had an urge to photograph a person or place, or an animal she hadn't yet photographed for her brother, Timmy. She stayed home when she felt the need to work on her portfolio. She had found a darkroom in a camera store in town, the owner willing to rent out time. On weekends, Margaret might sign up for six or seven hours, depending upon what she thought she could afford.

Margaret still had so much to learn—about light, about equipment, about developing prints. If Patrick had come to the country to research equatorial diseases, Margaret had inadvertently undertaken her own research as well: to learn as much about photography as she possibly could. She yearned one day to illustrate a book about Kenya, though it might not be one the average tourist would want to buy. There wouldn't be, in this imaginary book, a single shot of an animal (though Margaret did love photographing them) but rather a series of portraits and candids of the Africa few tourists seemed to know about.

At the *Tribune*, Margaret was still assigned to Rafiq, who was writing longer features only. She worked with him on a piece about widows (photo: a pregnant woman with her hand over her eyes, standing in front of her husband's grave, the markers of a thousand graves behind her); a portrait of the famous Kenyan writer Ngũgĩ wa Thiong'o (photo: the man, midspeech, brows furrowed, eyes flashing—a man of righteous anger); a piece on why female circumcision should be abolished (photo: two women bent over a young girl lying on the ground in protest, as if they might be going to do something to her—actually a setup with locals willing to play the parts since Margaret refused to be party to an actual circumcision); an intriguing piece about children from a remote village in the Narok District voluntarily gathering each morning to be taught to read and write in their vernacular and to speak Kiswahili (photo: children of many sizes in tribal dress in front of hut with disintegrating roof).

This last assignment required that Rafiq and Margaret travel to Narok, a distance of 150 miles. Because an overnight would be necessary, Rafiq had engaged a local driver who would act as interpreter. They had two rooms in Narok (Rafiq and the interpreter in one; Margaret in the other) at a hotel no tourist would ever stay in.

"I'm sorry about this," Rafiq said after he'd surveyed the premises. "But this was the best I could find."

"It's fine," Margaret said, noting the paint peeling from the stucco, the bars on the windows. She dreaded what she might find within.

Rafiq put his hands on his hips.

For the first time, Margaret felt an overwhelming desire to place her palm on the front of Rafiq's shirt. She didn't, but she couldn't remove her eyes from the place where she wanted to put her hand.

"Margaret?"

She raised her eyes to his. Did he know? There was a pause before he spoke, during which she thought he might. "I have to work during dinner to prepare the piece in time, so I'm afraid I'll have to leave you with David, the driver." He paused. "Will that be okay?"

"Yes," she said, still caught in a semitrance.

"Good, then," he said.

Margaret found Rafiq's behavior odd and yet not. It was as if he planned to announce to the paper and to the world (and thus to her) that he would be professional on any occasion during which he and she had to stay overnight together. She supposed she appreciated that, but she missed him all the same. Especially at dinner with David, a man whose eyes and heart were elsewhere. The driver/interpreter spent the night with his girlfriend, who lived in the village.

When on day assignments, however, Rafiq and Margaret would often break for lunch or take tea in a shop in Nairobi after all work was done. She came to look forward to these teas. Rafiq had a number of usual spots, but her favorite was the Golden Cup, an unprepossessing storefront that revealed inside a world of Middle Eastern culture: gold tea trays, thick wooden tables with polished surfaces, woven carpets of all colors underfoot, intricate weavings and carvings on the walls.

"This is wonderful," Margaret said the first time she entered the shop.

"It belongs to my cousin. He'll come out later."

"Do you have a lot of family?" she asked as Rafiq led her to a table.

"By Western standards, yes. I have cousins in Pakistan, London, Kampala, and here. If I went to London, for example, and didn't visit my cousins, I'd never be allowed to forget it. I have cousins who have the highest university degrees and cousins who are bookies. I have female cousins who have taken the veil and unabashed cousins who wear miniskirts and go braless. A great soup of cousins."

Margaret laughed. "I have three," she said. "One on my mother's side, and two on my father's. I feel impoverished."

"You are impoverished."

The cousin from the back room came out to greet Rafiq and Margaret. Rafiq introduced Margaret as a colleague at the paper, though whether that satisfied cousin Safeer was hard to tell. The two men spoke in English for Margaret's benefit. Before she knew it, an elaborate tea had been set before them.

"I hope you're hungry," Rafiq said when Safeer had left.

"What are all these?" she asked.

"This one here is falooda, the other motichoor ladoo, but my favorite is the malai khaja."

"They all look delicious," Margaret said.

"They'll completely ruin your dinner."

"I don't think I care," Margaret said.

"My cousin will take offense if we leave any crumbs."

The pungent flavors, the incense, the sight of Rafiq sitting back in his chair with his posture relaxed and his collar open, all contributed to a sense of having entered a temple of exotic serenity. Margaret felt a kind of intimacy there she hadn't felt in some time.

"There's a story I need to tell you," she said.

Rafiq turned to her.

"It's about something that happened to me while I was on Mount Kenya."

Margaret explained the climb in all its complexity, including the parts about Arthur. She related the last night in the banda, the holding of hands. Diana's behavior in the morning.

"We had to cross this glacier," Margaret continued. "It's called Lewis Glacier. It was steep, and I think we were all a little afraid of it. The guide had to carve footsteps out of the ice for us to walk in. It was probably two hundred feet across. We were all clipped to a rope with the guide at the front and a couple of the porters at the back. I looked down once."

Rafiq had set his teacup on the table. Why had she felt it necessary to tell this story? she wondered.

"It was terrifying," Margaret said. "Utterly terrifying. I started to pray then. I kept my eyes glued to the porter in front of me. When he moved forward, I moved forward."

Rafiq nodded.

"We were doing fine, and then we were in the middle of the glacier. I became aware of something odd happening, and then several people began shouting. Diana had unclipped herself from the guide rope and had gone above us and was carving out her own footsteps."

"She was completely unhooked?"

"Yes. Her intention, as always, was to get moving. She was exasperated with the guide's pace. By the time I looked up and understood what she was doing, she was just overtaking the guide but was about ten feet above him." Margaret shook her head. "And then she lost her balance and missed her footing. I can't even say what I saw and didn't see. I'm pretty sure I saw the guide reach forward to grab the edge of the hood of her jacket, and I can't believe it even now, but he missed it. Diana just slipped through his grasp. It was horrible, Rafiq. Horrible. We all went down on our knees, and Arthur was howling with grief. He was so crazed, I was sure he would jump and take us all with him. We watched Diana spiral away from us. She just kept on going. It was like being in the room of a tall building with a group of people when one of them decides to open the window and stand on the sill, and before you can barely tell her to stop, she jumps."

"I heard about this," Rafiq said.

"You did?"

"It was in the papers. It just said that a white Kenyan woman had died on a glacier while climbing Mount Kenya. I assume it was the same woman."

"When was the story?"

"Last—I don't know—January, February?"

"It's the same person."

"I'm sorry."

"I felt I had to tell you this story," she said. "I believe I caused Diana's death."

Rafiq was silent.

"Diana was impatient, and she couldn't stand the guide's careful pace. Fine. But I don't believe she would have unclipped herself if she hadn't been in a rage."

"A rage?"

"About what she thought she had seen between Arthur and

me. Yes, he'd been hovering. And, yes, I let him take my hand. But there wasn't anything between us. Far from it. I was always a little afraid of him. He could be mercurial—with you one minute, then dripping with condescension the next. I let him take my hand. I didn't pull away. Diana saw that."

"Thus the rage."

"Yes."

"I think this is all in your head, Margaret. I really do."

"No, Rafiq, it's not. There are others who blame me as well."

"Who?"

"Saartje did. She as much as told me so right there on the mountain."

Rafiq poured hot tea into their cups. "Then I think you should have another talk with her about this."

"I can't. She left the country. So did Arthur. But after the memorial service, which was the last time I saw him, he looked at me. It was a meaningful look. We didn't speak, but I believe he was trying to say that we were both to blame."

"And your husband?"

"Well, that's the terrible part," Margaret said, realizing she was crossing a line in revealing something of her marriage. "On the mountain, Patrick howled, too. The cry was meant for Diana, but the rest was meant for us, for our marriage. The next morning at breakfast, he made it plain that he considered me responsible."

"Margaret."

"It's complicated, and I don't want to imply that Patrick didn't have perfectly good reasons. He did. That's what was so awful about it."

"But surely that is behind you now."

"I don't know," Margaret said. "It did something to the

marriage. I've been trying to fix it, and I think Patrick from time to time tries to fix it, too. But it's gone so deep, and it's been so poisonous, I don't know if we can."

"A marriage can founder but still be worth the effort to save it," Rafiq said.

"How do you know that? Have you ever been married?"

Rafiq shook his head. "A lot of cousins. A lot of marriages."

Margaret nodded.

"Listen," Rafiq said. "If one particular cousin weren't spying on us right now through a certain tiny window that is behind us, I would hold your face in my hands and I would tell you that you are a wonderful, complex woman. I watch you on every assignment. Your heart is very big."

"We're being watched?" Margaret asked, a smile forming.

"Most assuredly."

"Why?"

"Safeer didn't believe me when I told him you are 'just' a colleague."

Margaret blushed and eyed the sweets set before them. "I think we'd probably better start eating," she said.

Rafiq and Margaret lingered there long into the afternoon. Sometimes they chatted, and at other times, Rafiq was silent. Though Margaret yearned to know his thoughts, she didn't ask for them. When finally they left that room of wonders for the bright bustle of the street, Margaret felt the sunlight as a punishment.

One afternoon, after a particularly trying day of attempting to capture the success story of Ruaraka Enterprises (a vast auto-parts complex) in words and pictures (the photos were unsuccessful; Ruaraka had to submit a line drawing of the complex), Rafiq and Margaret felt as though they'd been bludgeoned by the heat, the brutal glinting sun, and piles upon piles of scrap metal. The task had been physically exhausting and intellectually numbing. Rafiq shook off his jacket, tossed it into the back of the Citroën, and said, "Let's go look at the animals."

"Great idea," Margaret said. "Perfect antidote."

"We'll just look," he added as she got into the car. "We don't even have to talk."

"Sounds like heaven to me," she said.

On their way to Nairobi National Park, Rafiq stopped and went into a duka and returned with cold sodas and bags of crisps.

"How did you know that a cool drink and salt were just what I needed?" Margaret asked.

Fortified, they drove into the park and paid the entrance fee. Margaret tried to contribute, but Rafiq wouldn't let her. "My idea," he used as an excuse.

When Patrick and Margaret had been in Boston, one of their favorite pastimes had been to take drives into the countryside on weekends. The idea was to get out of the city but, more important, to relax the eyes, have no agenda, and stop to eat whenever they felt like it. They would drive to prime tourist attractions (Concord and Lexington, for example) but not actually get out of the car. On the other hand, they might stop beside a farm and take a hike in the owner's field. They might find a cozy inn and eat a ploughman's lunch by the fire, or they might stumble upon a diner in a mill town that served greasy hamburgers and thick milk shakes. Those drives almost always worked to remind Margaret and Patrick that there was life outside of hospitals and congressional meetings.

It had been a while since Margaret had gone to "look at the animals," which had never, oddly enough, been a high priority for either Patrick or her while in the country. It wasn't that Margaret didn't like them (they were often thrilling, and the pictures she sent Timmy thrilled him in turn); it was that the safari Land Rovers they inevitably encountered reminded her that the creatures existed for the tourists.

Still, the animals were magnificent, and even if the occasional picture Margaret took looked like a cliché, she never failed to be excited by the sight of herds of wildebeests or elephants, or a lone cheetah.

Rafiq drove at the slow speed demanded on the sign at the park gate. The idea was to look, not to race around the mostly deserted roads. Though it was not advised, they kept their windows open for air.

Rafiq steered with one hand, occasionally eating a crisp or taking a sip of a cola that was no longer cold. For the most part, they were silent. Margaret had ample opportunity to examine the man when a giraffe or a zebra was to the right of them, outside his window. Something tense in his face and posture had relaxed. Again, she wondered at his thoughts. There was, beyond his affable and intelligent demeanor, something inscrutable she might never discover.

She held a camera in her lap and wanted from time to time to snap a few shots but was unwilling to disturb the lazy, hot peace inside the Citroën. Taking a picture would inevitably remind them both of work, a subject they'd gone to the park to avoid.

Rafiq let a giraffe get close to the car. He held out his hand with the remainder of the crisps, but he couldn't get the animal to bend that far and lick the salt away. Still the giraffe eyed them with perfect calm, more intrigued by the funny-looking yellow vehicle, Margaret thought, than by the inhabitants inside. Once, Rafiq stopped to view, through her window, a small herd of elephants about a hundred feet away. Margaret felt that she had license then to take a few pictures. They both knew how fast an elephant could charge and that a yellow Citroën would be no obstacle to the animal's rampage. Rafiq was as alert as she to any sudden movement or trumpeting in their direction. The herd, however, seemed to want a little peace and quiet as much as they did, and hardly moved from the small pond they had found.

The savanna was arid—they were nearing the end of the dry season—and there were many animals in the park looking for water. Margaret and Rafiq drove so slowly as to be standing still. If Margaret let her eyes relax, she could see the heat shimmering above the earth, the flat-topped acacias spreading outward as if for water. A herd of dik-diks scampered in front of the car, and she felt as if she were watching a Cinerama from her childhood. All around them were the sounds of insects, but Rafiq kept just enough speed to prevent the bugs from entering the car en masse. Occasionally, Margaret had to swipe at a curious fly. The smell of the place reminded her of hemp.

At one point, they stopped, and within two minutes, they were surrounded by baboons. Margaret and Rafiq rolled up their windows. She knew that baboons were predominantly vegetarians, but they were also aggressive. She suspected it was in their DNA to look upon vehicles as good sources of food. Though it was expressly prohibited, many of the tourists would feed them.

Baboons also loved campsites. Once, when Margaret had gone camping in Amboseli with Patrick and a colleague, she had stayed behind at the site while they went in search of fuel. This she told to Rafiq.

"Ten minutes after the men left, I saw the first baboon. I got up from this small collapsible table I'd been using as a desk and tried to wave him away. I was a little frantic. I was trying to remember if the food was in the Peugeot or if any had been left in the cooler in the tent. A second baboon arrived, and within seconds I was surrounded by at least a dozen baboons, each moving closer and closer to me. I picked up a cooking pot and began banging on it with a metal utensil."

Rafiq laughed.

"I had no idea what the baboons might do to get to what they thought was food. When they advanced closer, I began to sing as loud as I could."

"What did you sing?" Rafiq asked.

"'The Star-Spangled Banner.'"

Rafiq threw his head back and laughed again. Just looking at him made Margaret smile.

"The baboons, you'll be interested to know, were indifferent to my singing," she went on. "They kept creeping toward me. One would slip closer to me on the right while my attention was on a baboon to my left. I considered getting into the tent..."

She could see Rafiq shake his head already.

"…but then realized it was a terrible idea. Being trapped in the tent while baboons crawled all over the canvas would be more than I could handle."

"I imagine it might be," Rafiq said.

"So, in the distance," Margaret continued, "I could see this single line of natives walking toward me. I didn't know who they were or what their intentions might be, but from where I stood, they looked like help. As they got closer, I could see that they were Masai women and that each held a bundle of sticks on top of her head. I couldn't think of the word for *help* in Swahili, not to mention Maa, but my predicament must have been obvious. As they approached the camp, they broke apart and ran wildly at the baboons, waving their arms and shrieking. Shrieking. The baboons, naturally, disappeared. I put down the pot."

"Then what happened?"

"When my husband and his friend pulled into the campsite, they found me anchoring one side of a sheet on which I had put everything that remained in the cooler. Anchoring the other sides were six Masai women. Though we couldn't understand one another, the Masai women chatted among themselves while eating cornflakes, banana chips, triangles of La Vache Qui Rit, and Tetra Paks of milk. I'd have given anything to have known what the women said."

"Cornflakes?"

"Cornflakes. When the men got out of the car, the women stood, put their bundles back on their heads, and left, again in single file."

"So," Rafiq said, pointing to the baboons, "you want to get out of the car and shriek?"

"Why don't we just put the car in gear and speed off?"

"Funny-looking, though, aren't they?"

Margaret and Rafiq had driven for almost forty-five minutes, encountering zebras, rhinos, and warthogs, when Margaret said in a low voice, "Stop the car."

He glanced at her, and she pointed out the windshield. Not sixty feet in front of them, a leopard lay on the branch of an acacia tree. The animal twitched his nose and stared, and Margaret knew he had spotted them inside the car—probably long before she'd noticed the leopard seemingly lazing in the shade of the twiglike leaves. Perfectly camouflaged. Almost.

"Roll up the windows," Rafiq said quietly.

Margaret did as she was told, but she itched to get out of the car and take a shot. Catching a leopard this close was a rare opportunity, and she wanted to try. The danger, of course, was that any move could cause the sinewy animal to leap out of the tree and attack. The trick, she'd been told by a colleague at the newspaper, was to keep the passenger door open and watch the leopard with the unencumbered eye while trying to frame the shot with the one behind the camera. One shot. That's all you could hope for. One shot with a zoom lens, and back in the car as fast as you could possibly get.

"Don't do it," Rafiq said.

Margaret was silent.

"Not worth it," he added.

She raised the camera and thought about trying to get the shot through the window. The angle was off and the lens was catching the rays of a lowering sun, which would destroy any photo of the animal. She would have to get out and stand maybe seven feet from the car.

She turned to Rafiq.

"No," he said.

"But a shot like this is so rare. Particularly if you can get the light right, which I think I can. I just have to get out of the car and move seven feet to my left."

"No," he said. "Let someone else do it."

She bit her lip. "Would you listen to me if I said to you, 'No, don't write that story; let someone else do it'?"

He didn't answer her.

"Rafiq," she said.

"Ten seconds max. Get out of the car, take the shot, get back in."

"Thank you."

"I won't get out to save you."

"Fair enough."

Margaret thought a long time before she opened the door. She would have seconds to complete a series of actions, the most important of which was to frame the shot and get it. She rehearsed the moves she would have to make.

"I'm going now," she said when she had the camera ready.

She opened the door, moved the seven or eight feet she needed, and raised the camera. The leopard seemed to be looking vaguely in her direction, but it made no threatening moves. The angle of the sun had created a pink light that highlighted the leopard on his branch. Margaret took another step to her left, to make sure she had the sun fully behind her. She knew Rafiq would be going wild in the car, so she didn't turn to look. It occurred to her that the angle of the sun might partially blind the leopard, but she noticed his eyes move as she moved. She was now ten feet from the car. She raised the camera.

She took as many shots as she could. She was outside perhaps twenty or thirty seconds.

"Don't move," Rafiq said behind her.

A knife sailed past Margaret's peripheral vision even as the leopard rose on its impressive haunches. The knife nailed a snake to the ground. Rafiq put one hand over Margaret's mouth, the other on her shoulder. The shock of his touch silenced her. He dragged her backward and to the side with his arms and hand.

"Get in the car."

She did as she was told with the speed and agility of an athlete. She couldn't get the door closed fast enough, though she noticed that the leopard hadn't moved from his high-alert position. Exposed to danger seconds longer, Rafiq ran around the back of the car, slid into his seat, and shut the door. He exhaled a long breath. They waited.

"He's looking at the snake," Margaret said.

"It was his concern all the time. The closer the snake got to you, the more danger you were in — not only from the snake but from the leopard, who might have attacked it, with you as collateral damage."

"What kind of a snake?" Margaret asked.

"A black mamba."

"It was silver."

"Yes, it was."

"Deadly?"

"Lethal. The most deadly snake in all of East Africa."

"How do you know all this?" she asked, beginning to shake from the scare.

"I'm African," he said.

Margaret had never thought of Rafiq as an African, though

of course he was, just as Diana had been. With his three-country allegiance, he'd appeared to Margaret to be a citizen of the world.

Rafiq never took his eyes off the leopard as he put the car in reverse. He backed up ten feet and then shot forward over the long snake, crushing it.

"Your knife," Margaret said.

Rafiq glanced at her with disbelief.

"It's just that you've had it with you always. You saved my life," she said.

"I told you I wouldn't save you from the leopard. But since I hadn't promised you anything about the snake," he said, smiling, "I felt that I couldn't abandon you to what would have been a terrible fate."

"Why is it called a black mamba?"

"It has an inky mouth. It's so deadly because it can rear up and strike its victim many times, and the toxin from just one bite can kill between ten and twenty-five men."

Margaret felt a pressure at her chest.

Rafiq glanced at her. "I think what happened back there was more a case of you, rather stupidly if I may say so, risking your life for not a hell of a lot."

"And I risked yours as well."

"Yes, you did."

"I'm so sorry and so grateful." She reached out to touch Rafiq's arm to show him how much she meant her apology. She could feel the heat through the cloth of his shirt.

She couldn't shake the thought of Rafiq's hands on her shoulder and covering her mouth. Though the moment had been startling, it was a feeling she did not want to forget.

"I think we'd better head back," Rafiq said.

The sun lowered, and the shadows stretched. The larger birds were black silhouettes against the sky. Rafiq drove for a long time.

"I think you should stop the car," Margaret said.

Rafiq slowed. "Are you all right?"

"Yes. No."

They stopped. "What's wrong?"

Rafiq glanced through all the windows. He got out and opened her door.

She stood, and he pulled her to him. He put his fingers in her hair and held her head steady. Margaret thought, *Thank you*.

He let his hands fall from her hair as he pulled away. Margaret immediately knew that something was very wrong. Rafiq turned his back to her.

"What?" she asked, bewildered.

"I can't do this," he said.

"Do this?"

"Be together."

Margaret was shaken by his words and his tone. "I don't understand."

But she did understand.

Margaret leaned back against the car. Something large was ending before she'd quite admitted to herself that it had ever begun. The loss of that barely acknowledged entity began to push its way into her chest. "I so wish you hadn't said that," Margaret said.

Rafiq stood beside her.

"How long have you felt this way?" Margaret asked.

"That it had to end? Just now. When I realized how much I wanted to make love to you."

"No," she said. "That there was an *it* at all."

"Shortly after I met you."

And Margaret had known it, too, hadn't she? When she watched him as he jogged to his car? When her eyes happened to fall on the skin of his hand against the white cuff of his shirt? When Rafiq had called the house that night? All those times at tea? And especially when he had put his hand on hers?

"Margaret."

She nodded.

"I have a story to tell you," he began. "At the Golden Cup, you told one. Now I have one."

She waited.

"When I was in London," he said, "I had an affair with a married woman. I loved her very much. It was all joy and pleasure for me, but even from the beginning, I could see that it was something else for her. She loved me, but she hated the secrecy and the betrayal. After a time, it became hellish for me, too." He paused. "Do you understand what I'm talking about?"

Margaret couldn't answer him. The revelation of that earlier affair was unexpectedly painful.

"I can't do it again," Rafiq said. "I promised myself I'd never do that to anyone. Because I know how it ends, and the ending is terrible."

"We didn't even...," she said.

"Kiss? Make love? No, we didn't." He was silent for a minute. "I know this hurts you. It hurts me. I'm sorry. I'm going to ask Solomon not to pair us together."

"Oh, please don't," Margaret said.

He put his arm around her. "The less we talk about this," he said, "the better off we are."

Margaret searched for the right words. "It feels as though I've lost something wonderful before I even had it," she said. "Before I even had a chance."

"To do what?" Rafiq asked gently. "From here on out, what we had between us would have had to be something very different. And I'm not sure you would have wanted that."

"I *would* have wanted that," she protested.

Rafiq again turned away from her. A sharp, rosy light lit up the savanna. Margaret didn't care if she and Rafiq ever found the gates. She didn't want to get into the car. She didn't want the car to move. *Surround us with leopards and lions,* she thought, *but don't let the car move.*

"Let's just stand here a minute," Margaret said.

The light abruptly left the grasses. Night fell as it always did—a curtain lowering itself. Around them, animals were out and foraging. Soon they would find the yellow Citroën and surround it. None of them would harm Margaret and Rafiq, though, because they'd be able to see, even in the dark, that harm had already been done.

The stars came out and then the moon. Margaret thought of trying to talk Rafiq out of his plan. She thought if she just turned and kissed him, she would be able to seduce him. But did she really want that? Part of her ached to make love to the man standing next to her, but part of her knew that Rafiq was right. She hated it that he was right.

After a time, Rafiq opened her door and helped her inside. He put the Citroën in gear. Margaret felt the wheels move beneath them.

As they passed through the park gate, Margaret turned her head away from Rafiq and stared at the lights of the city through her side window. Patrick would be wondering what had happened to her.

"Where have you been?" Patrick asked as Margaret walked through the door.

They had no servant to cook the meals, so they went out to dinner more often than they used to. But today Margaret could smell something savory that her husband had fixed up.

"You look like hell," he added. "What happened?"

"I'm sorry I'm late," Margaret said. "I had things I had to do."

"Such as?"

She could hardly think. She had little patience for this interview. "I don't know, Patrick. Things."

"I called your office."

Perhaps her face registered a small ping of alarm.

"Solomon said you'd done some work in Ruaraka. But he didn't know where you'd gone after that."

"I told you," she said evenly, "I had errands."

"Solomon said you'd done the assignment with Rafiq."

"What are you implying?"

"I don't know. Why don't you tell me?"

Margaret faced her husband squarely. "I. Did. Errands."

Patrick flipped a large wooden spoon above his head and let it fall to the floor. "If you want to be like that," he said.

"I think this is what you want to know," Margaret said. "There is nothing between Rafiq and me. Absolutely nothing. That couldn't be a truer statement."

His face relaxed from anger into puzzlement. "Are you okay?" he asked.

"As a matter of fact, I'm not. I'm sorry you went to all that trouble," she said, pointing to the dining table. "And I'm sorry I'm late, but I think the best thing for me is to go lie down."

How ironic, Margaret thought as she left the living room, that she would not have to lie about Rafiq. Margaret felt anger, and she felt an overwhelming ache. She needed a dark room and a bed.

That night, she drifted in and out of sleep. Each time she woke, she knew that something was wrong, and then it hit her. Fresh news. Again and again.

And questions. Would she have had an affair with Rafiq? Yes. She had no doubt. Would she have suffered? Yes, probably. Would it have ended well? Inconceivable. Margaret was angry at Rafiq for his arrogance in thinking he could know or predict anything about her. Would it have been better if he had just slipped away from her without having delivered his devastating pronouncement? No, she didn't think so. She'd have been confused, and it would have been all she'd thought about. She would have had to ask herself, again and again, *Why is Rafiq avoiding me?*

She hoped Patrick would think that she had been insulted or belittled at the newspaper and that she was trying to regroup.

Regrouping, however, was more difficult than Margaret had ever imagined. She was baffled by how enervated she felt. Having a bath seemed an enormous task. Margaret took to spending weekends in her bathrobe: she couldn't summon the will to get dressed. Mostly, she wanted Patrick out of the flat so that she could think.

She returned to the office the following Monday. She had been reassigned to Jagdish, punishment enough. She thought of quitting, but then what would she do all day? A dilemma more exhausting to think about than getting dressed. Occasionally, Margaret saw Rafiq. They were civil but not especially friendly. She felt that everyone in the office sensed a change. If they hadn't known before, they certainly knew then.

And then there was a second loss, one that flattened her.

As she stepped out of the bathtub one morning, she slipped and hit her hip on the porcelain rim and then again on the floor. She had tried to brace herself with her hands. She lay on the tiles, gingerly feeling her hip. But she was more concerned by a sudden strong pain in her abdomen. Had she torn a muscle? She held on to the toilet as she stood up. When she was on her feet, she reached for her lime-green terry-cloth robe and went out to sit on the bed. Patrick had already walked to the hospital, and Margaret had been getting ready to go to work. She thought she should call Patrick and have him come home. Or maybe she should just pull herself together and try to go to work. Another strong cramp took hold of her. It was like having a period but not. The pain was too sharp, too defined, not achy. Margaret needed to see someone, probably her gynecologist, a doctor she had once visited for a yeast infection.

Margaret slipped off the bathrobe and let it fall back onto the bed. She walked to her underwear drawer and then began to rifle through her wardrobe for a cotton dress that was clean and hadn't been worn recently. A cramp bent her at the waist. She whirled around and put her hand out, trying to reach the bed for support. As she did, she saw the bright-red stain on the terry-cloth robe.

Margaret was taken not to Nairobi Hospital but to a Catholic hospital, where her gynecologist had his practice. She had called the doctor, who had in turn called an ambulance. She arrived at the hospital in her bloody bathrobe. Patrick couldn't be reached until he returned from Dagoretti, where he was holding a bush clinic.

She'd been only six weeks along, her doctor informed her. Margaret tried to grasp what he was saying. She'd been pregnant? Was he sure? Yes, he was sure. He patted her hand.

She laid her head back upon the pillow and stared at the ceiling. She had been put into a private room with a window near the bed. It resembled a room one might have encountered in London in 1918: a pristine white-iron bed, capable of being shut off from the rest of the room by a long white linen screen; a porcelain water pitcher on a bedside table; no sign of any technology whatsoever, though there were holes in the wall, which she assumed powered various portable machines. The sisters wore their white nursing habits, and on the wall across from the bed was a large, gruesome crucifix.

The sisters cleaned her up, and her doctor examined her. Margaret was prepped for a D and C. When she woke from the twilight sleep, she had no control over the tears. Another new beginning lost before she'd even known it was there.

She first became aware that Patrick was in the room when he bent down and kissed her. He immediately told her she was young and there was plenty of time later to start a family. Besides, Patrick added, it was for the best.

"How can it possibly be for the best?" Margaret wanted to know.

"It's better that we wait until we get home," he explained. "Nairobi is no place for a baby."

"You don't believe that," she said, staring into his pale-blue eyes.

"I do, and I don't."

"You're just saying that to help me through it."

"Maybe. Is helping you through it such a bad idea?"

"Crying would be a better way to help me through it," she said.

He took her hand. "I'm sorry. I don't know what I feel."

A baby would have cemented them, Margaret thought.

Patrick let go of her hand and bent to the floor. "Brought you your favorite thing. A vanilla milk shake."

"Where on earth did you get a vanilla milk shake?"

"I found the kitchen and talked the cook—a nun, by the way—into it. I had to walk her through the steps."

Margaret took a sip. "Thank you, Patrick," she said, managing a smile.

"They'll keep you here a couple of days," he said.

"A couple of days. Why?"

"It's not abnormal. They have to watch out for infection."

In truth, Margaret was glad for the respite. Though she wasn't fond of the nuns—they were rough and no-nonsense; not a compassionate bone among the lot—the idea of lying on a bed with nothing expected of her seemed a kind of safe haven. A place where she could finally think.

She noticed that Patrick's knee was knocking up and down. He was anxious, she thought. Why? Anxious to leave?

"By the way, a lot of people want to visit you," he said.

"Not today."

"No, but okay if I tell them tomorrow?"

Margaret turned toward her husband. He smoothed her hair. She closed her eyes. After a time, she heard Patrick push the chair back and stand. He touched her cheek with his finger, and then he was gone.

Margaret rolled in the bed and stared through the window. Outside, it was dark and dry. The rains were late this year and hadn't yet come. Nearly everything was parched. The mud had turned to dust; vegetation had wrinkled to brown. Bodies were harder to keep clean. Dirt wreaked havoc with engines.

She had been pregnant for six weeks. She tried to figure out the moment of conception, but much of those early weeks had been a blur. She tried to imagine what it would have been like to be told she was pregnant. She imagined joy. Would Patrick have made them leave the country at once?

Margaret thought of Rafiq and his pronouncement. He had been proved right yet again. To be with Rafiq but to be pregnant with Patrick's child would have been unthinkable. And what if Margaret hadn't known who the father was? The anxiety of having to wait for the birth to find out would have been all but unendurable. She would have had to tell Patrick in order to prepare him.

And yet she would have undergone all of that. Margaret had never ached to hold a baby, but she did then. She couldn't sort out whether it was her mind or her body that wanted this. Did the desire come from the body, which didn't need to be told anything?

Margaret allowed herself to imagine a baby, a boy. She felt

what it would have been like to pick him up from a cradle and hold him, his head bobbing at her shoulder. Hadn't shoulders been designed for that precious purpose?

Margaret thought of Rafiq and his face, of his wonderful brown eyes, his Welsh jaw. Of the body she had barely had a chance to touch. Of the sound of his voice, the British accent strangely comforting. She wondered if he knew, if Solomon had told him. Or if he'd overheard the news from a nearby desk. She wondered if, when he'd heard, he'd turned his face away. Or whether he had thought of her and wished the child his.

Margaret thought of Patrick, who'd laid a thin blanket over his feelings. Who saw his role as her protector, her medical manager. In the face of helplessness, he wanted control.

And Margaret thought, as she stared out the window, of Africa, of the country just beyond the screen. It had been her constant companion for nearly a year, teaching her, scolding her, enveloping her. It was in her lungs and blood now. She'd thought she wanted to absorb Africa, but the continent had absorbed Margaret. She could not imagine ever wanting to leave.

Margaret lay parched like everything else in Kenya. She drank a lot of water, on nurses' orders and on her own. Nothing could slake the thirst. She thought of how everyone would be searching the sky each day, waiting for a telling breeze or a drop. There would be celebrations during the first good soaking rain — muddy festivities marked by dancing, the roasting of goats, drinking, and giving thanks to whomever they felt grateful to.

Flowers came, and cards. The next day, Solomon Obok arrived bearing books: three novels by Kenyans about Kenya, one of them by Ngũgĩ wa Thiong'o, the author Margaret had once photographed. During Solomon's visit, the sisters brought tea, a remarkably kind gesture Margaret hadn't anticipated, one that encouraged Solomon to sit and talk. But though they spoke of many things—his wife and children; a recent article about Thomas Oulu, who was still being held without benefit of trial, that was causing a stir; and even of people in the office—he never mentioned Rafiq, a sign that Solomon knew, that perhaps he'd known all along. He told her a Kenyan proverb about seeds that didn't sprout and of seeds sowed later, and about how this second set would always be the stronger of the two.

Margaret laughed. She told Solomon he'd made it up, and he sheepishly confessed. They spoke of weather conditions in which the first seeds wouldn't take, but the second set would.

"You must come back to work," Solomon said as he was leaving. "Jagdish is lonely without you." This produced another good laugh. It physically hurt Margaret to laugh, but it was worth it.

Moses surprised Margaret that afternoon with a basket of avocados from the garden of the Karen house. Margaret marveled at the speed of the bush network. She was moved by his visit and said so, and he was pleased. She worked out that it would take him, to and fro, at least two hours' traveling time, and she thanked him for making the journey. She asked him how life in the burgled house had been after she and Patrick had gone, and he said that much of the furniture had been recovered from a shop in Eastleigh. In its "visit" away from home, the furniture had been polished and even repaired. The relationship between the Australian mistress and Moses had improved markedly once the pieces had been returned.

Patrick came with necessities: a nightgown and new bathrobe; a mirror and a tube of lipstick; that morning's edition of the

Tribune. The miscarriage had followed so close upon that period of Margaret's lassitude that she believed Patrick had begun to blur the two events. He was confident that when she was up and about, she would regain her strength rapidly. To that end, he had signed them up at the tennis club. He had a hankering to take up the old sport again.

At dinner, she tried to locate her feelings for her husband, but they eluded her. Though she knew Patrick to be a good person, she couldn't help but wonder if damage hadn't been done by both of them.

The next morning, Margaret was surprised by a visit from James and Adhiambo. She thought about their journey to the hospital and back, one that would have been even more difficult than Moses's. As they came closer to the bed, Margaret saw that they were holding hands. Her eyes must have widened, because they both began to laugh. James looked as though he had a canary fluttering inside his chest, and Adhiambo couldn't stop smiling. They pulled up chairs beside the bed and handed Margaret a package wrapped in butcher's paper and tied with twine. They wanted her to open it before they'd even settled in for a visit. As she unfolded the cloth, she searched for the line drawing beneath the beads and seeds. It took a few seconds to register, but when it did, Margaret gave a little yelp. It was of a woman with a camera to her eye. In the distance was the outline of a city.

"This is wonderful," Margaret said with genuine awe. "It's a treasure. Thank you."

"We have news," James said.

"I guess so," Margaret said, glancing at their hands.

"We are living in my house in Lavington, and Adhiambo is

making the cloths all the hours of the day and selling them on Kimathi Street."

"On Kimathi Street," Margaret said with surprise.

"In a shop with crafts," Adhiambo explained. "A woman is seeing your picture of the cloth in the newspaper and is finding me. She is with..."

She turned to James.

"The Women's Collective," James said.

"And she is offering to sell everything I make."

"The Collective is taking thirty percent," James said, "but they are making good prices for Adhiambo's work."

Margaret could hardly believe she'd inadvertently done something that had helped another person — though the credit had to go to Rafiq, who'd asked to do the story.

"You will tell Mr. Rafiq," James said.

"Yes," Margaret said without missing a beat. "I will tell him. I'm so happy for you."

Margaret guessed that the Germans had decided that one woman in James's small house was better than a woman with four children. James might sometimes have access to extra food, she thought, and he could go home each night to a companion. Margaret wondered about the wife in Kitale but remembered she and the children visited once a year, so perhaps that would not be a problem. In any event, it wasn't Margaret's problem. As for Adhiambo and her children, maybe her visits home would be more frequent now that she was making money again. Margaret hoped that she was earning more than Arthur and Diana had paid her. Most of all, she was thrilled to see her so happy and out of that dreadful slum in which she had been imprisoned.

Margaret had a strong urge to call Rafiq immediately and tell him the good news, an urge she ignored.

She told James and Adhiambo that she would show the cloth to Patrick that night, and he would take it back to the flat for safekeeping. By the time she returned home, it would be on the wall in their living room.

Margaret sat alone in a chair by the window. Patrick had come and gone. By hospital time, it was late, well past visiting hours; in real life, it was just before nine o'clock. The air smelled slightly different than it had the previous night. She couldn't identify the scent, and after a few moments, it went away. She climbed back into bed and pulled the covers up and was reaching for one of the books Solomon had brought her when she saw a shape in the doorway.

He walked to the bed and stood over Margaret. He had on a jacket and tie and held a bouquet of long, straight yellow roses.

"I stole them from Parklands," he said.

Rafiq handed the flowers to her, and she realized he'd de-thorned them as well. Eight stems of perfect roses.

"You got another knife," she said.

Rafiq emptied a vase of drooping lilies and filled it again with fresh water from the sink. He set the bouquet on the nightstand and took the chair beside the bed.

"I am sorry for the loss of your baby," he said. "I had to say this to you in person."

She put her hand over her eyes and tried to gain control of herself. "It's hard to comprehend," she said. "Not there before I even knew it."

He nodded. The echo.

Rafiq would have waited for Patrick to leave the parking lot in the Peugeot. She wondered how he'd managed to slip past the nuns. She didn't know what, if anything, his visit meant.

"I need some water," she said.

Rafiq rose and found a glass and filled it to the brim from the pitcher. Margaret drank it.

"The whole country is thirsty," he said.

"I thought I smelled something different in the air," she said, nodding toward the window.

"They say the rains will come tonight."

"I've never felt this before," she said. "The yearning for rain."

"No one can escape it. For many people, it is already too late."

"Farmers."

He nodded.

The lights in the corridor went dim, signaling *lights out*. Rafiq got up and closed the door. The nuns had been by earlier to check Margaret's vitals, and she prayed they wouldn't feel the need to drop in again.

"I have to dim my own light," she said, "or they'll come in to see what I want." She turned on the reading light close to the bed and had Rafiq flip the switch for the overhead.

He took off his jacket and slid it over the back of his chair. He rolled his sleeves and sat down.

"I have some news," Margaret said in a whisper. "James and Adhiambo were here earlier. They were holding hands."

Rafiq tilted his head.

"They're living together in James's house. Adhiambo has had the best luck, and she asked me to tell you because she thinks you and I made it happen. A woman read your article and saw the picture of the wall hanging. She located Adhiambo and asked her to become part of the Women's Collective."

"I know that organization."

"She makes as many wall hangings as she can and gives them to the Collective to sell. The Collective takes thirty percent. I'm dying to go in and see what they're asking for Adhiambo's work. The best part is that she's out of that hellhole." Margaret paused. "We did good, Rafiq."

"Sometimes it happens when you least expect it."

"I've been wondering about James's marriage."

"James said he sees his wife only once a year. A marriage of convenience in the city is not so uncommon."

Margaret nodded.

"He's a smart guy. He'll figure it out."

Margaret looked away, through the open window. The leaves fluttered as if a wind had picked up.

"You are wondering why I have come," he said.

"Yes."

"I couldn't stay away once I heard the news," he said. "I kept telling myself it wasn't any of my business. And it isn't. But I wanted to tell you in person how sad I am for you."

Rafiq wouldn't tell Margaret it was just all right. He wouldn't gloss over the pain and skip immediately to the future where she would still be young and could have many children. Even James and Adhiambo, no matter how welcome, had tried to be a distraction. Rafiq would always tell the truth.

He stroked Margaret's arm with the backs of his fingers. Everything inside her that had been tense began to loosen.

She wondered what his touch meant. And then she thought that it might mean nothing. She was learning to live like the Masai. When something was there, it was there. When it left, it was gone.

The loosening became a yearning, deeper than the desire for rain.

"I don't know what to say," she whispered.

"Don't say anything."

He ran his fingers up the inside of her arm and then let them drift down to her hand, which he held.

"Don't go," she said.

"No."

Despite Margaret's desire to stay awake and talk to Rafiq, she could feel herself drifting off. The nuns had given her a sleeping pill. "Stay here until I fall asleep," Margaret said. "I don't think I could stand having to watch you walk out that door."

"I'm going to turn out your reading light now."

After he did, he bent over and kissed Margaret lightly on the lips.

Margaret lay in darkness. The dim light in the corridor had been switched off as well. In Africa, there was seldom any ambient light, particularly when there were clouds, as there were that night. She tried to make out the features of Rafiq's face, but she could see only his shirt, a ghost settling itself. He still held her hand. She knew that if they were caught, the nuns would tell Patrick. She didn't care. She just wanted Rafiq not to leave.

Sometime during the night, while Margaret was sleeping, the rains started. She woke early, flooded with a sense of tremendous relief. She sat up and looked around. There was no Rafiq and no note.

He had been there, and now he was gone.

The rains soaked the earth, and the country celebrated. Everywhere, there were smiles, even on the faces of the nuns. Though the heavy rains created impassable roads and caused filthy footprints everywhere, the earth now had its long-awaited drink. The change in the landscape was almost instantaneous. When Margaret walked out of the hospital, a panorama of green buds greeted her. The world had been rinsed and felt clean again.

Patrick was solicitous, cutting back on his workload for two weeks. He stayed home on weekends. She was allowed to be—just be—for which she was grateful. She was trying to swim her way up from the bottom of a pool. On many days, she was successful; on other days, the lost days, she couldn't get out of bed.

Later, when the lost days became fewer and fewer, Margaret began to mark out her life in milestones. First good walk. Check. First drive into the city. Check. First day back at the office. Check. First visit to the tennis club. Check. When she dared to hit a ball around a court and then swiftly wanted a match, she knew her body was physically healed. Patrick had been waiting for that moment. Not only did he return to his routines but, a few nights later, he asked to make love. Margaret didn't feel ready, but she had no good excuse. Her doctor had given her the all clear, and Patrick knew that. All of which might have been fine had Patrick not said, as he was unbuttoning Margaret's blouse, "You're sure you took your pill today?"

For a moment, Margaret was confused. What pill did he mean? She was taking a lot of them.

"You know, those little pink pills in the case?"

She pulled away so that she could see his face. "You think I neglected my pills, and that's why we conceived?"

"Well, I can't think of any other way it could have happened."

"You think I deliberately didn't take them?"

"No, no," Patrick, up on one elbow, said. "Though you'd been mentioning children here and there."

"Once, if I recall."

"Well, yeah. Maybe once."

"Are you going to feel the need to remind me to take my pill every time we make love?"

"No, I'm not," he said. She saw a slight roll of the eyes before he caught himself.

"Can we do this tomorrow?" Margaret asked.

"So we're making appointments now?"

She shook her head, more dazed than anything else.

"Fine," Patrick said. "Tomorrow."

In the morning, he woke Margaret from a sound sleep. It was still dark out.

"It's tomorrow," he whispered into her ear.

Margaret took the assignments Solomon gave her, but photography no longer felt like her passion. She was back on the "grip-and-grin" beat, which, for once, she didn't mind. Each time she entered the *Tribune* offices, she felt anxious. She would know, within seconds, if Rafiq was nearby or expected soon. When thoughts of him rose to the surface, Margaret pushed them away. As for the loss of that small beginning on the bathroom floor, that seemed not to leave her but rather to burrow deeper into her belly. She felt helpless to stop it.

If Margaret couldn't venture full bore into the Kenya she had begun to know, she could at least play tennis. The club was mixed race, and she made a number of new acquaintances. One could get a decent lunch there, and in the early evening, after the last matches, whoever was left could be found at the bar, a modest setup that nevertheless sold bia baridi, ice-cold Tuskers.

The tennis club, with its formal rules and dress on the court, became a kind of second home for Margaret. It held no memories, and she was getting better at a game she hadn't played since high school. She entered a tournament and placed well. Because the event had been an all-day affair, a buffet was served after the last match as a kind of celebration. Margaret was in a personal-best kind of mood and enjoying herself. Each time Patrick looked at her, he smiled. In those moments, Margaret thought he believed her completely healed, both inside and out.

One night, as she and Patrick were sitting down to dinner, the telephone rang. Patrick had to answer the phone each time it rang, no matter how inconvenient. Margaret could tell from the tone of his voice that he was speaking not to a friend or a colleague but to someone with whom he had a more formal relationship.

"It's Lily," he said, covering the mouthpiece. "Shall I tell her to call back later?"

"No," Margaret said, getting up. "I'll take it."

Patrick handed the phone to her and went back to his meal.

"Lily," Margaret said.

"Margaret, there is much chaos here. Mr. Obok has been detained. Rafiq is being deported."

"What?"

"We need you to come in as early as possible tomorrow."

Margaret was aware of having to keep her voice businesslike and neutral, though she could hardly breathe.

"Why?" she asked.

"Mr. Obok and Mr. Rafiq are accused of attempting to libel certain government officials. They were working on a story about a mass grave where students who were shot were buried."

It wasn't a rumor after all, Margaret thought.

"Of course I'll help out," she said to Lily. "Did you say the airport?"

There was a slight pause at the other end while Lily dealt with the non sequitur.

"Yes, that is where they are taking Mr. Rafiq just now. He is not allowed to go home to get his suitcase."

"Oh, Lily."

"So will you come in?"

"Yes, absolutely," Margaret said.

She settled the receiver into its cradle. She had to invent a credible reason for leaving the house.

When she turned to Patrick, she felt completely calm. "Obok has an assignment for me. It has to be done now," Margaret said.

"Now?" Patrick asked, incredulous. Margaret hardly ever worked at night.

"Yes. He's been trying to catch a Pakistani diplomat for a shot all day, but the man was always on the move and too busy. Just now an aide called Solomon and said that if he could get a photographer to the airport, I could get the head shot."

"I'll drive you."

"No, no," Margaret said. "I'm perfectly fine. One of us has to eat this wonderful chicken you've made." Margaret picked up her camera from its place on the sideboard. "Save me some. I'll be right back. I can't waste a minute."

Patrick, looking as though he were trying to translate a foreign language into English, said nothing, and Margaret was out the door.

The necessity to get to the airport was all-consuming. In the elevator, Margaret pictured the route in her head. She gave George, the watchman, a quick wave, ran to her car, and sped off. She realized she'd never heard of a police car stopping a speeding motorist in Kenya. Besides, she knew she wouldn't stop even if they made an effort. More than likely, it would be a ruse to steal the car or worse. As she merged onto the motorway toward the airport, she tried to imagine what she would do in that circumstance.

Do exactly what she was intending to do, she thought, and hope for the best.

Margaret parked in front of the international terminal. She slung her camera over her shoulder. She slowed down once she pushed open the double doors. As casually as she could, she asked the military officer near the entrance where immigration was. He pointed the way with his arm. Margaret held her keys in her hand and walked briskly in the direction he'd indicated. It was an effort not to run.

When she arrived at the entrance to immigration, she felt assaulted by bodies. Some people were saying good-bye, others were merely waiting, and still others appeared to be asleep on makeshift beds on the floor. There were Africans and Chinese and French and Indians and Americans and Arabs waiting for their flight number to appear on the overhead electronic sign. Margaret searched for Rafiq but couldn't see anyone resembling him. She began to panic, certain that she'd arrived too late. She wandered the periphery of the throng, methodically penetrating it, to search for a tall man with black hair. She searched until she thought she'd seen every person in the waiting area.

Margaret found a vinyl chair at the edge of the crush. She couldn't bring herself to leave the airport. She watched every face that passed by her.

Rafiq deported? To where? Not to Uganda, surely. Would he go to Pakistan then, to be with his family? To London with all the cousins? If he did, would he come back? Once you were deported, *could* you come back? Had Margaret seen his face for the last time in the hospital? And then she thought about Solomon. What had he and Rafiq discovered? How had they been caught? Where was Solomon now?

In the distance, three men approached the entrance to immigration. Margaret stood up. Rafiq was flanked by two military police, both of whom had handguns in holsters. Rafiq had no luggage and no briefcase. His tie had been yanked down, and one tail of his shirt had come loose from his belt. He caught Margaret's face, and she moved to intercept him. He shook his head in tiny movements. She held back. Rafiq stared straight ahead. Just as he was about to pass Margaret, he took a quick glance in her direction. He mouthed the word *Solomon*. Margaret nodded. She ached to say something to him, but he was already walking away from her.

Margaret watched numbly as the two soldiers and the man parted the throng. And then they were through the door and gone.

Margaret made it back to the vinyl chair and sat as still as she could. She breathed slowly and shallowly, in and out, in an effort to gain control. The sight of Rafiq and then the immediate loss of him had happened so quickly she felt as though she had been punched. She stared at a patch of tile just beyond her. She heard nothing. She saw only Rafiq. His message had been clear. *Do something for Solomon.*

Margaret put her head in her hands. Since she'd arrived in Kenya, she'd been robbed, caused a woman's death, been saved from a lethal snakebite, realized a love that was over before it started, and lost a baby. Now she'd just been silently asked to do something for someone whose life was in jeopardy. She'd had to watch a man she loved walk through a set of doors and out of her life.

When Margaret felt that she could stand, she made her way back to the place where she had left her car. She nodded at the soldier at the entrance and stepped outside. Another soldier stood next to her car, peering in the windows.

Oh God, Margaret thought.

She walked to the driver's side, knowing she couldn't avoid a confrontation.

"This is your car, miss?"

"Yes, it is."

"It is illegal to leave your vehicle here."

"I just had to run in to say good-bye to someone. I am here now. I'll get in the car and be gone in a second."

"I must reprimand you for a serious offense."

Margaret said nothing.

"What is your name?"

She told him.

"We will need to search your vehicle." He signaled to the soldier just inside the door.

"Why?" Margaret asked.

Neither of the men answered her. She'd been in the country long enough to know not to protest, though she bristled when she was asked to step aside, and the other soldier stood guard beside her. The soldier inspecting the car asked for the keys, and she tossed them to him. Inside, he found a jacket of Patrick's and an old Fanta bottle with a dead fly inside. There were crumbs and candy wrappers and, in the trunk, Margaret's old raincoat, which she'd been searching for. He asked her for her camera, and she reluctantly handed it over. When he opened the camera and ripped out the film, Margaret flinched as though someone had torn a bandage from her skin.

The soldier shut the doors and trunk and handed her the keys. "May I see your passport?" he asked.

"It's at home," Margaret answered, instantly anxious. Where would this end?

"Do you have any other identification?"

Margaret thought. The car registration was in Patrick's name. In a slim pocket of her camera bag, she kept a check for emergencies. That would have her name on it. But if she handed the check to the soldier, it might be misinterpreted as an attempt at bribery.

"May I look at my raincoat?" Margaret asked.

The soldier nodded.

She opened the trunk and riffled through the pockets of the coat. She found a ten-shilling note, a receipt for groceries she had bought, a set of directions in her own handwriting, and a pay stub. She wrestled for a moment with the quandary of revealing the pay stub with no work permit to back it up. But it was all she had.

She handed the pay stub to the soldier. He examined it and looked at Margaret.

"What do you do there?"

"I sometimes sell photographs — on a freelance basis only."

"And when does your visa expire?"

"Next May," she said, though that was wildly untrue. She had no idea when their visas expired. Patrick kept renewing them.

The officer handed Margaret her pay stub and waved her on her way.

When Margaret opened the door to the flat, Patrick stood up from the vile green sofa. "Where the hell have you been?" he asked.

"What time is it?"

"It's almost one o'clock in the morning."

She put her hands on the back of a chair to steady them. "I was detained," she said.

"Detained? By whom?"

"Soldiers at the airport. Two of them. I'd parked my car illegally, and when I went back out to get it, they interrogated me."

"About what?"

"Everything," she said. "They searched the car."

"Jesus, Margaret. You must have been scared to death."

"A little nervous," she said. "I was sweating."

"You're lucky they let you go."

"I guess so." Margaret did not feel lucky at all. She knew she couldn't bear it if Patrick crossed the room.

"I can't imagine on what grounds they could have held me,"

she said as she headed toward the bedroom. "I'd like a hot bath. And then a good, long sleep."

"Nothing to eat?"

"No, I'll have it tomorrow for lunch."

In the bathroom, Margaret turned on the taps and watched the tub slowly fill with water. She knelt in front of it and laid her head on its rim. She could hear Patrick moving around, then making his way into the bedroom. She heard the thump of his shoes, a belt buckle falling to the floor.

Her husband was just a few feet away from her, and yet she'd just sped to the airport to catch one last glimpse of another man. A man she wouldn't see again. Margaret didn't know what would become of Rafiq. She didn't know what would become of her.

Lily was rigid when Margaret got to the office the next morning. As she approached the desk, Lily flicked her eyes toward the armed policemen standing twenty feet away.

"You must go home," Lily said in a low voice. "We are not needing you here."

"What's happening?" Margaret asked.

"They are arresting one other reporter."

"But surely I am safe."

"Not at all. When they search Rafiq's records, they will see your photo credits accompanying his stories. You do not have a work permit. You must go home and stay there. You must do nothing until someone calls you. You might not be called."

"My God," she said.

"You must go now," Lily urged.

"Are there people trying to help Solomon?"

Lily leaned closer to Margaret. "Yes," she said, "but he is in serious trouble."

Margaret learned later that afternoon via the *Tribune*'s competitor that Solomon Obok was being held without benefit of trial and was thought to be imprisoned in a hole near Gilgil. Rafiq Hameed had been deported to London. Obok was accused of treason, a capital offense. No charges had been levied against Mr. Hameed, but his Kenyan passport and all his files had been confiscated.

When she left the editorial offices, she could do little more than walk the streets. She passed by the shop where she'd once admired a gold-colored teapot and by the restaurant where she'd had a lunch of Samosas. She walked past the Woolworth's in which one could still buy a Cuisinart. The beggar woman and her children were gone, which alarmed Margaret. She looked for them farther along Kimathi Street but couldn't find them. Had they been taken in and sheltered? Arrested? Gone back to the slums? She wondered, too, about the parking boys who had once threatened her. What had happened to them?

But mostly she thought about Solomon and Rafiq. She would go home and write letters to raise awareness of Solomon's plight and perhaps help to pressure the Kenyan government to release him. But Rafiq? There was nothing she could do for Rafiq. Perhaps he would be happier in London. She thought it right but nevertheless unsettling that he had chosen as his last word to her the name of Solomon. If only there had been time for two words or five.

When Margaret arrived home that evening, Patrick had both the *Evening Standard* and the *Tribune* on the dining table.

"What do you know about this?" he asked, jabbing the photograph of Solomon.

"I just learned about it when I went into work today."

Patrick moved in front of the table and leaned against it, arms crossed. "You were called out on assignment last night to photograph a Pakistani diplomat."

"Yes."

"This would have been after Obok was arrested."

"I guess so."

"Yet you said nothing to me last night."

Margaret set her camera case on the side table. "I didn't know until this morning," she repeated.

"I find that hard to believe."

"Believe what you want."

"And I noticed another thing in the *Tribune*," he said, picking up the paper.

"And what is that?"

"There's no photograph of a Pakistani diplomat."

"The soldier ripped the film out of the camera last night."

"They say that your friend Rafiq Hameed has been deported."

"Yes."

"How do you feel about that?"

"How do I feel about that?" Margaret asked incredulously. "I feel terrible."

"What did you do all day?"

"You know what, Patrick?" Margaret said. "I think I'm tired of being interrogated each time I walk in the door. I'm going to answer this one question, and then I'm not going to answer any others. If you want to know what I did all day, I'll tell you. I walked the city streets. I've been fired, Patrick. I had a lot to think about."

Patrick studied his wife for a long time. Margaret kept her face impassive.

"Maybe it's time to get you home," he said.

Part Three

In her bathrobe, her hip resting on the sill, Margaret examined the untended garden. The leaves had a sheen on them, and she heard the clicking of drops falling, a rain following a rain. She could still make out the design of the original garden, a diamond set within a circle set within a square. How many months or years had it been since a gardener had weeded the walkways, thinned the bougainvillea, clipped the lilies? Long, thick stems of roses lifted above the fray, a single blossom of pale cream quivering at each end. Patches of small, furry yellow blooms lay nearly buried beneath roving vines. Margaret saw, in a corner, what might be a statue, though she could make out only parts of stone or cement.

If she had the energy or the courage, she would call the Sikh and offer to bring the garden back to life. She would need help—someone stronger than she with good tools to prune the heavy branches—but Margaret had resisted even stepping into the garden for fear of snakes. The blossoms and layers of leaves seemed a perfect place for lurking reptiles. Still, she admired the chaos. She preferred it to the manicured gardens of the houses in Langata and Karen. At least this sad, messy patch of vegetation was honest. How long would it be before no blooms at all were visible? Would the vines burrow under the house and wreak havoc with the shallow foundation? Would the bougainvillea scramble up the building and poke its way through the casements?

Patrick had been working in his study since early morning. Margaret knew his routine even better than she could predict her own. Each weekend day, he got up at seven, washed his face with hospital soap, and fixed himself a pot of coffee and a bowl of Weetabix. He took his second cup and a plate of toast with pineapple marmalade into his study and did not emerge for hours. Today, he would come out in time for Sunday Lunch at the home of another doctor and his wife, both newly arrived from London. The Sunday Lunch seemed still to be de rigueur among the Brits, a rite more sacred, Margaret thought, than attending church. She had offered to make an apricot cheesecake for the lunch but hadn't been able to summon the energy to find the springform pan, never mind sift the ingredients.

At the image of the sifter, Margaret thought of her mother. She felt a small twist inside her chest. She and Patrick had been away for fourteen months, and though her family sent tapes, called at Christmas, and wrote at least a letter a week, Margaret ached to see them again. Her parents had talked about coming out to visit Patrick and her, but the trip was almost prohibitively expensive for them. The cheapest solution would have been for Margaret to fly home, but then her parents would miss out on seeing Kenya, which seemed to Margaret at least as important as visiting her and Patrick.

Dishes crowded the sink and spread along the red Formica counter. The dining table had not been cleared from the night before. Margaret's polyester robe wasn't clean. Her inertia over the weekend had become a near paralysis. When Patrick emerged from his study and saw the mess, he would be annoyed. He expected, after hours of his own work, that Margaret would have done her share, which truly was not very much. She examined the beige and pilled cuffs of the white robe. Margaret had to drive to a commercial laundry. She wore her shirts two and three days at a time to stave off the inevitable.

For weeks, Margaret had been writing letters to senators and representatives at home, to friends who might have political connections, to Amnesty International, to the *New York Times,* even to her old paper. She wrote that Solomon Obok had been detained and was said to be living in the most appalling of conditions, in a dirt hole in one of the most hellish places in Kenya. From what she had been able to infer from the other Kenyan newspapers, he wasn't allowed either visitors or books. She wondered if the man had a bed to lie on or a table and chair at which to eat his meals, the dirt hole too closely resembling a grave.

Obok's location seemed to change each time she read another story, and perhaps his whereabouts were deliberately altered every few days so that there could be no hope of rescue. After that first report in the *Evening Standard,* there hadn't been any further mentions of Solomon having pursued a story about fifty students buried in a mass grave. No charges as yet had been filed.

A Kikuyu had been appointed editor of the *Kenya Morning Tribune,* an appointment followed by mass firings, all Luo, Lily among them. It was, Margaret thought, a kind of silent takeover. The party in power now controlled all of the news media and thus could present its own picture of Kenya to its people.

As good as a coup, to Margaret's way of thinking.

She hadn't yet heard from anyone at the paper about an assignment, and she doubted she would ever be asked again to take a picture. She hadn't told Patrick of the letters she had written, although any day now she was expecting replies, and he would see the return addresses and ask her about them. Would he dare to open the letters himself? He might. He would say that he was worried about her safety, and he would be. But he would be worried about his own as well. More important, he would be concerned about his ability to complete his research.

On that awful night, after Margaret had lost her job and had returned from walking the streets of Nairobi all day, Patrick had said it was time for them both to go home. He hadn't mentioned it since. What he had meant, Margaret thought, was that *she* should go home, and he would follow. And who knew how long he might take to leave the country himself? One night at dinner, he had talked briefly about traveling to South Africa to attend a conference, but nothing had come of that either.

When Margaret let her surface worries slide away, she understood she was still in mourning for her stay in the hospital, itself a time of mourning. She wanted only to remember Rafiq's last visit—the dimmed lights, the rhythmic stroking of her arm, her intertwined yearning both for rain and for the man—afraid that if she stopped thinking about it, the memory would fade and vanish. Deported, like Rafiq himself.

She had heard nothing from Rafiq. She didn't think she ever would.

The anniversary of the climb approached. Margaret sometimes guessed that Patrick's increased moodiness could be attributed to that upcoming milestone, one that neither of them had mentioned.

She turned her eyes back to the garden. The chaos on the surface belied tenacious roots beneath. Wasn't a marriage much the same? If she and Patrick could clear away the wild vines and tendrils, mightn't they return to what they had once been? A couple who loved each other and intended to stay together all their lives? She realized they had spent more married months in trouble than they had happy.

Patrick, balancing a water glass, a cup, and a plate, opened the door of the study. He paused, as she had known he would, to take in the counter and the table and Margaret in her bathrobe. Instead of sighing or setting a cup down too hard, however, he gently put the crockery on the dining table and came to sit across from her by the window.

He took her hands in his. "What's wrong?" he asked.

Margaret shook her head.

"Margaret, please."

Margaret couldn't tell Patrick the truth about what was wrong without ending the marriage right there.

"I'm sorry, Patrick. I don't really know what's going on. It might still be the baby. Mostly, I worry about us."

"Yes," he said, "so do I."

"And without a job, I question why I'm here, what I'm supposed to do. I've been writing letters to representatives and senators and different organizations to help Solomon Obok."

"I know you have," Patrick said. "Mail came for you at the post office box. I forgot to bring it home on Friday."

"You forgot?"

"Maybe I forgot."

Margaret studied Patrick's face. "You weren't angry?" she asked.

"I was at first. But then I understood. Of course you're writing letters on Obok's behalf. What else could you do?"

"Did you open them?"

"No," Patrick said. "I didn't. If you want, I'll go get them now."

His black hair was still flattened on one side from sleep. His pale-blue eyes were slightly red-rimmed from so much reading. "I got a letter from my mother," he said. "I wrote to her because I couldn't understand what was going on with you. She said to give you time, that losing a pregnancy, no matter how brief, takes a while to get over." He paused. "It was a terrible time. I'm sorry."

Margaret realized she had her hands on her belly, protecting what was no longer there.

"Can I get you a coffee?" Patrick asked.

"Water," she said.

She could hear the cupboard open, the tap running. Margaret took the glass from Patrick and drank. He stood behind her and massaged her back. She thought of her husband, baffled, writing to his mother for advice. She reached up and took hold of his hand. He came around and sat in front of her again. The chairs were a pair: blue-and-cream-striped upholstery on antique frames.

"The real problem is the climb, isn't it?" Patrick asked.

Margaret was surprised he had dared to mention it. "The anniversary is coming," she said.

"You've been thinking about it, too."

"I have," she admitted. "It's been almost a year, and we haven't been right together since."

Patrick bent his head and studied the floor. He rested his chin in one hand. They would have to talk about it, whether he wanted to or not.

Patrick tilted his head to the side, as if he'd just had an idea.

She waited.

"What we really ought to do," he said, "is climb the mountain again and get to the top." He thought a minute. "Maybe that's the only real way to put this behind us."

Margaret watched as Patrick looked at the windowsill and then over toward the red counter. He crossed his arms. She knew he was measuring an idea, tossing it about, looking at it from all angles. She needed to stop him before the idea turned solid.

"Patrick," she said.

"You know," he said, interrupting her. "You know, it might not be the worst idea in the world."

"Climbing Mount Kenya is the last thing I want to do."

"Well, think about it for a minute," Patrick said, cutting the air with his hand. "It would be just the two of us, with a guide and porters. Or we could ask someone we know well, people we like and trust." He stood up and put his hand to his forehead. "I think you're in much better condition than you were then. The tennis, for one thing. We could do it, we could cross the glacier, we could reach the top. And it would be done! It would be done and over with, and we'd have erased—"

"Diana?"

"No, not Diana. I don't want to do that. We'd have expunged that sickening feeling we had after the climb. That deadly silence. That devastating mistrust. We would be together every step of the way. You'd never be alone, Margaret. We would do this as a couple."

"Patrick," Margaret said, putting her palms out, "I *hated* climbing Mount Kenya. I hated every minute of it. It was physically painful, never mind the rest."

But Patrick would not be dissuaded. "That's because we pushed you to go faster than you were ready for. We left you alone. I was an asshole, Margaret. I admit that. I should have stayed with you every second. I shouldn't have let Arthur get within a ten-foot radius of you. If you look at it one way, the whole fiasco was *my* fault."

Margaret arched her back. She tightened the sash of her robe. She stood and walked to the sink to pour herself a second glass of water. She drank the water and turned to her husband, who sat in the chair, whose face showed every new idea and plan as it occurred to him. A twitch here, a blink there. He rubbed his neck.

"Margaret, seriously," he said. "We'll plan it for, say, a month from now. We'll still be at the edge of the dry season. That'll give you — me — a month to get ready. We know so much *more* now. We'll buy better jackets, or, if we hurry, we can have them sent from home. We'll hike the Ngong Hills every weekend. I know you're in better shape. You've been in the country for more than a year, and your lungs are stronger. We'll stay in Naro Moru for a couple of nights this time, just to make sure we get thoroughly acclimated."

"People will think we're crazy," Margaret said. "Disrespectful, even."

"Think what? Who think? No one knows anything about us but us. We'll be together the whole time, with the Africans and the mountain. We'll help each other up. Margaret, I really believe this is what we need to do. To break the..." He shook his head, finally at a loss for words.

Ice jam, Margaret thought. She had never seen Patrick so animated — not since before they'd left the States, when they were getting ready to fly to Kenya. Her husband was pacing the room now, a man with a detailed plan.

Margaret considered the idea. Her heart shrank at the memory of the bog and the scree and the rats. The grim, dark cloud overhead. But mightn't a physical challenge be just what she needed to clear her mind? A task so difficult it would wipe away whatever had gone before? She recalled how hard it was to think about anything else while on the mountain. Surely that in itself would be welcome. She and Patrick could pay tribute to Diana when they reached the glacier. They could remember her. And then they could continue on and reach the top. The idea, as crazy as it initially sounded, had theoretical appeal.

But Margaret shook her head. No, it was insane. If she couldn't summon the energy to wash the dishes, how would she ever have the energy to climb a mountain, a very difficult mountain? She lifted her hair over the collar of her robe. It was getting hot in the room, and she thought of turning on the fan.

"I think couples need projects," he said, "to keep them together."

Patrick had thrown down the gauntlet. To say yes to the mountain was to say yes to the marriage. To say no was to admit that it was as good as over, that nothing could be done. And then, in a matter of weeks, Patrick would leave. He would go to South Africa on the pretext of a conference. Or to China. Or to India. And Margaret would go home. Alone.

Did Margaret have the right to deny the marriage its one chance?

She put her hands on the counter and bent her head. She turned to her husband.

"So what do you think?" he asked again. The hope on his face was like a boy's. He had gone from unhappy puzzlement to seeming clarity in the space of a minute, two minutes.

"Okay," she said.

He sat back, as if he didn't believe her. Perhaps he had planned a lengthier campaign. "Wow," he said. "You'll really do it?"

"Yes, I'll really do it."

Patrick grinned. He opened his legs and spread his arms along the sides of the chair. "It'll be great, I promise you."

"I believe you," Margaret said.

Everdene and Kevin Winter turned out to be the perfect choice.

The four sat under an arbor of jacaranda while purple petals drifted to the patio stones around them. Everdene had arranged a picnic at an outdoor table. Kevin made generous pours with the wine. Margaret apologized for the nonexistent cheesecake, but Everdene smiled and said she and Kevin didn't need the calories.

The garden was a wonder, Margaret thought. More an orchard than beds of flowers, it had been planted with produce in mind. In between the straight rows of fruit trees, the grass was cut short, as if sheep had nibbled at it. At the end of the lawn ran a clear stream of water. Even from the table, she could hear the stones clacking over one another in the rushing water.

"This is a kind of paradise you have here," Margaret said to Everdene and Kevin.

Kevin smiled. "The owners had sheep."

"Do you have sheep?"

Everdene laughed. "No. Just the illusion of sheep."

"Hell of a lot less work," Patrick said.

When Patrick and Margaret arrived at the stone house in Muthaiga, Kevin gave them a tour. The building had once been a men's club, he said, which explained the grand spaces on the ground floor, the warren of tiny rooms upstairs. This room was once a bar, Kevin said. That one, an old smoking room. He pointed out the library and what had been the front lobby. "Used to be a desk here for the receptionist. A small area there for the porters. The bedrooms are small, just big enough to accommodate a single bed. It's where the early settlers came for parties or to get away from their wives. It would have been a long journey from Karen, say, in the days when all travel was by horse. If you came here for a dinner party, you probably stayed two or three days. Everdene and I had to knock down a wall upstairs just to fit a double bed and a chest of drawers into one of the bedrooms. Strangely enough, the couple who lived here before us hadn't done so. We often speculate about the nature of their marriage."

Patrick smiled.

Though Kevin was young, his face had weathered into the shape Margaret thought it would always be. His eyes seemed perpetually drafted into a squint. Everdene was lovely, the sort of unassuming, intelligent woman Margaret had occasionally met. Everdene had bangs and light-brown hair to her shoulders. She wore oversize black glasses. Kevin's specialty was diseases of the bone, Patrick had explained. Everdene, who had a PhD in economics, taught at the university. The couple had been in the country four months and had nothing of the cynicism of some of the expatriates Patrick and Margaret had met before.

Margaret hiked her yellow sundress just above her knees as she lay back in the striped-canvas chair. Kevin continued to pour, and Everdene brought out a plate of cheeses and fruit. Margaret drank a white that Kevin, miraculously, had managed to keep ice-cold in a bucket under the table. It tasted like a Vouvray, and she wondered how Kevin had come by the fruity French wine.

"Sunday Lunch is a brilliant idea," Margaret said to Everdene. "You don't mind if we borrow it?"

"A Sunday picnic, really," Everdene said. "We love them. Hard to come by in London because of the awful weather, which is why we revel in them here. When we first came out, I just couldn't get enough of the sunshine. Kevin straightaway forced me to wear a hat. He's right, of course, but sometimes I just love to put my face directly to the sun. Which you can probably tell from all the freckles."

"I don't think anyone leaves the country without freckles," Margaret said. She glanced at Patrick, who was deep in conversation with Kevin.

"Do you want some water to go with that wine?" Everdene asked. "The only drawback of the Sunday picnic, one discovers, is the headache at six."

"Water would be great."

Everdene picked up a pitcher and poured ice water into a wineglass, which she then gave to Margaret.

"God, it's wonderful here," Margaret said. "I'd never want to leave."

"We never want to leave, either. Though we do, of course, to go to work. The house has all sorts of oddities. I'm sure Kevin pointed them out. The garden at the back was originally meant for a croquet lawn, and they had garden parties under tents, which explains its size."

"How did you find such a fabulous house?"

"The parents of a friend were moving and wanted to rent it out. It's a little embarrassing to have so much space for just the two of us. Nominally, we're house-sitting, though we've been allowed to make a few changes, such as the wall upstairs. We could never afford to live here. When we leave, someone else will take it over, or the owners will sell it. Eventually, they'll have to."

Margaret murmured.

"At first I didn't like the idea of renting such a big house," Everdene said. "It seemed wrong, given that the expats are hanging on by a thread here. The house should go to an African or, better yet, become an African school. Can you imagine? It's perfect. But it's not for us to say, and when we got here...well...I think we just lost all our scruples."

Margaret laughed. "Don't think about guilt. It's not your guilt, anyway." She paused. "Let's not talk about all that right now. A day like this is so rare for Patrick and me, I just want to soak it in."

"You're right. Of course you're right. You live in Nairobi?"

"We do. We used to rent a cottage in Langata and then we lived in a house in Karen, but somehow we ended up closer to the city."

Did Margaret want to tell Everdene the reasons for having to abandon the cottage and the house-sit? No. All she wanted to do was to forget. It was as if her brain were full up with anxiety and needed a rest. She wanted to hear about the oddities of Everdene's house, let her eyes relax, even close them if she felt like it.

Patrick's posture revealed his ease as well. Had they truly broken through the ice jam that morning? If so, this was their perfect reward.

Margaret looked over at Everdene. "Tell me about your students," she said.

"What did you think?" Patrick asked Margaret in the Peugeot on their way back to their flat.

"I liked them. I had fun."

"I did, too. I was wondering about the climb," Patrick said.

"What about the climb?"

"I was thinking of asking them to go with us."

Margaret was surprised by the suggestion. Wasn't the climb meant to be a personal challenge for them both? To go alone would be one kind of trip. To go with Kevin and Everdene would be something entirely different.

"Another couple would help with expenses," Patrick said. "Cut them in half, in fact."

Margaret pondered the quandary and in doing so realized that she liked the idea of having another couple.

"Do you think they're climbers?" Margaret asked.

"Were we climbers?"

"Wouldn't they think the invitation abrupt? We've only had one lunch with them."

"I felt comfortable," Patrick said. "I felt relaxed. Say what you will about Arthur and Diana, I never for one moment was relaxed."

Patrick took a roundabout.

Margaret could agree with that, but she felt a small tug of reluctance at the thought of opening up the climb to others. The trek would no longer be an attempt to accomplish something greater than the climb itself. There was a purity in that idea, a sense of purpose. On the other hand, she thought, it would undoubtedly be more fun with Kevin and Everdene. It might be safer as well. If they made it to the summit, the other agenda would have taken care of itself, wouldn't it? The two plans weren't mutually exclusive.

"Why don't you talk to Kevin," Margaret suggested, "and feel him out?"

Patrick returned home the next evening with the news that Kevin was enthusiastic about the climb. He and Everdene had never considered climbing Mount Kenya, but Kevin took to the idea at once and said he would talk it over with his wife that evening.

Patrick and Margaret had already made the decision not to tell the other couple about Diana. It was a risk, since Kevin and Everdene might well hear about the tragedy from someone else in the expat community. To start off the climb, however, with that image in their heads would do the other couple a disservice. Why burden them with that? At times Margaret wondered if she and Patrick weren't using their new friends for their own ends.

After dinner, Kevin telephoned Patrick and Margaret. Everdene was thrilled with the idea, he reported, and had nothing but questions.

"We need a few practice hikes," Patrick suggested. "Why don't Margaret and I prepare a picnic to be had on the Ngong Hills next Sunday? We'll hike up, have the picnic, then climb down. While we're eating, we can talk. Bring paper and pencils. We'll have to make lists. And the first thing you both need to do is buy hiking boots so you'll have plenty of time to break them in. There's a good place in town. Hang on a second." Patrick turned his head away. "Margaret, what's the name of the place you went to?"

"Sir Henry's," she said.

"Sir Henry's," Patrick repeated over the phone.

Margaret thought how strange it was that she and Patrick were now the more experienced.

"Terrific," Patrick said, and put down the phone. He turned to Margaret. "So," he said. "It's done."

That week, Margaret cleaned the flat and took two trips to the laundry. Patrick bought a fake Christmas tree, which they decorated. Everdene and Kevin invited them for Christmas dinner, and on the day itself, Margaret and Patrick called both his family and hers. Toward the end of the phone call, Margaret asked her parents to drive to a ski store and send them the best parkas and gloves and silk long underwear they could find, including six pairs of silk socks. She impressed upon them the need to do this as soon as possible, since the climb was now slightly less than a month away. If they sent the package that day or the next, it might reach Nairobi before she and Patrick set out for the mountain.

Timmy couldn't help but ask when Margaret was coming home, and at the sound of his voice, she nearly said "tomorrow." In the end, he had to settle for "soon." Her parents said that she sounded a lot better than she had during their last phone call, when Margaret had been in the hospital.

Margaret did feel better, she insisted. She looked upon the climb as a challenge. She and Patrick would reach the top; she was certain of that. No mention was made of the previous climb, which her parents knew about. They didn't ask her why she was doing this again, and Margaret volunteered little.

After Margaret hung up the phone, she thought about how

much she might have to bury, to put away. She understood this might be foolish, even unhealthy, but she saw no other way to manage her life.

Margaret thought of Rafiq. For a few hours one day, she had convinced herself that Rafiq was just a crush she'd once had. She suspected this might happen all the time with married people: they had harmless crushes and then moved on. One didn't necessarily have to act.

But she knew that she was lying to herself, that she would never forget Rafiq. The only compromise, Margaret decided, was to live her life on parallel tracks, one moving inexorably forward, the other reserved for memory. She wondered if it could be done and what the cost to her marriage would be.

When she thought of Rafiq, she tried to picture where he had settled. Margaret imagined he had taken a taxi to a Pakistani area of London, perhaps to Brick Lane or Bethnal Green. He would have gone to his cousins', she guessed. While the women gathered in rooms to talk and mind the children, the men would watch television, passionate about cricket. Sometimes Margaret saw Rafiq so clearly it hurt, but she couldn't put him in a specific place or at a specific job. Would he be living with relatives? Or would he have left London for Islamabad? Would she have been comfortable living his life with him? If Margaret had been involved with Rafiq when he was deported, she would have followed him. Of that, she was certain.

Discovering that she was in better shape than the last time she'd attempted the Ngong Hills left Margaret exhilarated. She remembered that awful, desperate thirst, the struggle for breath. Now there was none of that. She recalled the red ants only long enough to warn Kevin and Everdene about them.

On the first trip, the four sat atop the first knuckle and made lists. On the second trip, they easily made it to Finch Hatton's grave, marked by an obelisk and words from "The Rime of the Ancient Mariner." On the third trip, they reached the end of the hills and then the car again in record time. Kevin and Everdene were in excellent physical condition, far better than Margaret had been in a year ago. Everdene had sturdy legs and always carried a walking stick, a practice Margaret soon adopted. Kevin's compact figure seemed built to propel him up a hill. Of all of them, he was by far the fastest. Patrick and Margaret would slow him down, they explained, and for good reason. They shared with their friends the horror stories of HAPE and HACE, the miseries of AMS.

Everdene, in particular, wanted to know more about the glacier, but Margaret found herself unable to answer her questions. Patrick took over and described the rope, the carved steps, the guide's careful pace. It would be easier, Patrick said, with four of them instead of six. Neither Margaret nor Patrick ever mentioned Diana, nor even the names of the people they had first climbed the mountain with. They admitted that they hadn't reached the top and that was why they were repeating what was, at the very least, a challenging climb.

Back at Everdene and Kevin's house, Margaret told them the story of the Kikuyu and Kirinyaga.

Sometimes Margaret thought she was living inside an echo.

"Did you get any of those awful conditions you told us about?"

Everdene asked at dinner after their third expedition on the Ngong Hills.

Patrick and Margaret looked at each other. Margaret said she'd had a touch of AMS just after the glacier, which is why they hadn't tried for the top. She felt light-headed at the thought that she was lying to a woman she now considered a friend. But by not being honest about Diana from the beginning, Margaret had boxed herself in. The lie might have to continue along certain unexpected tributaries.

"Do we tip the porters and guide?" Kevin asked. He'd come out onto the veranda in a V-necked sweater. Margaret's long white dashiki fell to the ground. She owned four of them in different colors and wore them whenever she could, for comfort. Everdene showed off her tan with a gauzy aqua shirt and a silver necklace. The sun set, and Margaret knew they might have to move inside soon. When the light left the lawn, the mosquitoes rose from the grass.

"I think we tip the guide," Patrick said. "And then he takes care of the others." He paused. "Or not."

"Do you know how much? I just want to make sure I've got enough cash on me at the end."

"Well, you certainly won't need any cash on the mountain," Patrick said. "I don't know, but I'll find out before we leave."

"Dying to see the lodge," Everdene said. "I hear it's wonderful."

Margaret thought about the impalas in the grasses, the buck bounding away. "Bring a sweater," she said. "It's frigid at dinner. It'll be cold the entire trip. Layers are the answer."

"It was exactly a year ago that you two made your first attempt?" Everdene asked.

"It was," Patrick said, not looking at Margaret. "Nearly to the day. There's a small window twice a year when climbing the mountain is at all feasible. You can't go during the rainy seasons. You'd never get up the mountain, for one thing; for another, you could get lost in a blizzard."

"A blizzard on the equator," Kevin said. "Still can't get used to the idea."

"You'll see snow," Margaret said. "Especially at the top."

The parkas and silk underwear had arrived from home just the day before. Patrick had to stand in line at the post office for more than an hour to retrieve the package. Margaret and he were used to the routine. At Christmas, the wait had been four hours.

Margaret wished she had asked for four sets of long underwear so that she could give Kevin and Everdene a pair. At least she could give them socks.

The three who worked were taking Friday off so that they could have the two nights at the lodge before setting out Sunday morning. Margaret wondered if they would have the same guide or porters. She hoped not. The guide certainly would remember Margaret and Patrick and perhaps say something to them, which might then be overheard by either Kevin or Everdene—a situation Margaret didn't want to think about.

Patrick, on the Sunday morning they'd decided to climb Mount Kenya again, had used the word *expunged*. Margaret had been pondering the term for weeks and had decided it was precisely the word for what she hoped to do with the memory of that first climb.

Margaret scrutinized the porters. She introduced herself to each one and asked their names. They smiled at her. She saw no familiar faces. When it was her turn to meet the guide, she spoke to him in Swahili and then in English. She shook his hand and asked his name, which he said was Njoroge. She wondered if he had misgivings each time he took another climbing party out. Since the last trip, Margaret had learned that half of all AMS deaths in the world occurred on Mount Kenya.

Margaret and Patrick had already put on their puffy navy jackets. They left some of the layers and the silk underwear in their backpacks for when the temperature dropped. Everdene had slipped into a red ski jacket that made Margaret blanch when she saw it for the first time. No white fur on the hood, but it was far too similar to what Diana had been wearing. There was nothing to be done about it. Margaret certainly couldn't say to Everdene, "Don't wear red."

Kevin had on a black ski jacket, and Margaret guessed that the couple had sent for the gear. She glanced at their gloves and reminded them to check that they had their dark glasses with them.

At the lodge, Patrick had taken Kevin trout fishing. When the men had returned with a good-size catch, they'd asked the cook to prepare the fish for their dinner. The delicate and flavorful trout had been perfectly done. The men's pride in providing food for their wives was funny to watch, though Margaret remained suitably reverent during the meal. While the men had been fishing, Everdene and Margaret had taken a walk (no impalas) and attempted a swim at the pool. Margaret registered a scum slick on the bottom and bits of what looked to be algae floating on the surface. That afternoon, in her room, Margaret took a long shower to rid herself of unwanted flora and fauna.

After dinner on the second night, Margaret and Patrick had

made love for the first time in weeks. He undressed her slowly and spent lavish amounts of time kissing her neck and shoulders, seductive gestures he knew she liked but he had often skipped before. Though Margaret could never set aside the notion that they were *trying* (and perhaps *trying too hard*), she attempted to put herself into a similar frame of mind. She was aware, as she did so, of withholding part of herself from Patrick. She doubted that her husband detected her reserve; it had been more than a year since Margaret had made love freely.

"I'll be with you every step of the way," Patrick reaffirmed to Margaret as they set out. He had determined the order. He and Margaret first, to establish the pace; Everdene and Kevin behind Margaret. Kevin and Everdene never went ahead, though sometimes the four clumped together when the conversation involved all of them. Margaret learned that she could talk and hike at the same time and marveled at the difference in the degree of difficulty of this trek compared to the last one. It wasn't that Margaret could have run up the mountain; she could not. Suspecting she was still the slowest of the four, she nevertheless handled the altitude better than she had the previous year. Kevin and Everdene appeared undaunted by the earliest parts of the climb. Neither one was in the least winded or tired. Margaret decided there must be a genetic disposition to acclimation that the British have and Americans do not. But then she thought the theory specious and abandoned it.

"This is the place where we encountered the buffalo," Patrick announced. "It was just fucking huge, and it had its eyes on us the entire time. Both the guide and the porters were amazed that it didn't charge us, because we had clearly startled it when we'd gone around a bend. We must have had the wind coming at us. A startled buffalo is a scary creature. More people are killed by buffalo on Mount Kenya than by any other animal."

"What happened?" Everdene asked.

"We backed up. Very slowly, so as not to call any more attention to ourselves than we already had. I don't know if you noticed that fork in the trail back there, but we retreated to the fork and then went the other way. Cost us an hour at least."

"So... how do we know there aren't buffalo all over the place?" Everdene asked, betraying the first hint of fear.

"We don't," Patrick said.

"The guide is very good," Margaret said quickly to allay Everdene's concerns. What was the point, she wanted to ask Patrick, of frightening Everdene before they'd hardly begun the climb? "They all carry pangas as well," Margaret added, referring to the porters and the guide.

A lot of good a panga would do, she thought privately.

"You're climbing amazingly well this time," Patrick said to Margaret when the four set off again. "You must feel better."

"I do. I kind of wish you hadn't brought up the buffalo. I think the less everyone worries, the better off we'll all be."

"You're right. Sorry," Patrick said in that way he had. Subject over. Subject done with.

Margaret gave her husband a quick kiss. He had complimented her, and she had scolded him. Not the best way to accomplish their joint goal.

She planted her walking stick into the ground. "Wish I'd had one of these the first time around."

"You had a stick on the bog," Patrick said.

"It was way too late by then," Margaret replied.

When the sun came out as they neared Met Station, Margaret was jubilant. "This is amazing," she said to Everdene. "When we were here before, we were covered in cloud and never had a view at all. Look at this!"

They stood well above the base of the mountain and could see the terraced land on the lower slopes falling away to the flat plains beyond. Margaret searched for Nairobi, but though she saw smaller towns, she couldn't find the city. On the side of the mountain from which they had a view, the sky was cloudless. If she turned, however, she could see a dark gray mound hovering over the mountain and obscuring the peaks.

"Please don't let us walk into that," Margaret said aloud.

"I'm afraid we're rather used to cloud," Everdene said.

Margaret wanted to tell her how a dark sky during an arduous climb could drain the spirit and rob a person of the stamina needed to keep going. The sparkling view they had before them seemed all the more precious for what would likely come their way the next day or the day after that.

The four reached Met Station by three o'clock and were eating a hot meal a half hour later. Afterward, Margaret climbed the short distance up to a ridge so that she could savor the view and the blue sky. She lifted her face to the sun. Who had said it? Arthur or Willem? That though the temperature was frigid, the sun would be even stronger than it was on the ground. She had her sunglasses on but knew she risked a burn.

When she returned to the station, the other three were deep in a game of gin. She remembered the previous climb, when everyone had been too tired or too dispirited even to lift a deck of cards. Margaret sat near the others and listened to Kevin as he asked Patrick if he'd heard anything about a new disease that caused its victims to starve. A few cases had been reported in Naivasha and Nakuru. The natives were puzzled and terrified. No one knew how the disease spread.

Patrick said he hadn't encountered it but was curious and would look into it.

While the group finished yet another hand with much boasting and moaning, Margaret walked over to where the guide sat—just a few feet away from where the porters had gathered to eat. She wondered if the guide always sat apart, to establish a proper hierarchy. The fire felt good. Margaret sat down next to Njoroge.

"*Jambo.*"

"*Jambo.*"

"*Habari yako?*"

"*Nzuri. Nzuri sana.*"

"There's something I want to ask you," Margaret said.

"Memsahib."

"When we get to the glacier, I want to stop in the middle for just a few seconds. Maybe half a minute. The last time I crossed the glacier, I didn't dare look down. It's a fear I'd like to conquer."

"You have been on the mountain before," he said.

"A year ago."

"And did you reach the top?"

"No, we didn't. Some of us got sick," Margaret said. It seemed the simplest answer.

"You must go to the top," the guide said. Even though the sun was in Njoroge's eyes, he didn't wear sunglasses.

"Well, I hope to," she said.

"Yes, yes," he said vehemently. "If you are able and do not get the sickness again, you must do this."

"Is it hard? The final summit?"

"The summit is steep. But it is short."

Margaret picked up a stick and began to scratch the dirt in front of her. In a gust of wind, the smoke from the fire blew in their direction. Margaret tried to wave it away. None of the porters seemed at all bothered by Margaret's presence among them.

"How long have you been doing this?" Margaret asked the man.

"I am five years doing this," he answered, nodding his head. She noticed that he had on the relatively thin blue jacket that all the guides wore.

"Do you like it?" she asked.

"It is a good job," Njoroge said. "It is paying well."

"And where do you live?" she asked. She thought it would be impossible to commute to this job from somewhere else.

"We are having bandas at the lodge. Did you stay at the lodge?"

"We did."

"Is very nice."

"Yes, we liked it a lot," Margaret said. "My husband went fishing."

The guide smiled. "And your husband, he is catching the fish?"

"He and that man there caught quite a few." Margaret gestured toward the card game. "We had them for dinner."

The guide laughed. "Ah," he said, "then you are lucky."

Margaret nodded. "There's another question I'd like to ask you," she said, "but if you don't want to answer it, that's perfectly okay."

Njoroge turned to her.

"Have you ever lost anyone on the mountain?"

"Lost?"

"I mean, has anyone ever died on any of your expeditions?"

"When people die, it is because they leave their guides. These people are guides of their own visits to the mountain. Two are dying with me. It is four years now."

"I'm sorry," Margaret said. "How did it happen?"

"When we reach Top Hut, the men, they have the sickness," the guide said. He put his hand to his brow and shook his head. "Is very bad. They have the sickness in the head."

"Headache?" Margaret asked.

"No," Njoroge said. "They are crazy in the head from the sickness. And they go up to the top when it is a blizzard and they are not telling me. It is almost half an hour before I am even finding out they have gone. I go out into the blizzard to find them, but I am not finding them. The rangers, they come, and we search for them. For two days, we search for them. But then I am running out of food and have to go down the mountain. In a week, when there is clearing, the rangers find the bodies very far from the trail."

"They got lost?" Margaret asked.

"Yes, memsahib. They are getting lost. I am thinking then that I am no good for this job." Njoroge shook his head. "Is like herding goats. I must herd all my goats and keep them safe. I must never let them go, or bigger animals will get them and eat them."

Margaret blinked at the image. "But, surely, the men deliberately went off without you."

"Is still my fault. I should have seen the sickness. I should be checking them always."

"I'm sorry that happened to you," Margaret said.

"Oh, and I am sorry, too." Njoroge again shook his head sadly.

"Well, I still don't think it was your fault," she said. "Stupid people do stupid things, and sometimes they have only themselves to blame."

"I am promising you that you will not get lost."

Margaret smiled. "Thank you," she said. "And please call me Margaret."

"And we are stopping in the middle of the glacier," the guide said. "But you must tell the others so they are not so surprised. Surprise is very bad on the ice."

"Yes," Margaret said. "I will do that."

"What was that about?" Patrick asked when he and Margaret were alone in the banda setting up their bedding. Kevin and Everdene had earlier taken the two cots at the far side of the door. Patrick laid their shiny purple bedding at the other side for privacy. When Patrick had asked the guide if there would be other climbers joining them, the guide had said no.

"I asked Njoroge to do something for me," Margaret said. "And I hope you don't mind. I asked him to stop in the middle of the glacier for thirty seconds, so that I could look down. I told him that I had been afraid to look down the last time, but now I wanted to conquer the fear. It's what I'll tell Kevin and Everdene, too, because they have to know that we'll be stopping.

I can't pay proper tribute to Diana—I can't even think about Diana—when we're trying to get across the glacier. I won't be able to take my eyes off the feet in front of me. You remember."

Patrick nodded.

"Oh, and by the way," she said, smiling, "we're goats."

In the banda, Margaret lay awake a long time. She thought of the year before, when her legs had twitched and she had fallen into an exhausted sleep shortly after she'd put her head on the pillow. Now, something excited her and made her anxious. She thought it must be the glacier. She felt in the banda what she imagined she would feel as she stepped onto the ice.

Margaret wished she and Patrick could have slept outside with Njoroge and the porters. She'd had only a brief glimpse of the stars when the lantern had been put out and before the door was latched. How wonderful it would be to lie on the ground and look up at a perfectly clear sky with as good a view of the stars as they would ever get. She thought it promising that there were stars at all. Perhaps the menacing cloud she'd seen earlier had backed off, gone away.

"Are you awake?" Patrick whispered.

"Yes."

"I'm having fun. Are you?"

"What a difference from last year. This was such a good idea."

"I love you," he said.

"Love you, too," she said.

The vertical bog in the sunshine wasn't physically any easier, but it did lift the spirits so that Margaret didn't feel defeated by the gluelike mud and the incline. So far, the cloud had stayed pretty much behind the peaks. Blue-black billows hovered near the top. A god watching them, Margaret thought. A not particularly nice god, either. With any luck, the cloud would move off the mountain and leave them alone.

Everdene had trouble with the mud. Margaret stayed close to her.

"Horrible," Everdene said, trying to smile.

"The pits," Margaret said.

"Dante might well have used this," Everdene added, a costly expenditure of breath.

"It's like hitting your head against a wall. You'll feel so much better when you get to the top."

"If I get to the top."

"Oh, you will. Don't worry."

Patrick and Kevin hadn't been able to help their pace. Repeatedly, they went ahead and then remained in place for Margaret and Everdene to catch up. Kindly, the two men let them rest and get some air before continuing on and then having to do it again. Margaret, in slightly better condition for this particular leg than Everdene, enjoyed the position of being *not last* but tried not to exploit it. She gave Everdene encouragement, keeping the banter light and often telling Everdene not to talk. The four had a water break in the middle of the bog. Margaret thought of Njoroge, who seemed camel-like in needing so little water to keep going—unless he was drinking it when she wasn't looking. Margaret thought this impossible: he was always ahead of them, and not very far ahead of them at that.

During a short breather, Margaret told Everdene that when they reached the glacier, the group would stop for thirty seconds in the middle so that Margaret could look down. She explained that she hadn't been able to do it the year before, and she felt it necessary to conquer her fear. The guide understood the plan, Margaret said, and only Kevin needed to be informed.

Everdene nodded, unable to utter a sentence.

At the top, both women sat at the edge of the bog, even though the area was still muddy. Patrick, recognizing that Everdene was in some trouble, signaled to the guide.

"I think we need a rest and some water," Patrick said.

Kevin sat next to his wife, and she laid her head on his shoulder. Patrick picked that moment to tell the story of those early Africans, on the mountain for the first time, who thought that the water in the cooking pot was bewitched when it turned to ice. Telling the tale was quite an accomplishment on Patrick's part, Margaret thought, since he was short of breath, too. Only Kevin, amazingly, seemed unfazed by the arduous slog.

"You're amazing," Margaret said to Kevin. "Your lungs must be enormous."

"Can't account for it," he said, shaking his head. "I'm as surprised as you are."

Njoroge, who was standing nearby, scrutinized the peaks. "The rainy season is coming to greet us," he announced.

As they approached Mackinder's, Margaret thought about the rats. Had they been eradicated in the past year? She thought not. She would sleep covered up and close to Patrick. She wouldn't take his hand, too painful an echo.

"Gosh," Everdene said when she looked inside the banda.

"Did you bring ground cloths?" Margaret asked.

"We did. Oh, it's awful."

"It's only one night." Margaret had intended to bring in her bedding and lay it out, but then she thought better of it. The idea of sliding into the bag with a rat in it was beyond imagining. "Listen," she said to Everdene, who had dumped her bedding onto a dirty mattress. "I'm going to tell you something that no one told me last year, and I wished they had. When we go to bed, there's a strong likelihood of rats."

"In the banda itself?" Everdene asked, incredulous. Her hair was pasted to her head from the sweating and her hat.

Margaret nodded. "I'm telling you because I nearly had a heart attack when one ran over my hand. Lay your bedding out just before you go to bed. Lift the sleeping bag as high as it will go over your face and keep your hands inside the bag. Though they frightened me, they never really bothered us. I think they just run around the edges of the banda, looking for food. They probably leave when they haven't found any. After a while you won't be able to keep yourself awake worrying about them, so you should just give in and go to sleep anyway. Do you and Kevin have bags that zip up together?"

"We do. We didn't use them last night because we had cots."

"That's your best bet tonight," Margaret said, thinking she and Patrick would do the same. "It's up to you, of course, as to whether you want to warn Kevin or not. Four of our party last year slept the night through and never even knew about the rats."

"I won't tell him," she said. "He sleeps like a stone. But thank you for telling me. I'd have screamed if I'd felt one."

"Your husband doesn't snore," Margaret couldn't help but point out.

Everdene laughed. "No, he doesn't."

"I'm jealous," Margaret said.

Despite the condition of the banda, Everdene seemed revived by having reached Mackinder's. Only Patrick appeared to be under the weather. His skin had turned white and blotchy. As he sat at the edge of the veranda while one of the porters washed the mud off the back of his parka, he seemed listless. Margaret sat beside him.

"You okay?" she asked.

"I think so. Just need a rest."

"No songs tonight, I'm guessing?"

"Do you know what the meal is?"

"Let me guess." She put a finger to her cheek. "Stew?"

"I'm not hungry anyway."

Margaret examined her husband more carefully. Bad color was one thing; no appetite was quite another. "This doesn't sound good, Patrick. Maybe you're getting AMS?"

"I say I need a little rest, and you jump to AMS?"

Margaret recalled advice either Arthur or Willem had given them the year before: often the person with AMS is the last to admit it. Margaret would watch out for Patrick. Perhaps a night of acclimatizing would help. It was always possible that he'd eaten something that hadn't agreed with him. He would be the first to suggest that one should look for the least-exotic answer first.

"I'm going to zip our sleeping bags together for tonight," she said.

"I'll do that."

"Well, if you want to lie down, and you don't feel well, just let me know, and I'll go in and do it."

"The rats," he said.

"Yes," she said.

And then she left the subject alone.

That night, the cards again came out, and Margaret took Patrick's place. They played gin until the sun set. At Margaret's suggestion, the three lay on their backs for a few minutes to look at the stars. Margaret had made up the double bed, into which Patrick had disappeared. Kevin had asked earlier, when Patrick hadn't eaten with them, if he was okay, and Margaret had said that she thought Patrick needed a rest, though they should all be on the lookout for signs of AMS in one another. Margaret said that she'd make an assessment of Patrick in the morning and that she could use Kevin's help. Once she told Njoroge she thought Patrick was suffering from AMS, she explained, the trek would be over. The guide would simply turn around, and even Patrick was wise enough to know that one couldn't trek farther up without a guide. He'd be furious, Margaret thought. Or would he be relieved?

"This is simply brilliant," Everdene said of the large swaths of stars overhead. "I promise you, Kevin and I have never seen anything like this. This is worth the whole climb."

"I wish I had a telescope," Kevin said. "I imagine other climbers have brought telescopes."

"I've been in different parts of America where the air was supposedly clear and there was no light pollution, and I've never seen this," Margaret said. "Of course, you wouldn't see this from the northern hemisphere. I'm no good at identifying constellations."

Kevin had some skill in this area, as a result of the Boy Scouts, he said. He named several constellations he'd seen only in books.

"Makes you feel small," Everdene said, surveying the dazzling panorama.

"We *are* small," Margaret said.

"You are small, and you must go into the banda," Njoroge said above them. "Tomorrow we are waking at three o'clock in the morning. Or did you misremember that?"

"I tried to," Margaret said, sitting up.

Njoroge looked up at the stars as well. "Ngai is answering our prayers," he said. "The rainy season wants to come to Mount Kenya, but he is making it stay away."

"Let's hope he keeps it away for at least another day," Kevin said, hopping up.

"Ngai will do as he wants to do," the Kikuyu guide said.

In the morning, Patrick made a tremendous effort, and Margaret thought that though her husband was still under the weather, his color was better. To show that he'd improved, he asked for a large breakfast. The cook wouldn't give it to him — they would have a proper breakfast after the glacier — but Patrick did consume two large hunks of wheat bread with guava jelly and two cups of coffee in the fifteen minutes before the guide made them head out. Watching her husband, Margaret was sure Patrick was forcing himself to eat — he did it with bravado, like a child — but she couldn't prove it. Stopping the climb for Patrick's sake would enrage him and make him redouble his efforts to convince her of his health. He would then curtly remind her that he was the doctor and not she. She knew he could answer all the questions any ranger would ask, and wasn't that the ultimate test?

"You think he's okay?" Kevin asked Margaret.

"Not a hundred percent, but okay enough. Let me just talk to him.

"Are you all right?" she asked Patrick as they were hefting their backpacks.

"Jesus Christ, Margaret, what are you trying to do? I'm fine. Anyone here would say I was fine. Are you trying to sabotage us?"

His attack came with the force of a blow. Margaret was sure he'd practiced his answer.

"No, no," she said. Everdene and Kevin had set out, wanting to give Patrick and Margaret privacy. "If you say you're fine, then you're fine. The last thing I want to do is sabotage us. Believe me, I want to get to the top as much as you do. Not at your expense, though."

"I'm fucking fine," he said.

Margaret turned and started walking.

The scree challenged Margaret as it had done the year before. Margaret remembered that she had hated every minute of the climb last year, the scree the worst offender. Again, she could see only cones of light from the torches above her. Patrick had taken off, in part, she thought, to prove that he was fit. She couldn't even muster enough strength to encourage Everdene, who kept pace beside her and, frankly, seemed to be having less trouble than Margaret. Everdene's strong legs helped her on this part of the climb, but she had the good manners not to try to outdo Margaret, thus upsetting the subtle hierarchy they had formed. Margaret liked the woman even better than she had before.

Margaret guessed that all experiences on the mountain would

be different, even if you climbed it every year—a thought that
seemed so grim, she banished it at once.

At the top of the scree, Margaret bent from the waist to be
able to breathe better. Patrick coughed. He asked for water, and
the porters allowed them each a drink and a cookie. Margaret's
throat hurt, and she tried to slake her thirst as best she could with
the stingy cup of water the cook gave her.

Though the sun had not yet risen, it was daybreak, and Ngai
was still working on their behalf. The day would be clear. The
dark cloud, as far as Margaret could work out, had moved slightly
off the peaks.

"Bloody miraculous," Kevin said beside her. "With this kind
of luck, we will make it to the top."

"No other choice," Margaret said. "Once the rains come, we've
had it. And it won't be rain at this height."

"I imagine snow blindness would be the problem, then."

The terrain between the scree and the glacier seemed mild after
the misery of the scree. When the sun hit the rocks above them,
Margaret was awed by the majesty of the mountain. No cathe-
dral could compete. If one needed to find religion, this would be
the place to do it. The sheer size of the peaks and the way they
sparkled suggested spirits within. How easy it would be to believe
in pagan gods, their might and strength and beauty so close at
hand. The black cloud that menaced, the nearly blinding sight of
the glacier ahead, the wind that picked up, the magnificence of
the rocks themselves—each seemed to be delivering a message.
All a group of people had to do was agree on that message, and a
system of deities would be created.

Just before the glacier, the guide spoke to them. They would pause, he told them, at the center of the glacier for just a few seconds of rest. Margaret looked at Njoroge, though he kept his eyes from hers.

Margaret took her first step onto the ice. Once again, they had been placed in order by the guide. Everdene behind Njoroge, then a porter, then Kevin, then a porter, then Margaret, then another porter, and then finally Patrick, followed by the cook. Patrick, whose face was washed out from the glare, had been given a pickax to dig into the ice in case of emergency. Margaret considered whether she had made a mistake in not telling the guide the true reason for the pause needed at the center. Would he have backed away from her as a harbinger of bad luck? Would he have had words of wisdom that would have settled her thoughts?

Margaret couldn't help but think of goats. The guide at the front and the cook at the back were shepherds trying to get their small herd across the ice. The image made her smile.

Margaret didn't dare look down. She was saving that for the pause in the middle. She hadn't even allowed herself to think about Diana's fall, though she could feel those memories crowding her at the edges. Margaret took in long, slow breaths to soothe her nerves, but she found that that made her woozy. Examining the feet of the porter in front of her, Margaret wondered if Everdene or Kevin or Patrick was frightened. Patrick knew what was possible on the glacier. He might have images similar to Margaret's.

They drew closer to the center of the ice, and Margaret considered whether her idea had been a foolish one. Why had she conceived of it? She didn't have to stop and look down, a notion that was beginning to terrify her. She could so easily have stood alone at the edge of the ice and said a silent prayer. No one would have needed to know, not even Patrick. Why this mawkish request for ceremony? The guide would think she was trying to conquer a normal fear. Patrick would think she was paying tribute. Would Everdene and Kevin, hapless participants in this absurd ritual, dare to look down? Or had they already?

She felt the line stop. For the guide and for Patrick, she would have to do her bit now. She had only thirty seconds.

Margaret braced her feet. The porter in front of her turned around as if to signal that, yes, this was the time.

She gazed below her at the steep swath of ice. She made herself take her eyes all the way to the dark ravine at its end. She wished she had planned some words for this moment. Thinking that something appropriate would just come to her, Margaret found she had only images instead. Slight bumps on the ice. Teeth desperately tearing off a mitten. A red hood with white fur. The guide reaching out his hand. The still body spinning down the ice.

The white glare hurt her eyes. Margaret tried to think of something to say to Diana. Behind her, she could hear Patrick call her name. She had to do this quickly. The way in which she'd braced her legs didn't feel natural. What could she say to Diana?

I'm sorry. I'm sorry.

A year of a life not lived. A year of not being a mother. A year of not being a wife. Soon it would be two years, and then ten and then twenty. In twenty years, Diana would have been in her midfifties. Margaret's own mother was fifty-one. For Diana to have lost all that time with her children. To have lost the chance of grandchildren.

All losses were the same loss. Each loss encompassed the others.

They grew cumulatively, triggering memories. Margaret thought of Rafiq. She thought of the baby. She thought of her marriage.

A moment of physical terror, a sense of losing her balance. Margaret wavered and then went down on her knees. She reached for the porter in front of her and for a moment felt the horror of nothing. She clung to the rope, and then the porter had her. He was clutching her arm, and he had dug his ax into the ice.

Safe in her footholds, Margaret felt the paralysis beginning. She knew she didn't have the courage to stand up. She had no idea how to do such a thing.

Margaret put one hand over her sunglasses and started to cry. Had she cried even once for Diana? In all the time that had passed? She cried for Diana now, and she cried for herself. The porter behind Margaret grabbed her at the waist. She heard Patrick say her name. Margaret couldn't answer him, because she was trying to stop the crying. She clenched her teeth and made a noise that sounded angry but wasn't. She told the porter holding her arm that she couldn't get up.

He shook his head; he didn't understand her.

"She can't get up," Kevin called ahead to the guide.

"Is she hurt?" Njoroge asked.

"I don't know!" Kevin shouted. "I don't think so. I think she's shaken."

"She lost her balance," Patrick called from behind her. "The porters have got her."

"Can she stand up?" the guide asked.

"I think she can," Patrick said. "I'm not sure."

"Nothing is broken?"

"Nothing is broken!" Margaret shouted. "I'm fine!"

The guide barked in his native language, giving instructions to the porters.

Njoroge called back to Margaret. "The porters, when you say so, will lift you. You must go loose in your body and not worry. They will save you if you are loose and do what they say. Do you understand me?"

"Yes," Margaret said.

She put her hand out for a moment to signal to the porters that she wasn't quite ready. Margaret thought of Everdene and Kevin and Patrick. The longer she remained on her knees, the more she exposed them to danger.

"Okay," she said to the porters.

She tried to stay loose, though it was nearly impossible. They raised her up, but she was still in an awkward position and wobbled. Neither of the porters let go. They let her find her own balance.

"Now you are just all right," the porter behind her said.

She waited until she knew she had solid footing. Then she shouted to the guide that he could go on.

As soon as they had all reached solid ground, Patrick unclipped himself from the guide rope and walked straight to where Margaret stood. He shook her once, hard, by the shoulders. "What the fuck?"

Margaret's head snapped back. She stared at her husband. Kevin stood just behind Patrick and put his hand on Patrick's shoulder. "What's going on?" Kevin asked.

Patrick released Margaret. "Nothing," he said. "Absolutely nothing."

Margaret could see that Kevin didn't believe Patrick. Who would believe a man who had just shaken his wife?

Everdene came and stood by Margaret's side. "I'm so sorry," she said.

"No, it's I who should be sorry," Margaret insisted. "I've done you both a terrible disservice."

Margaret told Everdene and Kevin the whole story. About the previous climb, about her need to honor Diana. "I had an agenda," Margaret said, "and I should have told you about it."

"You could have killed yourself," Everdene said.

"I worried you. You must have been afraid for yourselves."

"I was," Everdene said. "The whole thing was terrifying. But I think we were afraid for you most of all."

"It was stupid," Margaret said. "Just plain stupid."

"Look, you felt it was something you had to do. I understand that," Everdene said, putting her hand gently on Margaret's arm. "And I understand, too, that you didn't want to worry us."

"Thank you," Margaret said.

The AMS hit Everdene second. By the time they reached Top Hut, she admitted that she had a terrible headache. She staggered into the banda and lay on one of the bunks.

Bunk beds, Margaret thought. What a luxury.

Patrick had given up on the attempt to hide his malaise. He took a bunk across from Everdene and rolled over onto his stomach.

Margaret sat at the edge of Everdene's bunk and rubbed her back. "We'll go down in a few minutes."

"I just need to rest," she said.

Margaret got out the sack that had the meds and distributed aspirin to Everdene and Patrick.

"You might as well give me some of that, too," Kevin said. He sat at the edge of an empty bunk and held his head in his hands.

"Headache?" Margaret asked.

"That and other things."

"Let me know if you need Imodium. The AMS is supposed to go away as soon as you've made the descent. We'll leave in just a few minutes."

She poured water for the three of them, but Patrick wouldn't take his. Margaret went outside the hut and spoke to the guide, who had his hands on his hips.

"They're all a little sick," she explained.

The guide's expression didn't change. "Your husband is telling me of the woman who died last year."

Margaret clenched her hands together. "Yes," she said. "I'm very sorry. I know I should have told you."

"You must go to the top now," he said, pointing. "Ngai is inviting the rains soon."

Margaret looked up. The dark cloud was moving fast toward Lenana. "I can't go to the top," she said. "My husband and my friends are sick. They probably have AMS. I think we have to get them down the mountain as soon as possible."

"Yes, we will do that," the guide said. "But first they will rest. When they are resting, you will come with me."

"I think I should stay with them," Margaret protested. How could she make the summit without Patrick? Wasn't that as good as severing whatever was left between them?

"No," the guide said. "They will be fine. You have wronged Ngai. Am I mistaken?"

Had she wronged Ngai?

"Memsahib, the only way to make it right is to find the top."

"Now?" she asked.

"Yes," Njoroge said vigorously. "Just this minute we must go."

"I'm afraid," Margaret said, looking at the steep angle of the summit.

"You will not be afraid. I will lead you."

She gazed again toward the peak of Lenana.

"I'll just tell them I'll be right back," she said.

Kevin and Everdene were already asleep. When they woke, she would help them down the mountain—across the glacier, down the scree, along the bog. With any luck, when they reached the bottom, they would still be friends. With Everdene, Margaret would try hard.

Margaret bent to her knees so that her face was near Patrick's. She saw his eyes open.

"Njoroge says I have to go to the top. To atone."

"I figured."

"I'm sorry, but I would like to go."

"I don't really care."

"That's just the AMS talking," Margaret said.

"No, it's not. This was all a stupid idea anyway."

Margaret understood what he meant. They had set themselves a challenge—to reach the summit to save the marriage—when each of them had known that it might not be possible. Was it that a marriage that might have survived in America, among familiar surroundings, could not withstand the challenges and moral complexities of Africa? Or was it simply that she and Patrick—though each meant well—had fallen out of love?

She rubbed Patrick's back. "If I had a potion to make you better, I would," she said.

Patrick was silent, and his silence irked her.

"Did you have an affair with Elena?" she asked.

"You're asking me that now?"

"I guess I am."

"Does it matter?"

She thought a minute. "No. No, it really doesn't."

Patrick rolled his face away. "I didn't, for what it's worth."

Margaret touched the back of his head.

"Okay," she whispered as she stood.

The guide showed her how to put the crampons on and how to use them. He gave her a pair of ski goggles.

Margaret began to sweat almost immediately and could feel the prickles inside her clothing. The angle of the slope was much steeper than the rest of the climb had been. The air felt nonexistent. She was surprised she didn't have a headache.

The blizzard hit them halfway up. The snow stung Margaret's face where it was exposed. She thought the guide would turn around, but he didn't. She couldn't go back without him.

Margaret was shocked by how near the edge of a cliff of snow they climbed, how deep the ravine below it. Of everything she had ever done in her life, surely this was the most dangerous.

She marveled that the guide hadn't prepared her for the danger, and then she panicked that she might slip. Njoroge might not even know. Was this attempt at the summit meant as a punishment? From the guide? From Ngai? Margaret could barely see a thing in front of her; had she not worn the goggles, she would have been forced to shut her eyes.

Still, the guide went up and up. The struggle seemed relentless.

Margaret and Njoroge weren't connected by a rope this time, and there were no porters behind Margaret to catch her if she fell. Margaret focused on the red band of the guide's crampons so that she didn't lose him in the snow.

Her breath was so tight, she couldn't even call his name.

She began to crawl upward on her hands and knees like an animal. It occurred to her that she might die. Wasn't it pure hubris to attempt the summit in a blizzard? But Njoroge had been insistent. Why wouldn't he wait for her? His behavior was incomprehensible. When Margaret got her breath back, she would yell at Njoroge for frightening her so much.

No, she wouldn't, she thought. They all had to depend on him to get them back down the mountain.

Margaret was barely crawling now. She began to pray.

Still on her knees when Njoroge held out his hand, Margaret struggled to her feet. He had on a bandanna that covered his face. "And now you have made it," he said.

She looked around her.

"This is the summit?" she asked.

"The summit, yes," he said.

She put a hand on his shoulder to catch her breath. He waited patiently until she could stand on her own.

"Here is where they are sometimes putting flags," he said. "Do you have a flag?"

"A flag?" She shook her head.

"Is all right," he said. "The wind is taking them away anyway."

Margaret planted her feet and stared into the view, but she could see nothing. Maybe one day she would tell Rafiq that she had finally climbed Mount Kenya.

"Ngai will forget about you now," Njoroge said.

Despite the sting on her face, Margaret stood for a long time.

How amazing, she thought. She had climbed an entire mountain known for its spectacular view, and all she could see were small bits of white—and wasn't that exhilarating?

Acknowledgments

For Asya Muchnick, whose editorial letters should be framed; for Jennifer Rudolph Walsh, whose savvy and humor make her a joy to work with; for Michael Pietsch, a publishing gentleman and my gracious former editor; for Elinor Lipman, from whom I have learned much about being a human being, both in writing and in life; and for John Osborn, who with a single sentence of advice stripped away a large and potentially fatal part of this book. Without him, nothing would be possible.

About the Author

ANITA SHREVE is the acclaimed author of fourteen previous novels, including *Testimony; The Pilot's Wife,* which was a selection of Oprah's Book Club; and *The Weight of Water,* which was a finalist for England's Orange Prize. She lives in Massachusetts.

BACK BAY · READERS' PICK

Reading Group Guide

A Change in Altitude

A novel by

Anita Shreve

On a recent visit to South Africa, Anita Shreve talked with Michele Magwood of *The Times* (Johannesburg)

"Story is essential for me," says Anita Shreve. "I'm not one for, say, magical realism. When the flowers start talking I'm outta there! I am a realist."

Shreve is one of America's best-loved authors. When her novel *The Pilot's Wife* was selected for Oprah's Book Club in 1999, it catapulted her into the firmament of bestsellerdom and won her a devoted audience. Her near-annual books routinely sell in the hundreds of thousands and are a favorite with reading groups.

She is slim and forthright, with a peppery humor and a penetrating curiosity. "I'm driving my escorts here mad with my questions." She chuckles and says she has just started reading Harvey Tyson's novel *Blood on the Path,* about the founding of South Africa. While she may be filling her head with South African facts, it is an endless curiosity about the human condition that drives her work. She deftly assays the impulses and emotions, the secrets, betrayals, and jealousies, we all harbor within us, and which inform our responses to outside events.

"I'm fascinated by the human heart and how people react in extraordinary moments," she says.

In each novel Shreve buries a pivotal event, a cataclysm or mischance, which detonates in the lives of her characters, radiating fault lines through the story.

Sometimes the moment is small: in *A Change in Altitude* it is the mere holding of a hand that upends lives; sometimes it is more dramatic, such as the air crash in *The Pilot's Wife* that shatters the widow's world. In the compulsive *Testimony*, the story centers on a sex scandal at a private school in Vermont. A group of teenage boys are caught on film having drunken sex with a more-than-willing fourteen-year-old girl. When the tape finds its way into the headmaster's office, the entire campus begins to unravel.

Shreve strives to make each book distinctly different from the last, and in doing so she takes risks. In *Testimony* she tells the story through multiple viewpoints—teachers and parents, teenagers, cops, journalists, doctors—as the characters pick through the wreckage wrought by the sex tape. It is an immensely skilled novel, an ambitious, beautifully executed telling.

In *A Change in Altitude* she decided to set the story in Kenya in the '70s, a time when Shreve spent three years in Nairobi. "I had become obsessed by Barack Obama," she says in explaining her setting, "and I felt I had the tiniest edge because I know the Luo people—his father was a Luo—I knew where he came from. So I changed continents for this story."

Patrick and Margaret are American newlyweds who are posted to Nairobi for a year. Patrick is a doctor specializing in equatorial medicine; Margaret, a photographer. They move into the cottage of a colonial mansion owned by Arthur and Diana, a brittle, condescending British couple who invite Margaret and Patrick to climb Mount Kenya with them. That anyone would tackle this mountain without proper training or equipment is appalling, yet Shreve herself climbed it in the '70s "in sneakers! How stupid was that? And with no preparation!"

It is a brutal climb up, and worse coming down after a catastrophic accident for which Margaret is blamed. This lingering blame threatens her marriage, and she struggles to truly acclimatize to her new home. Early on Shreve writes that "In Africa, Margaret often felt dazed, as if something shiny had hurt her eyes."

For her, Kenya is violent and violating: she and Patrick are repeatedly robbed; a childminder is raped; students are killed and buried in a mass grave; and an editor is "disappeared."

Shreve was robbed eight times during her stay in Kenya, "but there was no violent crime then. I loved the people and I loved the physical country."

Although she has never been back, she follows events there and is especially sad about the current drought. "I couldn't believe it when I read there are Kenyan refugees here in South Africa. It's unthinkable! It was the model country at one time."

After this book tour Shreve will go back to one of several manuscripts she has begun. "I only know where I'm going with a story after fifty or sixty pages. In the old days I used to plot assiduously because I didn't know what I was doing! Now I follow my instincts."

Never at a loss for a story—"scratch any surface and you'll get an interesting tale"—she has no plans on easing up her prolific pace. "I don't think writers ever get to retire—unless we lose our faculties!"

This interview originally appeared in *The Times* (Johannesburg) on October 3, 2009. Reprinted with permission.

A brief conversation with the author of *A Change in Altitude*

What was your inspiration for the novel?

The novel is about how a single moment in time can alter the course of a person's life. We're all either worried about it or have had it actually happen to us. As a writer, I think it's intriguing to push a character up against the edge and to watch how he or she behaves.

How did you decide on this particular setting for the story?

The novel takes place in Nairobi, Kenya, where I lived and worked in the late 1970s. I suppose you could say this book has been thirty years in the making.

How did your experience of living and writing in Kenya help shape A Change in Altitude?

Though my book is fiction, it's based on a number of experiences I either had or witnessed. For example, I did have a cottage in Karen, I did work for a national magazine in Nairobi, and I did climb Mount Kenya. But what happens in the novel did not actually happen in real life. I can't think of a single scene in the book that's actually true. It's all well and good to recall experiences that have happened to you, but if you don't trigger the imagination, nothing will actually get written.

Did you think when you were in Kenya that one day you might write a novel set there?

When I lived in Kenya, I was years away from writing novels. I had wanted to write fiction as a child and as a student, but I don't believe I ever thought of it as a realistic career choice. So I turned to journalism for fifteen years. And it was only then, after I had that experience, that I began to write fiction.

Questions and topics
for discussion

1. How would you interpret the novel's title? Does the concept of "altitude" have significance in the story beyond its literal meaning?

2. During the drive to Mount Kenya, Margaret and Patrick talk about whether photography detaches you from the present or helps you immerse yourself in it more fully (pages 73–74). In your own life, do you find that taking photographs enriches experiences or prevents you from being fully in the moment?

3. When Diana brings Adhiambo to stay with Patrick and Margaret for the night, they disagree about how best to deal with the situation. Margaret seems more concerned about Adhiambo's emotional well-being, while Patrick focuses on her physical state. In what way do their differing perspectives reflect other aspects of their character? Do you think Adhiambo would have been better off if Margaret and Patrick had taken her to the hospital that night?

4. Throughout the novel, Margaret is struck by the way Kenyans use the phrase "just all right" (pages 65, 67, 187, 243, and 301). How would you interpret the meaning of this phrase? Why is it so surprising to Margaret?

5. How culpable is Margaret in what happens on the mountain? To what extent does the blame fall on others involved in the climb? Should a person be held responsible for the unintended consequences of her actions (page 122)?

6. Is Patrick right to confront Margaret about what happened on the mountain? Margaret argues that if he loves her and intends to stay with her, he should not have told her his opinion. Patrick, on the other hand, believes it is more important to be honest (page 123). What do you think is more critical in a relationship—total honesty or sensitivity to the other's feelings?

7. Why do you think Margaret feels so strongly about taking the photograph of the leopard? Are there parallels between this action and Diana's behavior on the glacier? Have you ever put yourself in danger because of a momentary impulse? What do you think motivates actions of this kind?

8. What is your definition of "infidelity"? Does Margaret's relationship with Rafiq constitute unfaithfulness to Patrick? Is there such a thing as emotional infidelity, or is physical cheating the only real infidelity?

9. How much of a marriage's success or failure do you think can be attributed to the love between husband and wife, and how much to external factors such as jobs, finances, location, and other people? Patrick says, "I think couples need projects to keep them together" (page 269). Is he correct that a couple must put in effort to make their marriage work?

10. If the accident on the mountain had never occurred, do you think Margaret and Patrick's relationship would have evolved differently? Would anything more have happened between Arthur and Margaret? Between Rafiq and Margaret?

11. Imagine Margaret and Patrick thirty years after the end of *A Change in Altitude,* looking back on their life together in Africa. How do you think each of them would describe the trajectory of the relationship during that time?

12. Describe your response to the novel's ending. Did you find it sad? Uplifting? Did you feel that things had worked out for the best?

Testimony

"A sex, lies, and videotape thriller set at a prep school. As scandal erupts, many are implicated, and blame is tantalizingly hard to fix." — *Good Housekeeping*

"Contrasting the sweetness of young love with the primal recklessness of lust, Shreve paints a chilling portrait of how bad decisions in brief moments can ruin lives." — Joanna Powell, *People*

"About as raw as a piece of fiction can get.... Shreve takes the reader inside the minds of everyone involved.... It's an ambitious narrative technique, but Shreve nails it.... There's no protagonist in *Testimony,* just as there is no antagonist. Shreve's too accomplished a writer to portray life that simply."
— Kate Ward, *Entertainment Weekly*

"Gripping....A thoughtful look at the ways people fail those they love.... *Testimony* will break your heart even as you race on to the next page." — Jennifer Roolf Laster, *Houston Chronicle*

"A tale that is mesmerizing, hypnotic, and compulsive. No one walks away unscathed, and that includes the reader."
— Bette-Lee Fox, *Library Journal*

Sea Glass

"A helluva read.... Shreve simply has the Gift—the ability to hook you from the first page and not let go until the final word."
— Zofia Smardz, *Washington Post Book World*

"Shreve's four-hankie plots are pure silk, and her characters are so real you can feel them sitting next to you on the couch."
— Michelle Vellucci, *People*

The Last Time They Met

"Shreve is careful in this story of an undying love affair to let the pressure grow slowly, compelling her readers to turn each page hungrily to gain a deeper understanding of the characters' lives."
— Rebecca Banks Zakin, *Providence Journal*

"A poignant novel . . . so astonishingly well-constructed that when you're finished you'll want to reread it all at once."
— Erica Sanders, *People*

Back Bay Books
Available wherever paperbacks are sold